The Unraveling

The Unraveling

VOLUME ONE
OF THE
Erotopian Chronicles

Carl Frankel

MANGO GARDEN PRESS

The Unraveling
Volume One of The Erotopian Chronicles

Copyright © 2019 Carl Frankel. All rights reserved.
ISBN: 978-0-9898138-7-7
Library of Congress #: 2019905488

First Print Edition: July 2019
Cover Art by Erin Papa (The Turning Mill Graphic Art Studio)
Interior Design: Tilman Reitzle

Mango Garden Press
27 Crown Street
Kingston, NY 12401
http://MangoGardenPress.com

This is a work of fiction. Names, characters, places, and incidents either are the product of the author's imagination or are used fictitiously, and any resemblance to locales, events, business establishments, or actual persons—living or dead—is entirely coincidental.

For more information about Carl Frankel and his work: CarlFrankel.com.

The universe, by definition, is a single gorgeous celebratory event.

—Thomas Berry

For the dreamers and the doers who are
bringing forth a wiser world.

Contents

Earth to Erotopia
11

Mirror, Mirror
37

The Welcome Waterings
63

The Wheel and the Cross
91

Something To Say No To
111

Lovebirds On the Wing
127

Beyond the Body
169

The Mother Of All Connections
191

In the Garden, With a Mosshard
205

The Pray Party
225

The Coming Together
257

To The Great Ones
271

Glossary
276

Acknowledgements
278

Earth to Erotopia

*"Sex on Erotopia is the cornerstone
of civic and spiritual engagement. Its
priestly class doesn't seek to save souls.
It celebrates the arts of pleasure."*

—Ulrich Von Zeitler,
*First Report to the Senate
Select Sub-Committee on
Intergalactic Affairs* (2049)

-Vala-

THE LANDING SPIDER ROTATED IN SLOW CIRCLES AS IT floated downward. With a rising sense of disbelief, Vala Cortes stared out of her porthole and took it all in. The thick northern forests rising into the high mountains with their craggy snowless peaks. The western prairies rich with crops and spotted by picturesque hamlets. Another quarter-turn, and through her porthole a vast eggplant-shaped body of water came spilling out from a narrow band—the Midriff Ocean, which girdled the planet at its equator and separated it into two roughly equal halves, Civside and the Wild.

She knew something, not much, about the planet's geography. Von Zeitler had briefed them before they left. He'd told them how places on Erotopia were named for body parts and soul parts, external geography pinned to interior experience. The two land bridges a dozen miles apart that joined the northern and southern land masses were called the Suspenders. The largely landlocked body of water between them was the Bay of Sighs. The watercourse flowing into it after tracing a serpentine course through the southern valleys, down from its source high up in the Shadow Mountains—the River of Forgetting. As she gazed down at the approaching planet, she wondered what the view had looked like before the massive engineering project that had transformed a necklace of lakes into the Midriff Ocean and separated what had been a conjoined land mass into two mostly separate continents.

The scrolling data readout had them down to seven thousand feet now. She looked back out the porthole, and the planet's capital city and only true metropolis came rising up to meet her. Kailara, 'our beating heart' in Erotopian, a sprawling cheery jumble of brightly-hued low-rise buildings, fields, meadows, trees and lakes, all luminous in the unpolluted air. There, to the north, was the Temple of the Divine Nectar, a magnificent Taj Mahal-like double-domed structure. Below it, at the city's geographical center, was the generous green space of Mosshard Garden, a bucolic gathering of meadows, gardens, and copses of thick trees.

Vala experienced an odd awareness: Her spirit was leaving her body. She felt waft-y, drifty, lighter. She knew it wasn't actually happening; she'd turned a sensation into a story. In truth, her spirit was about to come alive, not bail out on her—she was probably just releasing some of the anxiety that had been building up for months and now was boiling over. She couldn't help but wonder, though: Was this how people felt when they were dying?

She stole a peek at her travel mates, whose faces were glued to the other two portholes. Jahangir, the expedition's leader, was looking relatively chill. Her boyfriend Darius kept saying, "I can't fucking believe this is happening, I can't fucking believe this is happening."

After the fourth repetition, Vala thought, *I can't fucking believe you keep saying that.* She gritted her teeth and looked back out the window. They were no more than a thousand feet up now, and descending too fast for her liking. "Are you guys scared?" she asked into the porthole.

"Not I," Jahangir replied from behind her. "My butterflies are flying in formation."

"Hell, no," said Darius. "I'm a warrior."

Of course the guys wouldn't cop to being afraid. So here she was, on her own again. The closer their module came to touching down, the harder her heart banged up against her rib cage. Why had she said yes to this? Back on Earth, she'd rarely traveled beyond her home turf, and now she was about to settle down on a planet in a distant galaxy that everyone else called Erotopia, but she'd dubbed Fuck-o-Rama. A culture based on sex and pleasure—how would that play out? Things were sex-crazed on Earth too, of course, but people there tended to sweep it under the carpet, into the alleys, under the sheets of dark bedrooms. They didn't rub it in your face, and that was good; a person could get on with their life. Here they did it in the road. Literally, if von Zeitler was to be believed. *Jesus.*

For the millionth time, she wondered if she was overreaching. If there was one thing she was certain about, it was that she was living inside a chrysalis; it was her life's mission to bust free. But Fuck-o-Rama, with everybody watching? Not likely for a woman who specialized in shadows. She was screwed, and not in a good way.

Flags were coming into view, flags everywhere, dotting the fields and boulevards and roofs in a rainbow of bright colors. But no, she caught herself: They weren't flags, they were pennants. *Banderines*, not *banderas*. Flags were a call to team and tribe—they were martial and unitary. Pennants were diverse and festive. You marched under a flag—you partied among pennants.

The landing zone was circular, two dozen yards across, and surrounded by a meadow of blue-green turf that stretched into the distance on all sides but one, where it was bounded by a short ceremonial wall and, just beyond it, a densely vegetated area.

Three people, two pale women and a dark-skinned man, were staring up at the descending craft. One of them, the blonde, offered a small wave. Vala's heart went *ka-thunk*. But then she realized: This wasn't first contact. It was the Earthling Bree Tavendish.

The spider hit its mark dead center, pulled there by Erotopian technology that had Earth scientists totally baffled. The landing mat was rubbery and trampolined them into a soft landing. Bounces became shimmies became trembles, and finally stillness. Vala un-buckled herself, stood up, and shook herself clear of nervousness as best she could. Jahangir released the door lock and the thick portal swung open. She was the second person out, two steps behind Jahangir and immediately ahead of Darius, who kept pressing up

15

against her from behind. Her knees went wobbly as she stepped off the clanking metal ramp. She looked back to Darius for support, but his attention was elsewhere, on the vast excitement of their new adventure, on anything and everything but her. She returned her gaze forward. *Maybe Jahangir*—he seemed to sense what she wanted because he reached behind him without looking back and took her hand at exactly the same moment she reached out for his.

The newcomers lined up across from their welcome party. Bree was wearing an elegant ankle-length forest-green dress with cut-outs at the breast and crotch. Vala tried not to stare at the Earthling's vulva, which was thatched with straw-colored fur.

The two groups contemplated each other in silence. Then Darius leaned in toward Jahangir. Vala promptly mimicked the gesture from the other side—she wanted to know what he'd say. She immediately regretted the move. For one thing, it was none of her business, and for another, the two extraterrestrial members of the welcoming committee, those two sex-crazed Fuck-o-Ramans, were contemplating her with bland undecipherable expressions that she found utterly terrifying. She couldn't begin to decipher what they were thinking, or what plots and plans they might be cooking up. And now the first thing they were seeing was her breaking a rule, transgressing a boundary, eavesdropping on a private conversation. Thirty seconds in, and she was already fucking up. *Dios*, she could be stupid!

But the die had been cast, the crime committed. She'd heard what Darius had whispered to Jahangir. "Sweet Jesus, fuck me. Damn, this is gonna be good!"

Bree stepped forward. "Jahangir? You, of all people? We picked up your ship's signal a while back, but I never dreamed you'd be on it. What brings you here?"

"I applied and the Committee chose me," he answered with a smile and shrug. "They wanted an entrepreneur. They've given me a provisional license to explore the commercial opportunities."

"That had to be a compromise solution."

"That's right. The left wanted full diplomatic relations, the right wanted to invade. I was the man in the middle."

"You come in peace though, right?" she said carefully, as if to correct a possible misunderstanding.

His gaze flitted toward the Erotopians standing expressionless behind her, then back. "I come in peace and love," he answered smiling.

"Yes," she said, "I'm sure you do. What are they saying about me? There's no communicating through a wormhole—I'm on the silent end of a news embargo."

"You're globally notorious. Some people want to try you for treason. Others want to"—he looked down modestly—"well, you know."

"Fuck me?"

Jahangir's eyebrows rose a tiny bit. "That's right."

"I'm not surprised," she said, then added with a twinkle, "Which side are you on?"

Jahangir hesitated and said, "Neither. You're a person. You're my friend."

Bree's amused expression suggested that she knew the real answer and was fine with it.

"The *Post* has taken to calling you 'the Ex-Patriot,'" Jahangir said.

Bree shook her head. "Jesus, Earthlings. So happiness is treasonous now?"

"It's out of fashion, at a minimum. You're one of the reasons I was chosen. They thought I might be able to talk some sense into you."

"Good luck with that. But I sure am glad to see you."

Sharing a smile, they fell silent.

Vala decided not to rule out their having slept together. Jahangir had quite a reputation, and Bree was the sort of woman, attractive and accomplished, who'd attract his interest. They plainly had a good connection.

A butterfly was circling around Vala, the biggest butterfly she'd ever seen. It was a good six inches across, and its wings were iridescent, scarlet, gold and indigo. It seemed somehow intelligent, almost like it was checking her out, wondering if this strange creature merited alighting on.

A new wave of panic swept over Vala. Why couldn't she be like that butterfly? (Which appeared to have decided against her and was fluttering away.) She imagined how the scene looked from above, the clean and elegant geometry of it—the three Earthlings here, the two Erotopians there, and Bree in her right place in between.

"We're wearing our translation implants," Jahangir said. "Your people, too?"

Bree nodded. "We can do better than that, though. We'll chip you with Erotopian technology, which translates perfectly across all languages. You'll be able to talk with anyone. For now, though, this will work."

Introductions followed. Jahangir cleared his throat and said. "Hello, I'm Jahangir Persad." He gestured to his left. "This is Valentina Cortes, Vala for short."

Her heart bungeed into the basement at the sound of her name and then settled back in its usual place, pounding even harder.

Jahangir swiveled to his right. "And this is Darius di Selva."

Her guy hammed it up as she'd thought he would, dipping his knee in a theatrical half-bow. "At your service," he said, and laid his biggest and most dazzling smile on them. His red-carpet smile, Vala called it. It was weaponized—it bowled people over. She remembered the first time she'd seen it. She'd been dancing at the Limelight Club; it had knocked her for a loop. And now here she was, holding hands with Jahangir, and it was starting to feel awkward, disloyal at a minimum and on the edge of cheating. She wondered what the Erotopians were making of the odd imbalance—two of the Earthlings holding hands, and the third one completely on his own. For all she knew, they were reading a wildly false meaning into it. About status, maybe, or exclusion. There was simply no way she could know. There wasn't merely a culture gap between Earthlings and Erotopians—the abyss was galactic. Just that morning, barely an hour before they'd clambered into their landing module, Jahangir had showed her a checklist of possible problems he'd developed. His "Fuck-Up Manual," he'd called it. She'd noticed the second listing first because it was plainly about her: *Gratuitous Attacks of Modesty.* And then, immediately above it, Jahangir had written, *Cultural Confusion: We Say 'Tomato,' They Say 'Asparagus.'*

Bree was introducing the two Erotopians. "The High Priestess Kri'Zhalee," she said formally. "And the High Priest Kri'Bondai."

They looked to be in their mid-thirties. With her olive complexion, high cheekbones and full lips, Kri'Zhalee had the dramatic good looks of a Mediterranean beauty. Kri'Bondai was tall, broad-shouldered and square-jawed, with ebony skin and a penetrating gaze. Their bodies were draped in what Vala at first took to be thick silver-gray cloaks, but then she looked again and wasn't so sure. The material was shimmering and swirling—it seemed to be almost alive. And then she realized: It *was* alive. Kri'Bondai and Kri'Zhalee weren't wearing clothes; they were draped in their own energy.

Their cloaks shifted into higher gear. The swirling became more energetic, more animated, more erratic too. Their coverings dropped away to reveal, in the briefest of now-you-see-it-now-you-don't spotlights, different naked body parts.

Kri'Bondai's broad chest and six-pack abdomen.

Kri'Zhalee's firm and sizable breasts.

Her black-haired bush, which seemed to be enveloped in a low fog, her sex so rich and fecund that it was exuding an aerosol mist. (But Vala had to be imagining this.)

His large-side-of-average phallus, erect and pulsing directly at her. (And there could be no imagining here.)

And then the display was over. The cloaks calmed down and clammed up, leaving the High Priest and High Priestess draped from the neck down in shimmering silver-gray once again.

"I say, *goddamn*," Darius stage-whispered to Jahangir.

-DARIUS-

ONE OF THE GREAT DELIGHTS of Darius di Selva's life was seeing a beautiful woman naked for the first time. During his adult years, this blessed event had happened with bracing frequency. Women went for him—he had looks and charm, and persistence. He'd recorded his conquests while in college and in his junior year had stopped counting at one hundred—it had seemed like a benchmark of sorts. Since his graduation, his throughput had slowed, but the total had kept rising.

Kri'Zhalee's body rivalled any that he'd ever seen. That, plus her face and hair, put her in a category Darius called "museum quality," the Everest of a rating system he'd developed deep into a night of serious drinking with some fellow lacrosse jocks. Her bush was especially remarkable. It seemed almost alive, like a small vital animal breathing.

He wondered if he'd have sex with her. He hoped so, and figured the chances were good. Erotopians were conspicuously promiscuous; as a sexual High Priestess, Kri'Zhalee would, if anything, top the charts here, too. He recalled a quip of Jahangir's that he'd shared with them en route. "We're like the explorers who crossed the Atlantic on the Mayflower. Only they were the Puritans, and we're the Impuritans." The two men had laughed; Vala had gotten indignant. "I'm not impure," she'd protested. "I'm a goddess." Of course she'd go there; the poor woman had been schooled by nuns. A part of her still believed the ideal woman was a virgin.

The sight of Kri'Zhalee's body was still lighting up his brain. That extraordinary pussy, like a humid land in a misting cloud-for-

20

est! Everything about her was intimidating. How would he ever find the nerve to hit on her? According to Von Zeitler, they had alcohol here. Probably not tequila (back home, margaritas were the ticket), but liquor was liquor—he'd find something that would do.

-ᴋᴚI˙ᴢHꚉᴌᴇᴇ-

THERE WAS SOMETHING OFF ABOUT THE EARTHLINGS'
auras. They were shrouded and heavy, also fragile and
tremulous. There was sleepwalking in them, and cloudi-
ness, and grieving too.

Over the course of their long history, Erotopians had been visited nine hundred and seventy-six times by beings from other planets.
They'd welcomed blobs of gelatinous protoplasm, stick-like creatures three times their height and one-tenth their weight, beings
that were walking, talking sex organs. They'd encountered species
without bodies that were pure energy. Every one of these visitors
had raised for Erotopians the same threshold question. Should they
or should they not grant them entry? The three new Earthlings had
made it through the initial test, but now that the High Priestess was
experiencing their *l'shavas* in person, doubts had arisen again. There
was way too much confusion here—and confusion, when habitual,
tended to normalize lashing out. It metastasized into violence, and
violence was a virus. It could propagate.

Their l'shavas are worrisome, the High Priest mind-messaged her.

His words came through with bell-like clarity. *Are they hiding
something, do you think?* she responded, using the same modality.

From themselves, maybe.

Might they be Hagorrhs? Shall we verify again? A heartgasm?

His "yes" rang inside her like a gong. They began immediately,
in intuitive harmony, pulling into their heart centers alpine energy from above and equatorial energy from below. When they had
the two pleasures joined together—purity and passion, witness and
wetness—and the ball was spinning and golden, they propelled it
toward the Earthlings in a blazing flare of love.

Their heartgasms hit home. The Earthlings' *I'shavas* softened and flashed yellow light. A nervous system explosion shivered Darius's shoulders, coursed through his torso and wobbled his knees. Vala went rocketing up the arousal ladder to a shallow six. Jahangir's Inner Temple opened wide and snapped shut. His response was so intense that Kri'Zhalee worried for a moment that she and Kri'Bondai had overdone it—the Earthling was clinging to his breath like a man on the edge of drowning. But then he managed a deep inhale and his breath became normal again.

The High Priestess observed with a sense of relief. He was okay, and the Earthlings could love.

In a single voice, the two sex wizards said, "On behalf of the Nine, we greet you."

-Vala-

A GUST OF SOMETHING HOT, like a desert wind, blew over Vala. It had come from the High Priest and Priestess—yes, definitely from them. She felt a wild stirring in her body. She felt it where she had sex, and she felt it in her belly, just above and behind her navel, and she felt it most of all in her nipples, which had gone all erect and tingly and were straining at the lace of her bra.

Little quivering antennae—that's what they were, she decided. Scouts, sniffing out their new environs. Her anxiety started to evaporate, and the beginnings of a smile teased life into her lips.

She imagined her nipples sniffing the air, noting its musky, perfumed quality.

Her attention went to her hand, which was cocooned inside Jahangir's. She let her hand go soft, a small experiment. Jahangir noticed and wrapped it up tighter.

She liked this man, how he paid attention.

She wished she could tell him about her nipples.

She wanted to be touching someone—she wanted someone to be touching her. Her crotch felt stirred up and swollen. Back home, her body didn't work that way. There, if she found someone attractive, her heart expanded early and her spirit along with it, but her genitals didn't get involved until she and her new man had gotten horizontal and stayed that way awhile. And now here she was, barely landed on Fuck-o-Rama, and her body was already raring for action—and weirder and more disturbing still, she seemed unable to banish Kri'Bondai's sleek and muscled body from her misbehaving mind. She'd only seen it for a moment, but what she'd seen had sunk in deep. His dark chocolate skin, his sculpted form, his erect and elegant phallus. This last bit was especially jarring. She kept trying to shoo away the image—sought intervention from the Holy Mother, even. Nothing helped. Still Life with Cock had a will of its own. It resisted—it persisted.

Why? And then, in a flash, she had it. It had to be Lola's doing, Lola her alter ego whom she'd first discovered when she started dancing at the Limelight Club. Unlike Vala, who was more shy than not, Lola was an exhibitionist. She loved to tease guys—it thrilled her to display her body. She got turned on by the look they got in their eyes that told her their everyday reality had fallen away—they were in a new realm now, and all they saw was … *her.* When that happened, she wasn't a piece of meat in a strip club any longer. She was a dream come true, perfection made flesh.

Vala was a mortal woman—Lola was a goddess. She was shameless, and she was wanton. And now it was Lola who was saying, *Damn, that man is gorgeous!* Yes, Vala decided, that had to be the explanation. In a backwater of her psyche, Lola was yawning, stretching, saying hello. She was thrilled to be on Erotopia and staking out her right to be sexual. Preparing to claim dominion, even.

The High Priest was gazing at Vala as inscrutably as before. Fearfully, she hazarded a closer look at his face but made no progress—she couldn't begin to fathom what he was thinking. She asked herself: Could a High Priest mind-read? The notion seized her with panic. What if he was reading her mind right now? What if he knew that she, Vala—or, rather, Lola—was fantasizing about him like a sex-starved obsessive? She kept seeing his body, his hard penis. If he could see into her, if he could *actually* see into her, might Goddess strike her dead right there.

The High Priest's energy cloak sparked red light and spread open like a curtain. There, again, was that muscled body—and there *it* was again, his phallus in the actual flesh, in its standard upright position. Moments later the gates closed over again—modesty was restored unto the land. Vala breathed a sigh of relief because the sight of his body was gone, and also because the strange compulsion that had caused her to fixate on his body seemed to have vanished as well. Lola had taken mercy and backed off—Vala's mind was free to roam again.

A wild possibility occurred to her. Maybe the High Priest *had* read her mind—and maybe, even more incredibly, it hadn't been a bad thing. Maybe that reveal had been his gift to her. A naked message, you might say. *Thoughts and dreams never need to be hidden.* Maybe that was what he'd been telling her, this High Priest, this teacher. *Honor what is. Don't empower shame.*

Her eyes came up to meet Kri'Bondai's. Unblinking, he looked back. *Dios*, he was hard to read! But he seemed to be smiling now, and friendlier.

-Jahangir-

MEANWHILE JAHANGIR HAD GONE PALE. Until now, Erotopia had been strictly notional for him, a frothy brain concoction. Now that chapter had ended. This place wasn't an idea; it was reality. He could fall in love here—he could die. Nor was this the only reason he felt daunted. Forty years earlier, his parents had migrated from Jaipur to San Jose to start a new life. That had been their grand adventure. His was a hundred times more ambitious—a trip to another planet, not another country, with the eyes of all Earth on him. And to top it off, just now, there'd been the unexpected and unsettling unlocking of his sex vault. Jahangir loved sex; it was one of the reasons he'd come here. But what he'd just experienced, although it had lasted only a moment, had been positively alarming. Pleasure that intense could drive a man insane—it could consume him, strip him of his humanity. In the flames beyond the shadows, he'd sensed monsters.

Bree came up close and gazed into his eyes. "Are you okay?"

This close in, this tender, she felt more familiar now—an Earthling, not an Erotopian.

"It's just ... is this really happening?"

She leaned forward and kissed him on the lips, so lightly that his nape hairs stirred. "My dear, dear man," she said. "It is." She took his hand and brought it to her naked breast. "You are welcome here. Truly welcome. Can you feel it?"

He gave a tiny head-shake no. *All these doubts inside my head.*

"When I came here, I came home," Bree Tavendish said. "You're home now, Jahangir Persad." She placed her hand on his and pressed down. He felt the soft flesh and hard nipple in the palm of his hand, and began to relax. If this was home, he'd take it.

He was feeling aroused. He knew full well that Bree had offered him the mother-breast, not the sex-play version, but a soft lovely tit was a soft lovely tit, and he'd been wanting Bree for some time now. On Earth, their relationship had been strictly collegial. He was an investor in a natural-language translation company, she a key employee, and neither had felt inclined to sponge away those boundaries. Jahangir had noticed her looks—of course he had, an attractive person was one of life's delights, right up there with the satiny sheen of his bespoke suits and the creamy lattes he liked to brew up on his six-thousand-dollar Marzacco. Tall, with broad shoulders and a fit, athletic frame, Bree had an oval-shaped face, cornflower-blue eyes and thick, long flaxen hair that she liked to wear plaited in an elegant French braid. She hadn't lit his erotic fire, though—her looks spoke more to him of health than sex. They'd socialized twice after meetings, just the two of them sipping drinks together in a quiet, dimly-lit hotel bar, and he hadn't thought to hit on her.

He hadn't been surprised when she was selected for the maiden voyage to Erotopia. A communications expert was required, and no one was better versed than Bree in the translation system they'd be using. It had been the subject of her doctoral dissertation (*Like Esperanto on Espresso: The Social and Cultural Implications of a Universal Translation System*), and she'd helped write the software, too. He hadn't expected her not to return to Earth, though. Nor had he anticipated the enormous fuss her staying behind would cause. For close to a week, the entire global population had bubbled over with speculation. Had she been abducted by aliens? Shut down by a virus? Fucked to an Erotopian frazzle? Then the authorities had ended all the conjecture by releasing a letter von Zeitler had brought home with him. In it, Bree had declared her love of sex, her love of a man (an Erotopian man), her love of her new country—and her intention to stay. Her love affair with Wyldermon, she wrote, was one for the ages, the most romantic connection ever. Never before had Erotopians been visited by a humanoid species with whom sex was anatomically possible. In their two bodies, the two species had found each other at last, Erotopians and Earthlings, cosmic twins joined from far apart.

In her letter, she described a bout of wild lovemaking with him and three of his male friends that had produced something she called megagasms. "Goodbye, Mum," she'd written. Her final words. "I'll miss you."

What had come to be known as the Tavendish Manifesto was received with guffaws by some, envy by others, and much self-righteous outrage from the right. If one were to take all their huffing and puffing at face value, she was a deserter, a traitor—and, of course, a slut.

Jahangir had responded more positively. The letter had sparked his sexual interest and transported Bree across the invisible line that separates platonic friends from prospective bedmates. More than six months had passed since then, six months with him feeling a buzz of desire every time he thought of her, and now here they were together, here on Erotopia, and she was smiling at him guilelessly, and his hand fit perfectly on her breast.

"We don't do reassurance like this back home," Jahangir said.

"You barely do reassurance at all back home," she answered drily.

"And here, you do it all the time?"

"We do whatever it takes," she said. "The animal body cures damn near everything."

"I like how your animal body feels."

"I like how it feels, too." She smiled back.

They stood unmoving for a time. He was lost inside the bubble of the two of them and only dimly aware of the others with him. He wondered what it would be like to have sex with Bree. Fun and athletic, probably. There'd be lots of easy laughter and affection. Rewarding too, if those megagasms she'd referred to were real.

A vast sense of relief washed over him. Back home, his selection by the Committee had made him an overnight celebrity. Not one single thing about this had pleased him, and he'd been especially unhappy about the scrutiny his love life had drawn. He had two primary polyamorous partners, Jonah and Marie. Their non-exclusive arrangement produced a steady stream of lovers passing through his door and lesser numbers through theirs. He was totally comfortable with his lifestyle, but he hated, he absolutely *hated*, how he'd become tabloid fodder. A week before they'd left, *The Rag* had published a picture of him dining with a prominent Silicon Valley executive who'd shared his bed later that night. The attention felt obscene. Fame was like a jail to him. Here, his celebrity status was a full galaxy away. Here, he could be ordinary. Here, he could be free.

"Your provisional license," Bree said. "What will make it permanent?"

"Business opportunities that are likely to, quote, 'generate significant revenue without having a significantly adverse impact on Earth morals.'"

"And the opportunities they have in mind?"

"The Committee's public talk was about minerals, spices and such, but I'm pretty sure they've got their eye on tourism. Sex tourism. The Committee can't officially sanction that sort of thing, of course—they can't be publicly endorsing sin, but it makes sense, right? Erotopia may or may not have minerals and spices, but it definitely has women. Beautiful, exotic, sex-loving women. Guys go on sex tours to Thailand although sex workers are horribly exploited there. What would they pay to have sex with genuinely happy women who would tear down porn's fourth wall and give them, up close and personal, the perfect sex of their dreams?"

"Women will want it, too," Bree mused.

"If it feels right, they will," he agreed. "We've legalized gambling— we've legalized marijuana—the time has come for sex, it seems."

Bree nodded thoughtfully. "Erotopia would be the perfect way to do it. You're making money, and you're keeping all that immorality off-planet. Hell, you're keeping it off-galaxy!" But then a confused look crossed her face. "I get why the Committee would want an entrepreneur. I also get why they'd choose you. But Jahangir Persad, sex tycoon? I'm not seeing that."

"You're right, I don't want to run a sex tourism business. Or even launch one, for that matter."

"Then why did you apply?"

"I had a brain bomb." She looked at him puzzled, and he elaborated. "Four times in my life, I've had a really big idea—I call them brain bombs. Each of the first three launched a business; together they made me a wealthy man. When this one arrived, I had to pay attention."

"And the brain bomb was?"

"Reality programming. *X-rated* reality programming."

Bree's eyes widened. "Here. On Erotopia."

"That's right. Just imagine the demand—Earthlings having sex with hot extraterrestrials!"

She nodded thoughtfully. "You're right, it could be huge." She hesitated. "But I thought you were here to explore commercial opportunities, not launch one."

"I sold it as an add-on. I seized the moment."

"And the Committee approved? They're not exactly sex-positive."

"I had a memory lapse. When I pitched the reality show to them, I somehow forgot to mention its X-rating."

"Quite an oversight, that," Bree said, laughing. "What will you do, spring it on them when you get home?"

Jahangir nodded. "I'm thinking two versions, one for the kiddies and one for the grown-ups. Strange things have been known to happen back on Earth. The X-rated material may be stolen and distributed against my will."

"And you'll just happen to have a bank account on the Cayman Islands." Jahangir didn't speak—instead, he blinked loudly. "You criminal mastermind, you."

"Deals with the devil, darling." Jahangir shrugged. "Deals with the devil."

"X-rated reality entertainment," Bree mused. Her gaze fell on Darius and Vala. "That explains these lovelies, I presume?"

Jahangir nodded and turned to face his companions, who were standing alongside each other a few steps behind him. Darius's arm was around Vala, and he was whispering in her ear. His heart skipped again at the sight of them. His surprise surprised him—he kept being waylaid by how beautiful they were.

Vala heard Darius out, then tilted her face upward for a kiss.

"Scene One of *The Erotopian Chronicles*—'*The Lovers Arrive*,'" Darius announced when their kiss was done. "How was it?"

"Great," Jahangir answered. But he didn't mean it. He needed them to be lovebirds—this had looked chaste and tentative, like a kiss between strangers. And now, to make matters worse, Darius was looking a trifle unsettled, and Vala seemed terribly forlorn, as if her exchange with Darius had confirmed a terminally sad intuition she had about her prospects for happiness in this short life. Still, it was ungodly how good the two of them looked, how beautiful and sexy. Not too far into the future, if he played his cards right, their names would be in lights on the virtual marquee—their sweaty, undulating bodies on display to the world—their sparkling, ecstatic eyes lighting the way for billions of rapt and turned-on followers.

"You looked so beautiful, doing that," Jahangir said. "I'd love to see you kiss again. This time, though, please bear in mind this grand, romantic adventure that you're on. And better yet, you're getting to share it together!"

"Ah," she said, and her voice had an edge, "our famous fresh start."

"I think I get it," said Darius, nodding. "You mean, like, put some tongue in it?"

-Jahangir-

MAN AND A WOMAN JOINED THEM, arriving via the arched opening in the ceremonial wall. On Earth, he might have passed for Tibetan; he had straight dark hair that fell down to his hips. He was naked above the waist—his nickel-gray trousers contrasted sharply with the terra-cotta tone of his skin. She was slender with close-cropped orange hair, green-and-gold tattoo sleeves, and expressive sea-green eyes. Her peek-a-boo dress was a scarlet twin of Bree's green one. Hugs all around among the welcoming committee, concluded by a prolonged and tender kiss between the man and Bree.

"This," she announced when they were done, "is Wyldermon. He's a Wild guide, a Wild guard and my Best Beloved, the reason I am here."

"A Wild guard?" Vala quavered. "Why is guarding necessary?"

"Hagorrhs," Bree answered. "Renegade tribes still live in the Wild. Some of them badly want in."

"What's a Hagorrh?"

"They're us with a will to Power Over, us with a will to dominate regardless of consent."

A chill ran through Vala. Here was another fine fantasy gone. And to think that she'd thought she'd be safe.

Minutes earlier, the three eronauts had been outfitted with translation chips—the process had been no more painful than a pinprick. Jahangir had no trouble understanding Wyldermon, who bowed low upon being introduced and said, "May He be with you in His pleasure and His power."

He brought his hands to his pelvis and flicked them outward toward the new arrivals. It was, Jahangir realized with a start, the motion one makes when sowing seed.

"And this," Bree continued, "is Cymanthea. She's a second-degree Celebrant."

"A what?" Jahangir asked.

"A Celebrant. She's well along on the Priestess path."

The woman stepped forward. "Welcome." She cupped her small breasts and raised them in greeting. "May She be with you in Her pleasure and Her power."

Jahangir took the hint and sowed seed back at them, a gesture that was mimicked moments later by Darius and Vala, boldly by him and nervously by her.

"Wyldermon and Cymanthea," Bree said, "are here to help us with your Welcome Waterings."

"Our what?" Jahangir asked.

"It's a welcome ritual," Bree explained. "Things are very different here; we need to help you adjust. There's culture shock—and it's not just that. Like, there's the air."

"Yes, the air!" Jahangir echoed. He treated himself to a deep inhale. The scent was ambrosial and intoxicating, humming in the air and in his body. "It's amazing," he said. "It makes me want to fly. It makes me believe I *can* fly."

"It's what happens when millions of people, for hundreds of generations, have led rich and fulfilled lives," Bree said. "It's the scent of no suffering. The scent of human happiness. You'd have the same air on Earth if you'd made wiser choices."

"Emotional air pollution," Jahangir said. "I hadn't realized."

"That," Bree said. "And no petroleum. And no heavy industry."

"This is heaven, life before the Fall. That's what you're saying, right?" Jahangir inquired.

Bree disputed his assertion with a firm shake of her head. "That's what I thought too, at first. But then I came to realize that Erotopia isn't heaven, not as conventionally understood. Heavens

34

are steady-state, and Erotopia isn't. We're not under the illusion that we've 'arrived'—we're always seeking to become wiser. Heavens are safe—there's no negativity there. Here on Erotopia, we have Hagorrhs. And the shadows that live inside us, too." She paused and then added, "Don't misunderstand—these negatives are good. Heavens choke on their own goodness; they can't survive their perfection. It's the grit that makes the pearl."

Darius said. "I thought this was sex camp. That sure sounds like heaven to me."

"Ah," Bree said, "but we're not just happy boinking bunnies here. The sex is part of a larger scheme. It's one of the main ways we express our commitment to pleasure and our commitment to celebration. We're not a sex culture; we're a wisdom culture."

Kri'Zhalee stepped forward and addressed the Earthlings with ritual formality. "Visitors: Do you consent to join us for your Welcome Waterings? Anything you do will be within your boundaries of pleasure, comfort and safety."

Jahangir nodded yes.

Vala swallowed hard and spoke her first words since arriving. "Will it involve sex?"

"If you'd like."

A long pause followed. Then she nodded.

"Darius?"

"Duh," he said and looked anxiously at Vala.

A small battalion of butterflies escorted them to the wall, which was covered with deftly painted murals portraying people having sex, *lots* of people having sex, in positions ranging from the missionary-mundane to the miraculously acrobatic. Twosomes, threesomes and moresomes in bright hues, all turned with a fine artistic hand. One tableau in particular caught Jahangir's attention. A man was on his knees fellating a second man, this one standing, whose face was buried in a woman's crotch. Her thighs were scissored around his neck, and her back and neck were arched in ecstasy. They were circled by a ring of children who were holding hands and dancing. Jahangir felt a clutching in his gut. Weren't we supposed to be protecting kids from the sights and sounds of erotic high jinx, not inviting them to gather round the sexpole?

The archway was ornamented with bas reliefs of vulvar decorations—painted fluting lips along each edge and, at the apex, a sculpted oversized clitoris. Jahangir smiled at the sight of it—Vala grabbed his hand anew and put it in a death grip. They passed through the gate and arrived at a sea of vegetation that stretched out toward the horizon on both sides and rose up dozens of feet above them. Bright flowers—purple, teal, coral—winked at them through the foliage. Three narrow footpaths made their way left, right and center through the shrubbery.

A light breeze had come up, fluttering the leaves and tickling Jahangir's cheeks like a feather-soft brush. "Bree, you go with Jahangir," Kri'Zhalee instructed. "Wyldermon and Kri'Bondai, you take Vala."

The High Priest nodded, took Vala's hand and led her to the leftmost path. Kri'Zhalee and Cymanthea bracketed Darius and guided him to the path on the right.

"Thank you, Jahangir!" Darius called out as he headed into the greenery. "I'm a prisoner of love!"

"More like a prisoner of lust," Jahangir said quietly to Bree.

"Aren't we all?" she responded, and led him into the jungle.

Mirror, Mirror

Heart-blasted, the Cold Ones lose themselves
And wobble off, doomed to forever roam,
Adrift without coordinates,
Ghosts in space without a home.

—Translated from Vervi M'chani,
The Well and the Wall

-Jahangir-

THE FIRST TIME JAHANGIR saw Darius and Vala, they were poised in holo freeze-frame on a cushy white sofa in a well-lit apartment somewhere. His hair was tousled and blond, hers was straight, thick and jet-black. He had on blue jeans and a purple muscle shirt, she a rose-pink blouse, black mini-skirt and gold spike heels. Darius was smiling into the camera. Vala was looking down—maybe distracted, maybe shy—and picking something invisible off her top.

Jahangir clicked 'play' and the holo-vid sprang into life again. "Stand up and twirl," Darius instructed. Vala obeyed, spinning like a ballerina with her hands above her head. She had the looks of a runway model, but she was a bit too short for the job and a bit too curvy, too. Her complexion was café au lait and her eyes were dark chocolate. Her skin was glisteningly sleek and smooth—she looked spectacularly fit and toned. And those curves: shapely legs, elegantly rounded hips and a wondrous rear, two tight globes of perfection. A narrow waist and breasts bountiful enough to attract the eye of folks who look out for that sort of thing.

He rotated her image so he could see her from all angles. After much back and forth and over and under, he decided that she didn't have a bad side, not that he could see, anyway. He thought back to the time not so long ago when entertainment images had still been projected onto wallscreens in two dimensions. Some twenty years ago, when he was in his early teens, that had changed. Virtual reality had transformed the viewing experience into something immeasurably more stimulating and intimate. He felt his body stirring into life as he explored the contours of her body.

"My turn," Darius said on the holo-vid, and executed a slow bodybuilder's turn. He was very sexy, too. Blond, six foot three, with sapphire-blue eyes, a firm, straight-lined jaw, and broad shoulders that tapered in a sharp V to his waist, he looked as fit as Vala and unflappably self-confident. He was opulently muscular without looking steroid-pumped. His biceps swelled and rippled when he moved his arms—the cut contours of his abs were visible beneath his tight tee. And that killer smile of his, which erased everything but its own glory. Everything about him said, "I've got this!"

Their bodies left Jahangir feeling dizzy, as if it were he, not they, who'd just spun around. And Vala's eyes—Jesus, her eyes. Jahangir fast-reversed and replayed two, three times. Yes, it was as he'd thought: Every time she looked into the camera, her eyes seemed to be inviting him to dive down into their depths, down into their heat, down into their questions, down to where he saw, or thought he saw, her longing to be saved.

In the next scene, Darius and Vala sat at a round café table in the kitchen and shared some tidbits about themselves. He'd been born into nouveau Main Line money—his grandfather had been a successful restaurateur. He had a small trust fund thanks to Gramps. He'd moved to Hollywood after college, pursuing a career as an actor. Vala was the daughter of undocumented Mexican immigrants. Hers had been a mostly borderline existence, shadowy, impoverished, and concealed as much as possible from the authorities. Her last surviving close family member, her mother, had died six months ago. Now Vala was living in the Anglo, affluent Hollywood Hills with Darius.

"I'm on my own," she said.

"No, you're not. You've got me," said Darius.

"Of course I do," she answered and stared down into her lap.

They busted some moves. Waltz loops, salsa hip-shakes, a saucy jitterbug twirl. They moved well together—they might have had some professional training. Jahangir froze them in mid-spin, settled back into his burgundy leather lounge chair, and heaved a sigh of relief. There *was* a needle in the haystack, after all. He'd gotten thousands of applications, the vast majority of which hadn't merited more than a moment's look by his screeners. He'd gotten them from people who'd had too much to drink, from people who'd had too much to smoke, from people who figured they'd get chosen if they just said "fuck" and "cunt" enough. His team had culled the applications down to fifty and turned them over to him. He'd gotten up to thirty-nine and was starting to despair: Not a single one had come close. But then he'd clicked number forty into life and now here he was, staring at Darius and Vala in a daze of disbelief, as if he'd stumbled on footage of the actual real-life Santa Claus. And what a gift Saint Nick was bringing—these were the ones he'd been waiting for.

He watched the rest of their application holo-vid, praying they wouldn't blow it. And they didn't. In their closing scene, Darius and Vala clinked flutes filled with bubbly, then smiled into the camera with their glasses hoisted. Their message was clear: *We're the ones.* Jahangir froze them in mid-motion, went into the kitchen to brew an espresso, and tried to get sober about what he'd just seen. For some time, he'd had a mental checklist of the qualities he was looking for. *Charm and charisma*—check. *Physical beauty*—they were spectacular. And then there was a more subtle requirement—*contrast*. Here they didn't just hit a home run—they knocked it out of the park. He was rich, she was poor. He was white, she was Latina. He was outgoing, she was introverted. He was confident, she was shy. He was the privileged guy who people might want to see get taken down a notch, she was the Cinderella girl looking for "I am woman!" moments of empowerment.

He sipped his espresso and concluded that he could trust his instincts—he hadn't been deluding himself. Charisma, looks, contrast—they were the perfect couple.

He couldn't give them the job yet, of course. He'd have to do due diligence. Meet them in person, fact-check their resumés, contact their references, run their names through court and crime databases. For now, though, he could stop screening other applicants.

He turned off the holo-vid and said their names out loud, just to hear how they sounded. "Darius di Selva. Valentina Cortes."

He liked how the syllables rolled off his tongue. They were good names. Sexy names. Name-in-lights names.

Wow. That too, even.

He brought up his voice app and dialed them.

-JaHan9IR-

THEY CONVENED THE NEXT EVENING in their Hollywood Hills apartment—that white leather sofa they'd been sitting on was theirs. Two hours later, he emerged into an unlikely Los Angeles rain feeling keener than ever about his new hires but worried because he didn't have a done deal yet—they hadn't said yes to doing X-rated.

He'd waited as long as he could before sharing that aspect of his project. Initially, he'd hesitated because he hadn't wanted to put the Fundies in a lather—and then, having saddled himself with this small moral failure, he'd decided to hold off on telling Darius and Vala until enough trust had been established for them to be more open to his explanation. He'd waited until dessert, sopapillas that she'd made for the occasion, before swallowing hard and plunging in. Would they consider having sex on camera, with each other and with others, too? They'd be rewarded handsomely.

He laughed, she blanched. "How handsomely?" he asked.

"Millions of dollars handsomely. Many, many millions."

"That's mighty good looking," Darius said.

She turned to him, looking close to tears. His smile faded. "We'll have to talk about it," he said.

"Please do that," Jahangir said, "and let me know."

Ten minutes into his car-service ride home, Jahangir's cell phone gave its signature chirp. It was a two-word text from Darius, and it made Jahangir laugh. "Fuck. Yeah." The entrepreneur fist-pumped and texted back, "Fab! Dinner with Vala tomorrow night? And you the next? Make sure this is right for us all."

He settled back into the rich leather seat of the limo, allowed himself a satisfied smile, and ran the numbers one more time in his head. A hundred million sales at an average of four dollars per episode, a ten-episode season for starters—that added up to four billion dollars in gross revenue. Allocate twenty percent to sales, marketing and branding, subtract a very generous four percent for royalties (Darius and Vala would come out of this *rich*) and a round fifty percent for taxes, and he was left with more than a billion dollars. *Jahangir Persad, billionaire. Jesus.* What did a person do with all that money? How many yachts could one guy buy? He laughed aloud.

The driver looked at him sharply in the rear-view mirror. "I just thought of something funny, that's all," Jahangir reassured him. "I'm not crazy. No need to worry, friend."

"Good. You never know."

The driver was dark-skinned. Jahangir gave it a shot. "Where you from, *bai*?"

"Kolkata," the man answered easily. "And you?"

"Rajasthan via San Jose. What brought you to Los Angeles?"

"Chasing a dream. Like everyone, I guess. Dreams are good, right? When I dream, I see a three-bedroom house in Sierra Madre. A small yard, a park nearby where my kids can play. What do you see when you dream?"

Jahangir closed his eyes, asked himself the question, and saw Darius and Vala come in. Their bodies were joined in a single sinuous form, writhing as one while people watched around the world, billions of people watching with their hearts racing, watching and touching themselves, watching and touching each other, watching and coming, singly and together, as the dollars came rolling in to his bank account like waves rolling onto the shore.

The man from Kolkata was watching him through the rear-view mirror, waiting for his answer.

Jahangir said, "I see a mountain in the mists that's made of gold."

-Vala-

"**A**RE YOU QUITE SURE," Jahangir asked Vala, "that you're okay with doing X-rated reality entertainment? When I first mentioned it, you looked appalled."

They were sitting at a table for two at Chez Antoine's. White linen tablecloths, dim lighting, waiters who made you feel like it was an honor just to be there. The restaurant was her and Darius's go-to place for special occasions. Birthdays, the anniversary of their first time together, that time he'd landed a gig he was sure would make all the difference. She was wearing a knee-length black tulip skirt and a white silk blouse that was classically elegant yet snug enough to flatter her figure. Four-inch heels and an Akoya pearl necklace that had been one of Darius's first gifts to her. An extra open button at the breast. Stylish and sexy, that was the ticket.

She gazed into her bright pink cosmo and wondered how to answer. Her heart was skittering nervously. What had unfolded in her life over the last two days seemed fantastical, as dreamlike as winning the lottery. Yesterday she'd been invisible and scuffling, tomorrow she'd be rich and famous—the American Dream was blowing through her window like a hurricane. She discreetly pinched the skin of her forearm and got the sting she was looking for. "You're right, I was," she said, "but I'm fine with it now. That's what matters, isn't it?"

"What brought about your change of heart?"

"I decided to view it as an opportunity. I've dedicated my life to personal growth. What better way is there to challenge yourself than with sex? It defines us, don't you think?" She looked at him and asked, "Why did you go after civilians? Why didn't you do the obvious and hire porn stars?"

"I considered it," he acknowledged, "but only briefly. I decided that I wanted this to be a *reality* show, not a pretend show, and real meant all-natural and enhancement-free. No collagen, no implants—and no faked orgasms, either. I wanted real people and real sex. How likely was I to find that in Porn World?"

"Porn *is* phony, isn't it? Everything is prettied up—and so impersonal!"

"Exactly so—and that makes it less pretty to me."

"I can't stand porn," she said, nodding in agreement. "I find it ugly. But Darius—he loves it. He keeps hoping I'll watch it with him."

"Guys," Jahangir said, "they tend to be that way."

"Darius wants me to try a lot of things," she said.

Jahangir sipped his Connemara and placed it carefully back on the table. "Is Darius into personal growth the same way you are? Does he want you to grow and change?"

"The man gives me opportunities," she said and laughed into her empty glass. "I'll have another cosmo, please."

The waiter appeared with their main courses and was followed moments later by the wine steward, who showily set them up with two pricey half-bottles that Jahangir had selected without consulting him.

She was surprised at how comfortable she felt with him. She'd come into the evening expecting to feel terrified of not passing muster. She was poor, he was rich——he'd be the one judging her performance, not the other way around. In addition, if the tabloids were to be believed, he was quite the man about town. How many smart, beautiful women had he shared romantically-lit corner tables like this one with? Hundreds, she figured. Probably bedded them, too. But the actual Jahangir had proved to be attentive, unassuming, and easy to talk to. He seemed like a genuinely nice person.

"What about you?" Vala said. "Do you see yourself growing from this adventure?"

"Not particularly." He shrugged. "I like myself fine the way I am."

"Why are you doing it, then?"

"For the money. And the fun. And the adventure."

"Anything else?"

Now it was Jahangir's turn to sip and think. Eventually he said, "For thousands of years, Erotopia has been refining the arts of love. What do they know that we don't? I'd really like to find out."

So there it was: He was headed to Erotopia for the money and the sex. She fingered the stem of her wineglass and gazed into his eyes—he returned her look blandly, innocently. She liked his eyes, she decided tipsily. Yes, she liked them a lot. They were charcoal gray, and kind and gentle, and there were flecks of other shades there too if one looked closely enough. Emerald-green, and chestnut, and here and there a flash of gold.

"I'm so glad we'll be doing this together," Jahangir said finally. "I knew you were beautiful—I didn't know I'd like you, too."

"You do?" she answered, pleased and surprised.

He nodded. "You're honest. You're real. You want to connect."

She flushed. "Thank you." She grew silent and then said, "Relationships are tough, though. Once you lose trust, it's not easy." The dark-berry notes of the pinot noir Jahangir had chosen for her were swelling her mouth and gullet—she experienced a passing dizziness. "I'm intimate until he's proven guilty," she said and giggled into her glass.

"A sense of humor, too," Jahangir said. "Intimate until proven guilty. You're perfect for this. Damn."

He contemplated her approvingly—she felt warm and glowing all over.

"And you—you'll make a great boss," she said. Then she flushed and looked away. It was she, not he, who was being interviewed, she who was under the microscope. And now she'd gone and passed judgment on him. Had she seemed presumptuous? She didn't want him thinking that she didn't know her place.

He didn't seem at all put off. "A toast," he said and raised his glass.

"To Erotopia," she offered.

He expanded gently: "To *connection*, and Erotopia."

She riffed off that: "To connection, *on* Erotopia."

They leaned toward each other, touched glasses, and drank. A strand of hair had fallen over her eye. It made for sultry forties noir, and sultry forties noir was good, but it felt like an obstruction. She couldn't see out—he couldn't see in. With a slim finger, she whisked it away.

Her breasts in their tight white silk blouse were resting on the table—they'd landed there when she'd leaned forward to clink glasses. Propped up like that, they had to look plump and inviting, especially with that peek-a-boo buttonhole she'd left open. She considered sitting back and decided against it. He had beautiful eyes, and he was such a sweet man. She'd leave her breasts there just like that, laid out for him on the white linen.

-DARIUS-

"THE BEST MARGARITAS IN TOWN," Darius said, hoisting his glass. "Margaritas are my trademark. My brand, you might say. I'm the Margarita Man."

They were sitting at the bar of Chez Antoine's, facing images of themselves in a ceiling-high mirror that was fronted by long shelves of liquor. Shadowy banquettes and mahogany wainscoting were reflected in the spotless glass. A jazz piano was tinkling. Jahangir said, "Have you put 'Margarita Man' on your resume?"

"No, but I've considered it. It's a brutal world. A guy's got to differentiate."

"Your looks don't give you a leg up?"

"Everyone's good looking in this town—and like they say, looks aren't everything." Darius salted his finger, dunked it in tequila, sucked. He thought to himself, *Sure, go for it,* and added, "You've also got to have a big dick."

"Excuse me?" asked Jahangir, blinking.

"It's not enough to advertise—you've got to deliver the goods too, right? And you've also got to have a big pair of balls when you're just a piece of meat, which is what everyone is in this town. You've got to be willing to be told you're nobody, then get up off the floor and come back for more—and keep doing it again and again."

"Not your style?"

Darius made a face. "Apparently not. Vala thinks I'd do better if I"—he made air quotes—"'went out and scrapped more,' if I"—air quotes again—"'acted less entitled.' She wants me to be more aggressive and assertive—I should be one of those guys who takes

49

the hill no matter what. And who knows, maybe she's right. It's just not how I'm wired, though." He stared glumly into his drink and eventually came out with, "What do you think of monogamy, Jahangir?"

"As little as possible," the celebrated playboy answered and with a wry smile sipped his Connemara.

"Seriously."

"I decided some time ago that it's not for me. That doesn't make it not for everyone."

"Well, I think monogamy is unnatural. Men were put on this planet to spread their seed, not stay loyal and true. We don't fool around because we're treacherous and unfaithful—we do it because Mother Nature programmed us that way. It's how we propagate our DNA." He paused, swigged and resumed. Jahangir was listening with a cocked head and what seemed to be genuine interest. "And you know what else?" an emboldened Darius continued. "Women may tell themselves otherwise, but they actually want us to be that way. They work for Mother Nature too, right? The more men a woman has hitting on her, the better chance she has of landing a good mate. Men fucking around—and women fucking around, too!—is part of God's grand plan."

"Have you talked with Vala about this?"

"Not for some time now," Darius answered with a scoffing laugh. "She's fallen in with a women's studies crowd. You know the type. They're all 'patriarchy' all the time, except for when it's 'testosterone poisoning.' Just thinking about them makes me want to go to a whorehouse, light up a cigar, and get my dick sucked."

"Their grievances are real, though, don't you think?"

"Hell, yes! I'm all for genuine equality between men and women. Equal pay, smashing the glass ceiling, all that. But for equality to actually mean anything, it has to run both ways. Women deserve to be seen and respected—and so do men. Women deserve to have their feelings taken seriously—and so do men. And it's not like it's always the men who get the goodies and it's always the women who get screwed. Men don't live as long as women, and it's not just genetics—it's stress. Over three times as many men as women commit suicide. And don't get me going on how the divorce courts favor the so-called gentler sex." He paused. "Patriarchy fucks us all over. That's what women don't understand."

Jahangir's smile had been broadening as he listened. Now he laughed delightedly. "Who knew? You're a 'masculinist'!"

"I'm a what?"

"The male version of a feminist."

Darius thought it over, nodded. He was feeling grateful. Over the years, he'd come to expect so much hostility toward his perspective that Jahangir's polite interest was landing like applause. "I guess I am. I'm for male empowerment—our right to show up as we really are. People with penises—we're under siege, my friend."

Jahangir looked unconvinced. "Are we? I'm not so sure."

"Look: I get it," Darius answered promptly. "This is still very much a man's world. But that doesn't mean men aren't disadvantaged in some ways, too. The winds of feminism are blowing so strong that it's difficult for men's voices to be heard, especially about their loneliness and suffering."

"Are you lonely? Are you suffering?"

"Not a fair question. This is a job interview, not a confessional."

"It's an unusual job," Jahangir offered gently. "It's a job that calls for melodrama."

"Ah, well," Darius said, "you'll get plenty of that with me and Vala." He spun his glass between his fingers and said, "You've got dark skin, Jahangir. Dark skin, and a dick. Tell me—do you feel like a member of the dominator class?"

"The answer isn't yes or no," Jahangir answered with a shrug. "I don't relate to the framework. Politics isn't my thing. Not political politics, and not sexual politics, either. I'm into people, not groups or tribes."

Darius aimed a finger at his own chest. "Me, white man. Me, sinner. I have one duty only, to be 'woke.'"

"How do you feel about that?" Jahangir asked with a sympathetic nod.

Darius rolled his eyes. "Like a masculinist—that's how I feel. Like, I've got rights, too. Like, please get out of my fucking face."

"Masculinism *does* get a bad rap, doesn't it?"

"It sure does. But it's not about the right to be Neanderthal."

"What is it about, then?"

"It's about the right to have feelings. But that's not right, exactly—it's about the right to have feelings, *too*. Women get mad at us for not being in touch with our emotions—and then they get mad at us when we do experience them, and don't just soldier on and grin and bear it." He stared into his margarita and eventually said, so quietly and sorrowfully that he might have been talking to himself, "I get it, I really do. When people look at me, they don't see a survivor."

Jahangir couldn't help himself; he laughed out loud.

"There you go," Darius said. "You just proved my point. You haven't met my parents, dude. My silver spoon had shit on it." His voice rose. "What, because I'm white and come from money, I'm not allowed to have feelings?" He waggled his finger at Jahangir. "Don't be falling for their crap, my friend. Fucking identity politics."

"I think I get it," his companion said eventually. "You're not being insensitive to women's emotions so much as you're being sensitive to men's. You're sensing an unfairness that needs righting."

Darius nodded.

"You're a warrior for justice."

Again he nodded. "Thank you. Yes, it seems that way to me." He paused, searching for the right words. "It's like that's my job as a man."

"As a *real* man."

"Sure. That works, too."

"The real man sticks up for what's right and true. Is that what you're saying?"

"I suppose it is. The real man is a warrior for good. These are crazy times, right? All heat and no truth. The real man sees through all that and stays aligned with the sanity beneath."

"Can a woman be a real man?"

Darius pondered the question and said, "I suppose so, sure. But women are wired differently. They tend to be more emotional. I mean, Jesus, I feel guilty just saying that, but it's true—it's hormones. Sane women will tell you the same thing."

"What about you? Are you a real man?"

Darius signaled for another margarita and said, "I try to be."

"How about in the bedroom? What's the real man like there?"

"That one's easy." He took a bite of his grass-fed burger, brought his white cloth napkin to his lips and with uncharacteristic daintiness wiped it clean. "Real men take charge in the bedroom. Do you remember how, when you were in high school, you'd be alone with a girl, and you'd both be feeling awkward because kissing just might happen soon? The real man cuts through the uncertainty and kisses the damn girl."

"Or puts his hand on her breast?"

"Well, sure, if he wants to and he thinks it might be okay. There's this, like, quantum space between yes and no. The real man steps into the opening."

"He's courageous—that's what you're saying, right? The real man steps into the opening without knowing what he'll find."

"That's right. In a war, it might be a bullet. In the bedroom, it might mean getting his face slapped."

"How about in an elevator?"

"Like, with a woman you've never seen before?"

Jahangir nodded.

Darius's eyes widened; he felt indignant and aggrieved. "No, no, no," he answered sharply. "Real men step into the gap, but they never step over the line. Real men respect women—they don't grope."

"What about penises? Do they have bigger ones?"

Darius looked at him with consternation, then broke into a loud barking laugh. "What is this, a bozo test? A little Neanderthal is a good thing, but too much might be a problem? Jahangir, we're both educated men. We both know that dick size is a function of a person's DNA, not their 'manly'"—air quotes again—"values. If you have a big one, it's just dumb luck, kind of like winning the lottery." He fell silent. When he spoke again, it was more softly. "Jahangir, I've been wanting to tell you something ever since you asked us to go X-rated. It's a little personal, but"—he hesitated, his expression a mix of bashfulness and pride—"well, I happen to have a really big dick. Vala doesn't call me 'Monster' for nothing." He met Jahangir's steady gaze. "You're one lucky mother, did you know that? Oversized schlongs are ratings gold."

"Are they? I didn't know," Jahangir deadpanned.

"You don't? You're joking, right?" But then he decided to play along. "Of course they are. Just watch some porn. I'm so big I could be black, dude." Jahangir bit into his burger silently. Darius eyed his companion and said, "You're wondering why I say things like that, right?"

Jahangir met his gaze. "Yes, I am. You seem to like to misbehave."

"Dragging shit out of the basement," Darius said with a shrug. "It's just another something that we real men do."

They said their goodbyes outside Chez Antoine. A familiar momentary uncertainty was followed by a manly hug, two strong backslaps, and a concluding double-down handshake.

Darius felt heartened, happy, and a little bit tipsy. "Tell me," he asked, "did I nail the audition?"

"You did," Jahangir answered. "You da man."

"Damn, I'm stoked."

"Me, too," said Jahangir. He turned away with a nod and a soft smile. Darius called out "to be continued" to his departing back. He watched his new boss get in his waiting car. Then he whipped out his phone and called Vala.

-Jahangir-

ACK IN HIS HOTEL SUITE, Jahangir found himself thinking about Darius's late-breaking news flash about the proportions of his member. *I'm not a size queen,* Jahangir thought as he undressed. *In fact, I'm not into body parts at all! I'm not a tit man, I'm not an ass man, I'm not a leg man. What am I into, then?* He pondered the question and came up with a one-word answer: *Beauty.*

Yes, that was it. Beauty, which showed up in the bedroom in mysterious ways. He found it in his bedmates' lines and shadows—in the hidden crease at the inside of the thigh, in the ripple of a muscle rising up through supple skin, in the dark curve that separates the breast from the rest and then fades into nothing. He found it in his lovers' flaws—only two days ago, he'd been stunned into stillness by a C-section scar on the otherwise immaculate body of his latest playmate, a slender redhead named Yvonne. Most of all, he found it in his partners' glory. Nothing delighted him more than the stardust sparkle of a lover's ecstasy.

A shiver ran down his spine as he remembered his time with Yvonne. Her body had trembled from toes to temple when she came.

I guess that makes me a girly-man, he concluded with a wry smile. *Mister Sensitive, that's me. The Beauty Guy. Mister Artsy-Fartsy.*

Fortunately—he smiled again—he'd have Darius along to do the heavy grunting.

Yes, he decided, he was blessed. He'd really nailed it with his Chosen People. Darius and Vala had wonderfully contrasting personalities—and great relationship issues, too. And then there was their sexual politics. Step right up for your battles royal, the male view versus the female!

Won't that be fine for my wallet! Jahangir thought.

He corrected himself: *My pocketbook.*

He slipped on his silk pajamas and, smiling wryly, climbed contentedly into bed.

- Jahangir -

TWO RECENT PHYSICS BREAKTHROUGHS had made intergalactic journeying possible. Both had emerged from the improbable mind of Emmanuel Korski, a renegade six-foot-eight Jamaican physicist with thick rust-colored dreads and a savant-like capacity to penetrate the secrets of the universe. Korski's First Insight had produced the math that allowed physical objects to slip through wormholes; his second one, published six months later, ushered in the warp-drive speeds that compressed the trip into a manageable time frame by contemporary standards. There'd be no yearlong journeys for this crew of eronauts, and no cryogenic or deep-slumber interventions, either.

His discoveries had stirred massive public interest, much government funding, and greatly accelerated implementation schedules. Eight years to the day after Korski published his First Insight, and three weeks out from Earth with four days of travel still ahead, Jahangir emerged from his stateroom into the spacecraft's simply furnished common area to find Vala weeping on its one sofa. She was making stifled sobbing sounds, her chest was heaving, and her mascara had smeared into goth globs on her cheeks.

Until then, the three eronauts had carefully kept things low-key. They'd all seemed to understand that if they quarreled, they wouldn't be able to get away from each other, and so they'd steered a wide berth around difficult topics. Even Darius, who loved nothing more than to stir the pot, had exercised self-restraint. Jahangir and Vala had spent their time reading—biographies of entrepreneurs for him, romance novels for her. Darius had sketched and doodled. He especially enjoyed inventing superheroes, two of which he'd shared with

Jahangir. Flycatcher Girl had enormous breasts and a super-long prehensile tongue, which she used to dispatch pests and villains. SuperPenis swelled to outrageous proportions when aroused by injustice—his weapon was a thick fluid that he used to blind, bind and even drown people—his balls rotated like wheels and gave him cloud-of-dust acceleration.

And now here was Vala, who lost none of her beauty in her distress. "Where's Darius?" he asked cautiously.

She stopped sobbing long enough to say, "Fuck Darius," and started up again.

It was just the two of them, then. He plunked down next to her, said "May I?" and offered her his arms. She moved into them easily, sobbing into his shoulder and in due course mumbling into his chest.

"I can't hear you," he whispered from so close in that he could feel his breath against her ear.

"I won't have sex with him," she said. "It's been over a month now."

"Why not?"

"He cheated on me. With Roxy LaRue."

"Who?"

"A porn star. A famous deep-throat artist. He had a picture of her on his cell phone. She was staring up at the camera and had her mouth wrapped around him. That workshop I went to? I needed to be away from him. I needed to be with myself." She dissolved into a new round of weeping, then turned a woeful gaze on her companion. "Do you know why Darius and I are really doing this?"

"No, why?" asked Jahangir, who felt suddenly weighted down, as if she'd just attached a dumbbell to his chest.

"Because I'm on the verge of breaking up with him. This is his last-ditch effort to keep us together. You know, this 'great adventure.' I figured okay, why not. If it didn't work, I could say we'd tried everything. I could leave with a clean conscience—and a big fat nest egg to back me up. I'd be a celebrity, not another loser of a *chica* thrown out into the street." She shook her head sadly. "That workshop? I fucked the lead trainer."

"Ah," said Jahangir. His eyes grew wide as insight dawned. "And soon you'll be on Erotopia."

"That's right," she affirmed, nodding. "The land of the revenge fucks. Don't get mad, get even, right? *Dios*, I was stupid!"

Her floodgates opened and her many fears came pouring out. She should never have said yes to making this trip. She was a fraud, an imposter, the worst. Like with her looks: Men found her attractive, but she was a total dud in bed, your proverbial hot mess. She'd never let herself be ass-fucked. She couldn't deep-throat. She couldn't even come just from regular fucking!

"I'm a total idiot," she said and started crying again.

Jahangir was on the verge of offering reassuring words when Darius emerged into the room. It was a heartstopping view: blond hair and rippling naked muscles above tighty-whities and a pair of mismatched argyle socks. He looked from Jahangir to Vala, then turned back to him and said, "Did she—?"

"She did," Vala cut in, with an edge to her voice that could have cut glass. "She told him about how you fucked Roxy. She told him about how she fucked Zack."

"Zack," said Darius to Jahangir. "She fucked someone named Zack." He plopped himself onto a bolted-down metal chair. "I didn't fuck Roxy," he continued. "She gave me a blow job. She gave me the eye at a bar and offered me a freebie. Right then, right there, in her car, easy-peasy. What guy in his right mind would say no to getting head from the world's greatest cocksucker?"

"A guy who's in a committed relationship," muttered Vala from between clenched teeth.

Darius threw up his hands. "Jesus! Why do we keep having this conversation?"

"Because you keep cheating on me."

"That wasn't cheating! I went to the circus. I visited the sword swallower."

He and Vala turned imploring gazes on Jahangir, in their eyes the same request. *Tell me I'm right. Rule for me, please.*

Jahangir didn't rattle easily, but that's how he was feeling now. For the first time, he was having second thoughts about his choice of companions. He'd wanted a couple with ragged edges, but this one was coming apart. He pursed his lips unhappily. Why had he stinted on the due diligence? He should have done a thorough relationship assessment. Questionnaires, interviews, therapists. But he'd let his heart lead him, his heart and his dick. And now he was paying for it.

"This isn't good," he said. "I need you to come into Erotopia feeling in love and connected. You need to be lovebirds on a honeymoon."

Vala shook her head dubiously. "I don't know if I can do that," she said.

"I can," said Darius. "I can pretend. I'm a pro."

"What if we try this?" Jahangir proposed. "A middle ground, a soft up-ramp—you two spend our remaining travel days getting back on good terms with each other. Share laughs, start liking each other again. And then, when you get to Erotopia, commit to making a fresh start."

Darius turned to Vala. "What say, Mouse? Shall we?"

"I don't know," she said, shaking her head. "I am *so* pissed off at you!"

"Well, get over it," said Darius. "You're in show biz now. Be a trouper."

She opened her mouth to answer but was silenced before she could speak by an uncanny stillness that descended on the spacecraft. There followed a dim trembling in their tin-can shell and then a rumbling so faint that Jahangir wasn't sure he'd actually heard it. He tumbled into a black abyss, for how long he couldn't say. When he emerged, his skin was damp and his heart felt huge and hot inside his chest. Vala was sitting next to him and gazing at Darius adoringly. "Of course I can open my heart to him," she said. "I'm crazy in love with this man."

"Thank you," said Jahangir as his heart flooded over with emotion. "Thank you."

"No, thank *you*," Vala said, and there was so much gratitude in her voice that Jahangir was seized by the desire to bend her back in a kiss right then and there.

Her guy looked as gorgeous as she did. Jahangir wanted to kiss him, too.

Darius wasn't looking at either of them. He was staring with slack-jawed theatricality at his underpants, which were surging impressively at the crotch. "Boys and girls," he said, "behold. From out of nowhere. What the fuck?"

The Welcome Waterings

*"On Erotopia as on Earth, the mind apprehends
space in four directions. In Darwinian terms,
this translates into four strategies for survival
(forward/advance, backward/retreat, up/climb,
down/burrow), plus a fifth one, staying still.
Because of the mind's limitations, we see time
through much the same lens—we go backward
into the past and forward into the future.
This is the starting point of Erotopia's main
psychological paradigm. Space-time therapy
maps a person's space-time strategies against the
null point of perfect equanimity."*

—Ulrich Von Zeitler, *First Report to
the Senate Select Sub-Committee on
Intergalactic Affairs* (2049)

-JAHANGIR-

SUNLIGHT FILTERED THROUGH the lush vegetation, dappling Bree's back as she and Jahangir headed down the narrow dirt path. Her green dress fit snugly around her hips and legs but left her back mostly exposed. She had an athlete's firm, muscular haunches. His eyes kept returning to a patch of satiny down that spanned her sacrum like blonde moss and kept flickering in and out of shadow.

He thought back to something she'd said earlier. "You're home now." Until that moment, it had never occurred to him that he might not be 'home,' that he might not be anything other than deeply happy and fulfilled. Even here on Erotopia, it felt no different—he carried home with him, he inhabited it like a comfy shell. From his earliest days, he'd felt singularly blessed, and now, in his early thirties, his life felt damn near idyllic. Bree's words had him wondering if he'd been missing something. Might a mountain of happiness be out there beyond the hills he'd always known? He came up alongside her and tiptoed into the question. "Are you still as happy as you were when you sent us that letter, Bree?"

"If anything, I'm happier." Her next thoughts emerged from a deep and solemn place. "Jahangir, we all have a choice to make. We can choose to celebrate, or we can choose not to. We can choose bliss, or we can glaze over and forget about it. I know: 'Forgetting about it' may not seem like a choice, but it is. It's a habit, and habits are choices that have fallen asleep. When I got here, I woke up."

Her choice of words was a bit confounding—he couldn't really relate to all that business about being "asleep" and "waking up." He wasn't prepared to dismiss her out of hand, though. This was one smart woman, and that stirring in his gut was real. She might know something he didn't.

He asked her the question he was asking himself. "Were you happy back on Earth?"

"I thought I was," she answered easily, "but now I see, not really. I was always waiting for my next success to save me. If I could just get my Ph.D., I'd be happy. Then it was, if I could just get tenure, I'd be happy. Salvation was always in the future—it was never *now*, it was never *this*. Here, I don't look to tomorrow to save me. I save myself, every minute of every day. I save myself by taking all the pleasure I can in the gifts the Great Ones have given us. They want us to be ecstatic, Jahangir, and so I embrace the life ecstatic. Anything less would be—well, it would be disrespectful!"

"It sounds exhausting."

"Not really," she answered with a smile. "It's more like a warm bath than a party."

"Well, we're hoping to record you in your warm bath. You and your fellow Erotopians. Would you sign a consent form for me?"

"I would, but there's no need. I'm never going back to Earth, and I've got nothing to hide."

"And the locals?"

"Don't waste your time asking them to sign something. It will just confuse them." She paused. "How will you be doing the recording?"

"We're using nanocams and corneal implants. I'm wired up right now."

"It's not just Darius and Vala? I'd have thought you'd stay behind the camera."

"It's not my first choice," he said with a sigh, "but if that's what the show requires, I'll do it."

"Does all that rig make you self-conscious?"

"Less all the time. I'm getting used to it."

They came to a stone bench with a pair of butt cheeks painted on it in bright pink. Jovially they settled themselves on the designated locations. She snuggled up against him and laid her head on his shoulder. "I'm so thrilled you're here," she said. "A friend from Earth! You close the circle for me."

"It's amazing," Jahangir said. "It all happened so fast. Half a dozen years ago, this would have been unthinkable. Earthlings in another galaxy. Earthlings on a distant planet."

"Climate change had a lot to do with it, don't you think? With the urgency."

He nodded. "The planet's been heating up way too fast. People are looking for an off ramp."

Bree nodded. "But then word came back about a faraway culture of sex and pleasure, and they were handed a delicious distraction. Exit anxiety, enter lust and greed."

"My two favorite vices," Jahangir said.

She laughed and put a friendly hand on his thigh. "Questions. You must have questions."

"I do indeed—let's start with this. You decided to stay. Why?"

"It was the hardest decision I've ever made; I agonized. I'd fallen in love, with Wyldermon and the entire planet. I'd been handed the rarest of opportunities, the opportunity to actually be happy. Erotopia may not be heaven, but it gives you a tailwind, not a headwind. To stay here, though, I'd have to leave behind people and a world I loved."

"What was the turning point?"

"When I decided that guilt was optional. I'd been beating myself up for abandoning my friends and family on Earth, but then I realized I could just as easily tell myself that I was being in service to them—I was modeling the pursuit of happiness. But that wasn't all; there was something else. A moment, really."

"Oh?"

"When Wyldermon finally got it through my thick head that I could actually stay. I'd been assuming that the day would come when an Earth crew came to quote unquote rescue me. They might come in black robes, they might come in camouflage, but they would come, guaranteed. I had nightmares about it. But then Wyldermon explained that Erotopians have a technology that turns away incoming hostiles." She turned to him and asked cautiously, "Did you by any chance have an odd experience while you were en route?"

He gave her a strange look. "We did. It stopped a disagreement dead in its tracks. The love bomb, we got to calling it."

"That would be it."

"The three of us came way too close to having sex."

"Yes, well." She blushed. "Ulrich and I actually did. We agreed to pretend it had never happened."

"So that thing that hit us was what, a long-distance hello from Erotopia? A great big blast of 'welcome!'?"

"Not exactly," she answered with a small wry smile. "It was a test. Erotopians know how good they have it. They're determined not to let bad actors in. That blast of love they sent you? It was their blocking shield. They send out a concentrated ray of love. If it's absorbed, the visitors are allowed in. In that case, it becomes their visa."

"And if it's not? What would have happened if we'd failed the test?"

"No one knows for sure, but we believe your circuits would have gone haywire. Your computer systems would have imploded, and your nervous systems, too. You'd have gone drifting off into untethered space."

"Forever?"

"Forever."

Jahangir raised his eyebrows. "That's mighty harsh treatment."

"You could also say they're just taking care of themselves. They're as hard as nails when they have to be."

"And now you're here, and you're pursuing happiness. How're your studies going?"

She laughed. "Wonderfully. I'm following the Way of the Orgasm."

"That's, what, a metaphor?"

"No," she answered, "it's an actual path. The sexual priestess path. I signed up for it when I decided to stay. My studies have been going great. I'm already an Acolyte, third degree. I seem to have a gift."

"That's like, what, a martial arts belt?"

She nodded. "We have four main levels—Acolytes, Celebrants, Priests and Priestesses, and High Priests and Priestesses at the very top. Cymanthea is a Celebrant. Kri'Bondai and Kri'Zhalee are a High Priest and High Priestess—they're two of the Nine."

"What did they do to get that far up the hierarchy?"

"They showed talent and they practiced diligently."

"Are the Nine a governmental body? Or maybe quasi-governmental?"

She shook her head. "No, more like they're our educators-in-chief. They're where wisdom and pleasure intersect most superbly." They sat silently for a time. Then she said, "Now I've a question for you."

"Go for it."

"May I put my hand on you?"

"You mean, my cock?"

"That's right."

He looked at her, startled. "Whoa, Bree. That doesn't feel right. We're not lovers."

"That's where you're mistaken. We are."

"We are? Did I get blackout drunk with you back home?"

Bree laughed and shook her head. "That's where you Earth folks have it wrong—we're always making love. We're making love when we have a great conversation. We're making love when we're sharing a joke. We're even making love when we're arguing! Arguing is a plea for understanding—it's an unskilled plea for love. We're loving each other when we're dancing, and we're always dancing, Jahangir—all of us, always. We're dancing to the music of Source."

Somewhere above them, a bird chirped. "Me-haw! Me-haw!" Jahangir looked for it, couldn't see it. Then suddenly there it was, as big as an eagle, sweeping through the canopy with a great whoosh.

He felt a sudden onrush of gratitude. The emotion seemed to have come from the bird—its wings had maybe tickled his heart.

He turned his head toward Bree and kissed her at the nearest available location, on her hair just above her ear where the thick, cool rope of her lowest braid began. He took her hand and placed it on him. "When in Erotopia," he said.

-Vala-

A NARROW STREAM JOINED VALA and her two companions
as they walked along, lending its merry chatter to the rustle
of their footsteps and the birdsong overhead. They crossed
a delicately arched wood bridge and arrived at a spread of
moss beneath a tree with susurrating silver leaves. The men slowed,
looked at each other and smiled. Vala's heart started galloping. This
would be the site of her disgrace.

They held hands and formed a small circle. She found the courage to look directly at them and took heart in their kind smiles. The High Priest said, "You are a perfect Vala."

At first his words rang insincere—the notion was ridiculous, absurd! But then she recalled the counsel of more than one workshop and said, "Thank you. I try to be."

"A massage, perhaps?"

She nodded.

"Clothes on or off?"

"Off, please," she responded, surprising herself with her boldness. It had to be Lola, she decided, doing her thing, popping her head up out of the jungle, practicing guerrilla liberation. She settled into her sassiness and took her sweet time taking her clothes off, treating the men to a slow striptease. She enjoyed her performance; she felt in her power; this was something she was good at.

The greenery felt soft and welcoming beneath her. Above her the blue sky was peeking through the shimmering leaves and the men's sunny expressions were beaming down on her. She shut her eyes and felt Wyldermon settle in above her head and the High Priest at her feet. They started at precisely the same moment. The Wild guide's fingers went to her shoulder ridges fore and aft and worked their way in deeper. His hands were intelligent, sensitive, skillful—the muscles began to release. Vala could feel nothing in his touch but a humble desire to serve. No covert agendas, no distractedness, no impatience, none of the stuff she'd come to expect from men on Earth, every damn one of whom seemed to view massage as a toll on the road to getting laid.

Whereas Wyldermon was constantly discovering her with his hands, the High Priest didn't need to. It was as if he already knew her, or rather as if his *touch* did—far better, in fact, than she knew herself. His thumbs found a tender spot among the tendons of her left foot's sole. She felt a sharp pain followed by an equally abrupt release. She gasped and her back arched into the air.

He traveled deliberately from her feet up her legs, ankles to calves to knees to thighs, working just the right spots with just the right amount of pressure. They rolled her over, Wyldermon took his hands off her, and the High Priest continued up her back, kneading her waist, spreading her scapulae. From there he worked his way across her shoulders. When he got to the edges of her neck he paused, then went deeper.

And deeper.

And she was nine years old and back in Arizona.

She's peering around her mother's blue-and-white pleated skirt, clutching the rough cotton fabric. The door is open and there's a large presence on the threshold, a man in blue with his hat in his hands and a big hairy mole on his cheek. She can feel her mother's fear pouring off her.

"You killed him!" Mamá shouts.

The cop answers in a quiet voice, "No, ma'am. He killed himself."

"Like he put a gun to his head and shot himself?" Alma is still shouting. "Look me in the eye and tell me that, you blue fucking son-of-a-bitch."

"He killed himself," the mole-man says a second time. "And ma'am? It wouldn't do to fuck with me."

Vala emitted a choking gasp and sat up. Kri'Bondai was cradling her from behind. She closed her eyes and shuddered. Then she went under again.

They're on an Arizona highway in their junker pick-up. Alma is white-knuckling the wheel, and Diego is sitting between her and Vala, who is hanging onto the door handle so she won't get bounced off the seat. At the crest of a low, scruffy hill, a tall object rises up against a high bright blue sky. It's a giant cross. She makes the sign and watches it go whizzing by. She brings her gaze back to the road and takes Diego's hand in her free one. Ahead as far as she can see, there is only desert and highway.

A wave of sadness broke over her, an emotional tidal wave that left her choking for breath. Then her body shook, and the wave started to recede. She opened her eyes and stared blankly ahead. "They said he talked back," she whispered while Kri'Bondai held her close and rocked her from behind.

Eventually her storm of sadness passed and she collapsed back onto the moss. "I don't know where that came from," she said, "but I should probably be thanking you."

The High Priest contemplated her and said in a gentle voice. "Would you like to have an orgasm?"

She laughed at the straightforwardness of the question—he might as well have been asking if she'd like a cup of tea. Her first impulse was to say no. The emotional release she'd just experienced felt deeply non-sexual; Kri'Bondai's offer to take her across the border into Fuck-o-Rama seemed sudden, harsh, arbitrary. But then she realized that the separation was much less than she'd thought; in truth, it was limited to texture and degree. She'd experienced pleasure in the form of a massage—now she was being offered pleasure in the form of an orgasm.

An image came to her: Lola, strutting her stuff at the Limelight Club. This would be like that, she decided, only better. She'd be displaying her body *and* her orgasm.

"Have at it, magic men," she said.

-KRI'ZHALEE-

AS KRI'ZHALEE WALKED alongside Darius and Cymanthea in the Wildgarden, she was aware of a rare sense of bafflement. Her intuition was usually luminous and infallible. She'd been unable to find clarity with Darius, though, and with his Watering only minutes away, that was worrisome. She could only love him wonderfully if she understood him deeply, and this was proving hard to do. People usually had more than enough receptors to latch onto, portals providing access to their deep nature. If Darius had them, they were hidden. His psyche glistened like a steel container—his armor was damn near impenetrable. What to do? She decided to try a space-time diagnosis. It would be hasty and disorderly, not at all the usual process, but she'd get glimmerings anyway; it was a powerful process. And so, as they walked along, the High Priestess left her body, traveled to the High Throne, and summoned the spirit of Darius in the time-honored way.

Come to me, O child of Source. Show me how you dance with time and space.

His spirit-body came to her promptly, transported inside a silver cage. He was glowing all golden—the yellow hair on his head looked like a crown. Moments later he was doing her bidding, hurrying toward the front bars with his breath held tight and high inside his chest.

Two small steps were all she needed for her diagnosis. *Fast, faster, fastest!* That was Darius in a tight nutshell. The Earthling was chronically ahead of himself, always knocking on the next door with the last one still wide open, perennially fleeing forward from the beast not left behind.

Thank you for your soul's display, she transmitted to him. Darius's spirit-body bowed, smiled that golden smile of his, and dissolved away.

Yes, helpful, Kri'Zhalee decided as she left the High Throne and came back into her body. She cast a sidelong glance at Darius, who was gazing at her like nothing had happened. She understood him better now, but not well enough yet to serve him well at his Watering. She still had time, though, and another technique to fall back on. Time-shafting hadn't failed her yet, and although she wouldn't be able to initiate it until the Watering was underway, she was confident it would point her in the right direction.

Her new charge was checking her out and pretending not to. Kri'Zhalee softened, dialed in. Darius was hoping she'd open her *da'yo*, give him another flash of her body. More Earthling oddness: Why be furtive about something like that? She knew how pleasing her body was. Of course a person would want more.

She was so looking forward to watering this man. She'd need to take it slowly, though—he seemed so very fragile. Maybe find one single secret place, love it into light. The idea of a happier Darius flowed like a raft on a river from her head into her chest, where it exploded into the rapids of a heartgasm. There were sparks of red in this one, along with yellow and white. She breathed the energy back into her body, then sent it down her central channel and into her swollen storage zone.

Her *tra'da* opened wide and pulsed. A burst of moisture misted forth, beneath her quivering *da'yo*.

-DARIUS-

"**W**HAT WOULD YOU LIKE?**"** Kri'Zhalee asked.

"What would I like?" Darius echoed disbelievingly. "What would I *like?*"

He was holding hands with the High Priestess and Cymanthea in a small round clearing in the Wildgarden. Greenery rustled all around him beneath a disc of bright blue sky. He was having trouble believing his good fortune. He was about to be pleasured by two very sexy women, two very sexy *Erotopian* women, two very sexy Erotopian women who were *both on the priestess path.* What he was about to receive would be one for the record books. He was on his way.

"Would you like us on our knees?" Kri'Zhalee asked with a beguiling smile.

"Uh, yeah," he answered and started unbuttoning.

"Allow me," Cymanthea said. She kneeled, dislodged him, and got the sucking started. He was taken aback; her performance didn't stand out. Roxy and others had been better.

Then it was the High Priestess's turn. She got down on her knees and took over. Now he'd surely encounter the deep sexiness of excellence! But again the woman let him down. She projected passivity, distance, even contemplation. A sense of confusion arose in him as she circled him with her thumb and forefinger midway down his shaft, squeezed lightly, then brought her mouth very slowly down to her fingers, and just as slowly back up again. She did it all in a mood of meditative stillness, as if she were searching for something.

She repeated the action three times. Then her mouth came off him and she gazed up at him directly. Her lips were quivering and her eyes were moist. Her energy cloak had pulled back and her breasts were open in a full reveal. Dangling from her left nipple was a glistening pearl of what could only be milk. He stared transfixed as it grew more pendulous, then splashed down onto her thigh.

Moments later, a second drop emerged, matched this time by a twin on the right. Neither fell. Instead they hung there, as if awaiting something. They looked like nipple jewelry.

He stared uncomprehendingly at the tragic mask of her face. What the fuck was going on? How could things have gone so wrong, and how could it have happened so quickly? He'd been counting on great gagging blow jobs from two hot horny sluts, and instead he was getting, what the fuck, *milk*? Like he was a baby or something? And then there were the High Priestess's tears. What was that about? A woman gloms onto his cock, his really big cock, and she starts feeling sorry for him? Like it's pathetic or something?

A sense of panic overcame him. He had to get things back on track, and he had to do it right away. He grabbed two fistfuls of Kri'Zhalee's hair. "Open your mouth, slut!" he cried out, more loudly than he'd intended. "Do it now! Do as I say!"

She gazed up with a mystified look, then her eyes glazed over and she obeyed. He slid himself into the High Priestess's mouth, grasped her face firmly between his hands, and started to pump, steadily, firmly, in and out. The familiar motion relaxed and reassured him. Now, at last, things would get back on track. Kri'Zhalee would be turned on by his mouth-fucking, and this would get Cymanthea going, who'd dive in for her fair share. He'd seen it in a thousand holo-porns, but his expectations were disappointed again, and this too was the High Priestess's fault—she wasn't responding as she should. Her mouth was soft and pliable, but there was a frozenness about her, a vast caution, that told him she wasn't having fun.

Not getting off on his mouth-fucking her?

That riled him up even more.

What, Earth men weren't good enough for Erotopian women?

Now he wasn't just angry, he was furious. "Open your throat! I'm going to fuck your throat!" he hollered and started thrusting harder. He'd barely gotten started when Kri'Zhalee did something to him that was both subtle and decisive, and that stopped him in his tracks. A pinch, a squeeze, a matter of timing—he missed the nuances and was only aware that it had frozen his body, switched off his thinking brain, and left the rest of him feeling dizzy, adrift and more disassembled than not, as if his neurons were coming apart. As he wobbled on his feet like a boxer about to go down, she reached her right hand up to his chest and tapped his breastplate once and then again with two precise fingers.

Cymanthea was kneeling alongside, watching. Orange hair, green-and-gold dragon tattoos, horrified sea-green eyes. Then everything went black.

-Vala-

VALA WAS LYING NAKED on the moss beneath the willow tree. Her eyes were closed and her arms were splayed out above her head. She felt relaxed and happy. She could hear the brook splashing by alongside, bearing its cheery message.

She was starting to feel physically aroused, which was distinctly odd because not a soul was touching her. She was quite sure about this, and even more so about her turn-on. It was all very confusing. Her body was growing warmer and her vulva was swelling. She opened her eyes, just to make sure, and was confirmed in her assessment. Wyldermon's hands were in his lap a few feet away, and while Kri'Bondai's were closer, one hand was in his lap and the other was a good six inches removed from her. He was strumming the air with it, making delicate threading motions with his fingers.

Ah—that had to be the explanation. Her body was an instrument, and he was playing it. *Remotely.* She was impressed. Years earlier, she'd decided that men were blundering boobs in bed. She'd come here hoping Erotopian men would be different, and this was *very* different. Kri'Bondai had plugged directly into her nervous system, and he'd done it without even touching her.

Her vulva had that yummy spongey feeling. "Ohmigod," she breathed out loud and opened her legs wider.

When would he put his actual hand on her? By now she wanted it there, badly. Then she felt it, the palm of his hand pressing down on the outer portion of her vulva and rotating it in small circles. Her eyes shot open and she looked. This time, he was touching her. She closed her eyes and her breathing quickened as his hand caressed her. When two fingers landed on her button, she gasped with pleasure. He rolled it not too fast and not too slow, steadily and steadfastly, as if time had stopped and he'd be perfectly happy to keep doing it forever. She moaned and twisted on the green-moss bed.

Two hands were poised above her breasts. She sensed them there from behind her closed eyes, their weight and heat and presence. She was briefly baffled—the angle was all wrong for Kri'Bondai. But then she remembered: Wyldermon was there, too. Those hands in waiting were his.

She wanted him, too—she wanted it all. She reached up, grabbed his hands and pulled them down onto her.

She felt his warmth pressing down through her skin. Moments later his fingers went to her areolae and squeezed them firmly and decisively, once, twice, and then again. Her eyes opened wide as bolts of pleasure fired down into her crotch. Then she was orgasming, her body shuddering its pleasure out onto the moss.

"Let me hear it," Kri'Bondai said. "Your delight."

She opened her mouth, intending to gift him with the sound-track of her pleasure. Instead she laughed. Her laughter came from deep down inside her and streamed forth irrepressibly. She didn't try to suppress it. She laughed—the laugh laughed her—she laughed so much that her sides started hurting. She laughed for the pleasure she was feeling, she laughed for the breakthroughs she was having, she laughed for her miraculous good fortune. And as she laughed, she was coming. Her delight fed her orgasm and her orgasm fed her delight. The wheel kept turning and she kept coming.

"Glee-gasms," Wyldermon said. "You gotta love 'em."

The High Priest laid the palm of his hand gently on her vulva. Her crotch bucked once, then relaxed into the comfort of his hand.

For a time, they said nothing. Her breath softened and a smile settled onto her features. Kri'Bondai said, "How was the Watering? Do you feel well watered?"

She heard his question and started to laugh. She laughed so hard that she had to sit up.

Then she started coming again.

-JaHangir-

A FEW MINUTES' WALK BROUGHT BREE and Jahangir to a modestly-sized clearing with blue-green turf that sparkled like diamonds in the sun. A chalk-white pedestal had been set up at its center. There was an inlaid box on it and a black lacquered stool alongside it. Bree brought him up to it, took his hands and addressed him with rare formality. "Jahangir Persad, do you choose to be watered sexually?"

"I do."

"In that case, on your knees, my friend."

She sat on the stool, opened her thighs, brought him forward so he was only inches away, and displayed herself to him. Her labia were fleshy and elaborately folded—her right lip was especially large and had a mottled, fluted petal. Her clitoral head was hidden away, tucked beneath the cowl of her hood. Her vulva looked like an island, he decided, an island with a forest, ridges and a cave, and surrounded by the ocean of her dress.

"*Ba'da* out, please," she said.

"My what?"

"Your *ba'da*. Your cock." She patted her exposed vulva once, twice. "*Ba'da*, meet *tra'da*." She reached into the inlaid box and emerged with a crystal atomizer. "This is lube," she said. "Special lube. Very special lube. Now keep your eyes on my *tra'da* and pay very close attention."

She misted moisture onto herself. Jahangir blinked, startled— the scent was overwhelming. Years of wine-tasting kicked in—he picked up floral scents, hints of apricot and shitake and, behind it all, the intense funky musk of female sexual arousal.

Bree paused, frowning thoughtfully. "What the hell," she said and spritzed Jahangir too.

"Ohmigod," he blurted out. He'd tried any number of oils and potions over the years, but he'd never felt anything like this. His *ba'da* felt like it had been set on fire, good fire, fire that straddled the line between pleasure and pain. His *ba'da* ratcheted upward like it was being hoisted by invisible hydraulics. He gasped as the heat spread down into his thighs and up into his gut and spine.

Bree pressed her fingers into the pads rimming her *tra'da* and stroked them languidly, up and down, up and down. Gradually she built up the pace, and as she did so, the flesh beneath her fingers swelled into crescent mounds. From there she moved on to her central channel, massaging it with two well-lubricated fingers. Her hand went to her clitoris, which she started pleasuring with the pads of three fingers, slowly at first and then more vigorously. She sighed ecstatically and moved her hand away. Jahangir looked, and admired. Her *tra'da* had gotten puffier and rosier, and her clitoral head had emerged from hiding.

Again she reached into the inlaid box and this time emerged with an elegantly curved blown-glass dildo that shimmered red and orange and blue. She spritzed lube onto the working end, brought it down to her *tra'da,* and slipped it carefully inside. She sighed with pleasure, took a deep inhale and started sliding the apparatus forward and then back, steady as she goes, back and forth along the roof of her vagina. She repeated the action a full dozen times, pumping with both hands in and out.

"Come closer," she breathed. "I'm not good at this."

Jahangir inched forward.

"An Acolyte, that's all I am," she gasped.

She was working the toy faster. Another moan emerged and was joined by a liquid sound coming in from below. "An Acolyte, third degree."

Faster.

"Open your mouth! Now!" she cried out and swept the toy out of her body.

A stream of clear liquid arced into the air and traversed the narrow space between them.

Female ejaculate. He knew it as amrita from his Tantric explorations. He got most of it in his mouth, the rest of it squarely on his face. He could feel it dripping off his chin.

He loved the taste—he always had. The faintest bit briny, more mild than intense, but somehow pure and holy.

Bree dropped to her knees and eyed Jahangir affectionately. "That was mighty good for me! How about you? How are you feeling?"

He ran a quick inventory. His head was clear, his heart light, his mouth and throat beyond contented. "Wonderful," he answered. But then, to the south, there was his member, his rabid member, his penis from another planet. The last time he'd felt this frustrated and aroused, he'd been fifteen years old and Becky Garcia was shoving him out the back door after a torrid evening of third-base sex. "My cock," he said, "I mean, my *ba'da*. Good God, woman, what did you do to it?"

She made a face. "That lube I spritzed you with? It's an aphrodisiac. A very potent aphrodisiac. I'm sorry, Jahangir. I wasn't thinking."

"Do you think it might be, um, possible to do something about it?"

An embarrassing question, but he couldn't help asking.

She kissed a drop of amrita off the tip of his nose. "I'm sorry, Jahangir. People are waiting for us. The day will come when we play, I'm sure."

He suppressed his disappointment. "What's next, then?"

"The Tower of Delight. It's a fifteen-minute walk away."

"Maybe we can fly. There's a dragon in my pants."

She laughed and said again, "I'm sorry."

"Cockzilla. His name is Cockzilla."

She took his hands and pulled him to his feet. "Bring him along," she said, "your handsome friend. It'll be good for him, too."

-JaHangiR-

THE TOWER OF DELIGHT rose hundreds of feet above the Wildgarden. Bree and Jahangir rode to the top in a circular glass-walled elevator, then emerged through a hatchway onto a round roof deck. Casual furniture was scattered about—love seats, slatted wooden chairs, and an unlikely trio of beds, one of which looked big enough to host a small army. The sun shone down like a huge, hot dime.

"Come," said Bree and led him to the leather-clad railing. "Let me show you my Kailara."

A panorama of brightly-colored two- and three-story structures greeted him, stretching out toward the horizon. At first something seemed off—then he realized what it was. There was no blacktop to be seen and none of the blights that come with it, either—no automobiles, no traffic lights, no malls, and not a single billboard. The unpaved streets meandered—there wasn't a straight line anywhere. Narrow bands of forest flowed like rivers through the landscape; their shimmering leaves put Jahangir in mind of schools of green and silver fish. There was open space everywhere, fields for farming and meadows for playing.

"Kailara is shaped like a human body," she said. "The design was intentional."

"Why the human body?"

"It's where everything starts. It's a reminder."

Pressing up against him from behind, more kitten-ish than sexual, she pointed out the city's arms, legs, torso, and head. They were at the groin. To the north, between what Bree described as the city's heart and belly chakras, he could see Mosshard Garden, a long, vaguely oval expanse of meadows and groves of trees, and just beyond it, the twin white domes of the Temple of the Divine Nectar, which Kri'Zhalee and Kri'Bondai called home.

Thus connected, Bree and Jahangir gazed over Kailara. A vast sadness descended on Jahangir. "Where did we go wrong, Bree?" he asked plaintively. "Why can't we live like you do here? Why do we have so much hate and violence?"

"I've been thinking about that a lot since I got here," she answered quietly. "I believe it starts with how you pray. You go down on your knees and bow your heads. You're basically pleading for mercy. You treat God like the biggest, baddest primate of all—you make it 'bend the knee, or die.' And so there all you Earthlings are, down on your knees begging the Big Man to be kind, and a sort of hive mind develops. A *slave* hive mind. That's no soil for a soul to grow in. A culture steeped in terror produces more terror—it knows no other way." She fell silent and then said, "Source wants dancing partners. Source didn't make us to be slaves."

A voice interrupted them from behind. "Hello, sailor." It was Vala, flanked by Kri'Bondai and Wyldermon. She looked radiantly happy. She went up to Jahangir, rose up onto her toes and kissed him. It was an affectionate kiss, not a passionate one, all very respectable, but it wouldn't have happened if Darius had been there. Jahangir could tell.

She spoke quietly so no one else could hear. "I'll be fine here. Please ignore all that crazy stuff I said last night. I was just being silly." Her eyes interrogated his. "Do you mind?" Before he could answer, her arms were around him and her body was pressing against his. She kissed him again and this time her tongue danced with his. "I've been wanting to do that for days now," she said when they were done. "And now I'm here, here on Erotopia!"

A shiver went slaloming down Jahangir's spine. And God Almighty, his *ba'da*! Which had started slavering again; it felt huge and on fire. And was it just his imagination, or were coils of red energy actually spiraling out from his crotch directly toward her groin?

Vala seemed to see it too. Her eyes were fixed on his crotch. "*Santo Dios*," she said, "what is going on down there?"

"Damned if I know. It was my Watering."

"Mine was amazing, too," she said.

They were gazing into each other's eyes, their souls adrift on a sea of questions, when Darius came stumbling onto the Tower of Delight, trailed by Kri'Zhalee and Cymanthea. He looked dazed, and his body was being racked by spasms. He drifted over to the leather-clad railing and leaned over it without speaking.

Kri'Bondai eyed his companions, concerned. "You didn't—"

"I did," said Kri'Zhalee. "A *kri'lashö*."

"She had to," Cymanthea hastened to explain. "We had ourselves a situation."

"I tried to calibrate it," the High Priestess said, "but I don't know if I got it right. What's an Earthling's tolerance? And I was adrenalizing—I may have overdone it."

Jahangir felt a pang of compassion for Darius—plainly, something unpleasant had happened to him. But he also felt elated. A favored story line had been launched. *The rich guy gets his comeuppance.* He was eager to learn the specifics of what had happened, which he could do at his convenience. The poor sap's cameras had been rolling; there'd be footage to review.

Darius's spasms were growing more frequent and intense. Grunts emerged from him, animal-like and reflexive. His eyes were lidded, his expression leaden.

"He looks like he's having energy orgasms," Jahangir whispered to Bree.

"That's right, *kriyas*," she answered. "But he doesn't look like he's having fun."

"It looks like he's getting little shocks."

"Or in shock. That's different."

Through her swirling, silver-gray garment, Kri'Zhalee placed a hand on her crotch, inhaled deeply and released it in a shuddering long exhale. "I'm fine now," she said. "He took me by surprise, that's all. She turned to Bree. "How'd your Watering go?"

"Very well. I squirted like you wanted me to!"

"I believe in you, Bree—I knew you would." Her attention turned to Jahangir and a concerned look came over her. She went up to him, took his hands between hers and gazed into his eyes. Then she held a palm out toward his groin. "Oh, my," she said, and turned to Bree. "M-sap?"

Bree's face twisted into a grimace that had both "yes" and "oops" in it.

"Oh my," she said again, and addressed Jahangir directly. "Would you like to bless the Tower before we leave?"

"'Bless?'"

"That's right. Bless."

"I—I guess so," he answered.

"Excellent!" she exclaimed, and crooked a finger at Cymanthea. "Would you come lend a hand or something, please?"

JAHANGIR WAS FEELING AWKWARD. He wasn't used to performing publicly, and Cockzilla had been pounding away for some time now without getting closer to coming. What should have been a brief diversion was becoming a main act. His friends would be growing impatient.

At first, he'd hesitated when Kri'Zhalee made her offer. He wasn't one for sex in public or with strangers. But this was Erotopia, where the rules were different, and Cockzilla was on the rampage, so he'd decided to proceed. At his request, they'd positioned Cymanthea on her hands and knees on a bench by the railing so he could see the city laid out beyond her backside. The High Priestess had instructed her to prepare herself; he'd watched from behind as she worked herself up with her fingers. When she pronounced herself ready, he'd slipped his fire-breathing friend inside. (She'd felt just like Earth women—he'd been wondering.) And now, after a promising start, he was flatlining.

"Hmm," said Kri'Zhalee. She came up to them and placed one hand under Cymanthea's crotch and the other just above the base of Jahangir's spine. She stepped back and shared her professional assessment. "Extreme arousal, but no ejaculatory trajectory. There is inhibition. The walls have sadly closed in." Her next words were directed at the Celebrant. "Cymanthea, you'll come with him, right?"

"Of course, *Tsh'kiva*. I've been waiting."

The High Priestess's hand fell lightly on Jahangir's brow, rested there briefly, and was removed. He felt it hovering over his sacrum. Moments later, great waves of heat came streaming into his pelvis, spread north and south through his body, and promptly turned into his orgasm. He raised up off Cymanthea's back and fired into her with long shuddering explosions that came from where the heat had started. She met each spasm with a loud cry and clamped down on him with her inner muscles, summoning the next release.

An image came to him—a vast chasm of white light just beyond the tube of tissue that was squeezing down on him. The abyss seemed alive, like a conscious presence, calmly and patiently awaiting its due.

The orgasmic energy had claimed his brain; the top of his head was blowing off. White light streaming toward the stars. Again and again he fired into her. At last he stopped shuddering and collapsed onto Cymanthea's back. She lay beneath him motionless and eventually muttered something he couldn't quite make out. He grunted and she said again, more loudly this time, "The Hungry Python. Did you see it?"

He gave her neck a small affectionate kiss and tumbled into blankness again. Eventually a new voice penetrated his stupor. "*Dios*, that was hot. You're a crazed fuck-beast, Jahangir!"

Vala. He'd completely forgotten she was there.

He roused himself enough to glance in her direction. Vala, shy Vala, was touching herself. She was doing it through her dress, but she was touching herself, Vala who only the night before had sworn Erotopia would be too much for her.

"That's right, Jahangir." She laughed delightedly. "I'm playing with myself. In front of you. In front of everyone!"

He collapsed again onto Cymanthea. What an orgasm that had been! And damn, but Vala looked spectacular! With a light breeze fussing her hair, a wild ecstatic look in her eyes, her hand busy, busy at her crotch, and her nipples saying hi through her thin cotton tee.

And all this against the backdrop of Kailara.

In a flash, he saw it: This was the poster promoting their show. *Vala on the Verge*, he'd call it. It would be an instant classic, right up there with King Kong and Fay Wray.

Cockzilla stirred—Cymanthea moaned. Jahangir raised up, yowled and started firing again. He couldn't tell if his orgasm was wet or dry; he could barely believe it was happening at all. When he got to five, he stopped counting.

And then, at last, it was truly over. He groaned and fell back on his bony bed.

The Wheel and the Cross

"The Erotopian religious system lifts its objects of veneration from the deep psyche—shapes, energies, archetypes, which they project onto the external unseen world carefully and consciously, more as artifacts of the collective unconscious than as actual deities or sub-deities."

—Ulrich Von Zeitler, *First Report to the Senate Select Sub-Committee on Intergalactic Affairs* (2049)

- Vala -

ALA LEANED BACK AGAINST the Tower of Delight's railing
and took in her companions. Bree, Kri'Zhalee and Kri'Bondai
were benignly contemplating Jahangir and Cymanthea, who
were lying collapsed in a two-backed heap. Darius was hanging over the rail. He seemed not to have noticed anything at all.

Of course he hadn't—he was Mister Clueless. And now he'd
become Mister Even More Clueless—that *kri'lashö*, whatever it was,
had really done a number on him. She felt a passing pulse of pity for
him. He was a cad, but he meant well, and Jesus preached forgive-
ness. But she also *didn't* forgive Darius because he'd wronged her too
many times to count or forgive. And it wasn't only his philandering.
She'd thought she was teaming up with an up-and-comer, but the
man she'd hitched her wagon to had gotten stalled in a Hollywood
rut, and he'd shown himself over time to lack the gumption to dig
himself out. He groused and whined instead of doing. She'd seen
him do it again and again and had concluded long ago that it was a
character weakness. She attributed the deficiency to his upbringing.
Rich kids didn't need that extra gear.

Jahangir roused himself off Cymanthea's back. "Wow," he said,
blinking. He looked directly at Vala. "And wow," he said, "to you, too."

"Thank you," she said, and flushed.

Now, *this* man—he was different. He wasn't self-absorbed, he
paid attention—he was a great listener. He actually achieved things
rather than sitting around waiting to be anointed. He'd built and
sold three successful businesses during a time period that had seen
Darius land five small roles in B movies and change acting coaches
half a dozen times. He was richer than Darius, gentler than Darius,

humbler than Darius. He was also darker-skinned than Darius, and the child of immigrants.

No, she decided, it wasn't even close. She had a lot more in common with Jahangir than with trust-fund Blondie. But it was Darius whose hand she took as they headed downstairs from the Tower of Delight, Darius who was still her boyfriend for the time being, Darius with whom she was committed, more than not, she was pretty sure, to working things out with. Resolved to think kindly of him, she recalled what her lover Zack had told her after she'd shared her body with him, and after that her boyfriend problem. "No one is evil—there are only bad strategies."

Zack had been right. Darius wasn't evil; he was clueless. She started repeating the phrase to herself. *"No one is evil—there are only bad strategies."* By the time she and Darius had made their way down the Tower of Delight's spiral staircase, her mantra was starting to pay off and she was seeing her guy's positive qualities. He was gorgeous, he was funny, he could be charming, he could be sweet. He had money. She gave him a solicitous look. "How are you doing, sweetie?"

"I've been better," he said as a new round of *kriyas* seized him.

They passed through a vaulted archway into the Tower metro station. Paths laid out with mosaic tile wended their way among shade trees and flower gardens. There were stone benches and a low terraced hill for sitting, and a thatched lean-to for when cover was needed.

A man and a woman were absorbed in conversation in the shade of a gray-barked, white-blossomed tree. She was wearing a sundress—he was naked. She'd popped her breasts out and was holding them out for her companion, who was stroking and squeezing them as they talked. As Vala walked by, she heard the woman say, "Never the nipples until I'm at seven or higher."

"What was that about?" Vala asked Bree after they'd gotten settled on the grassy rise above the station.

"That reference to the number seven? We have an erotic arousal scale, zero to ten, from nothing to orgasmic."

"That, and that thing about the nipples."

"She was teaching him how to pleasure her breasts."

Vala blinked. It had never occurred to her that she could say to a man, "Touch here, touch like this, and for God's sake never do that." Guys hated being seen as ignorant or incompetent. There wasn't a man on her list of lovers who wouldn't have freaked out.

"Before Wyldermon and I made love the first time," Bree said, "he asked me to show him how I like to be pleased. He watched while I played show-and-tell. My breasts, my *tra'da*, that spot behind my ear that drives me wild." She laughed and shivered. "God, it was good. Like, the best foreplay ever."

Wyldermon said, "We call it the Tour de Pleasure."

"Erotopian culture is totally organized around maximizing pleasure," Bree continued.

"Of course it is. Erotopia is sex-positive," Vala said.

"That's true, but I was thinking of something else."

Kri'Bondai spoke up in his rich baritone. "I believe Bree was referring to our grid. It's powered by erotic energy. Our electrical system—erotic energy. Our engines and machines—erotic energy. We've learned how to harness the power of love. People are erojoule production factories."

"Sex is the centerpiece of our lives," Kri'Zhalee said. "It's how we pray to Source. It's how we give back to the We. It's how we sustain our economy."

Confusion arose in Vala. Erotopia's economy was fueled by erotic energy—a culture couldn't be more sexualized. But the Fuck-o-Rama of her imagination was a scary place, and Erotopia wasn't frightening at all. She felt excited, full of anticipation, and—she couldn't help but notice—a bit aroused as well.

A pneumatic whooshing came from the south. Then there it was, the air-train, hurtling through the station inches off the ground and braking smoothly to a halt, a spotless, glistening marriage of what looked like glass and chrome, but was probably an alloy she was unfamiliar with.

She sat between Darius and Jahangir on a soft bench that ran the length of the seventh and last car. The others stood. No hand-hold was required as the train pulled into motion. The ride was so smooth that Vala wouldn't have been sure they were moving had it not been for the scenes of Kailaran life that unspooled before her as the train zipped silently along. There flashed through her field of vision brightly painted houses, hardpack winding roads, stretches of field and forest, banners flying, and the occasional silver-flecked river. People were everywhere, walking, working, zipping along on scooters and bicycles, dancing. Everywhere people were dancing.

A woman with enormous breasts and a generous belly was in the car with them. She smiled a friendly hello to Kri'Zhalee, sowed seed toward the others, and made her way to a silver pole at the center of the car, where she took a deep breath and dissolved into a full-body shimmer.

"Her name's Zhay'rih," Kri'Zhalee said to the others. "She's a student of mine, and a Celebrant."

"I believe we're about to see the three-breath orgasm," Cymanthea volunteered. "She's contributing erojoules to the We."

Zhay'rih took another deep breath and expelled it with a loud "Aah." She inhaled again, pulled the breath up, and released it down-ward with a rolling sonorous exhale. After her next breath, her body started trembling and quaking, and her face lit up. An ecstatic light came into her eyes.

"Huh?" said Darius.

"She's having energy orgasms," Kri'Zhalee explained in the exaggeratedly patient tone people use with children. "You've been having something similar; you've been feeling the energy, but you've been blocked from the pleasure." She turned to him. "You could run energy with Zhay'rih. It's pouring out of you. It wants to be happy. It wants to be sexual."

Bree said, "The Erotopian term for running energy is *zhun'ha*. The literal translation is 'orgasm-dancing.'"

Darius made a face, then lowered his voice and said, "I don't want to. She's fat."

The High Priestess gave him a baffled look. "She's beautiful," she said.

"No. Fat."

Kri'Zhalee studied Darius intently and then said, "May I?"

A nervous smile flitted across his face. "May you what? A *kri'lashö*?"

"No," she reassured him. "This will be gentle."

"If you say so," he answered nervously.

She placed two fingers on his brow, went still for a long moment, and then removed her hand.

"What do you see now?"

"Wow," Darius said, "she's beautiful! Damn, that's a lot of woman!"

"That's right. Now go play."

"But what do I do?"

"Let your instincts take over. It'll come naturally."

Darius wiped his hands nervously on his trousers. Vala grimaced upon seeing this. It was probably the move that launched him off his barstool when he hit on one of his Bimbos of Los Angeles.

"Check in with her first, though," Kri'Zhalee said. "Get her consent."

"Like, ask if I can buy her a drink?"

"What a strange way to show interest. No, ask if you can do *zhun'ha* with her."

Moments later, Darius and Zhay'rih were eye-gazing, shaking and shivering together. Darius looked perplexed—he plainly didn't understand how this could be happening—but he also looked happy for the first time since his *kri'lashö*.

Vala's shoulder was pressed up against Jahangir's. Slowly, carefully, and oh so discreetly, she placed her hand on his thigh. Not too high and not too low, a good six inches from his *ba'da*. She was pretty sure Darius wouldn't notice, but it would be better if he didn't. As her mind went back to Jahangir and Cymanthea on the Tower of Delight, it dawned on her that the three eronauts had committed a monumental blunder in the run-up to this trip. They'd been so focused on the mechanics of filming, on the contents of the show, on the upcoming encounter with all things Erotopian, that they'd neglected to consider the erotic code of conduct among themselves. In the silence, a narrative had emerged: Darius and Vala were the sexual beings while Jahangir was a bystander, an observer.

She could feel the heat streaming off his *ba'da*. Yes, she decided, neutering Jahangir had been a mistake, definitely a mistake. She pressed up against him, delivering a flirty smoosh of the breasts, and whispered, "May I tell you something?"

"You most certainly may."

"I loved how you were with Cymanthea." She could feel herself blushing. "Would you like to be that way with me?"

"Are you saying you want me to make love to you?" A broad smile spread across his cheeks. "What a lovely notion!"

Not quite the answer she'd been hoping for. She tried again. "Jahangir, do you find me desirable? Would you like to make love to me?"

He laughed aloud and turned to face her directly. "Jesus, Vala, why do you think I chose you? For your accounting skills?"

"You've wanted me from the beginning?"

"From the very first moment I laid eyes on you."

A warm glow filled her chest. This rich, successful man wanted her. Her, Valentina Cortes, the invisible daughter of illegals from Nowhere, Arizona!

"Well, then—is that a yes? Will we? Shall we?"

He frowned, paused for a long moment, bit his lip, frowned some more, and finally said, "Of course, we'll have to get Darius's permission."

Oh, right. That. Her flush deepened. "Of course, with Darius's okay. That's what I meant."

"Good. That's decided, then," Jahangir said and gently placed his hand on hers. He said, "I am looking forward."

Vala cast a nervous eye Darius's way. He was still running energy with Zhay'rih and seemed not to have noticed anything.

Jahangir's hand on hers felt like a statement—*you and me, girl, we're a team.* She sighed happily and settled back into her seat. They sat alongside each other rubbing shoulders for the rest of the trip, admiring her handsome hunk of a boyfriend as he danced orgasms with Zhay'rih.

-ᐯᗩᒪᗩ-

THE TROUPE DISEMBARKED INTO the parklike setting of Power Central station and set out from there to their lodgings at the Treegarden Pod in Mosshard Garden. Wonder arose in Vala as she absorbed the sights and sounds of Kailara.

A nude woman, lying on the grassy verge with her legs spread wide and her arms sprawled over her head, basking in the midday heat—a sun angel.

Half a dozen people holding hands in a circle and kicking up their heels. At their center, a naked man, quiveringly erect and having full-body *kriyas*.

A man and woman wearing peacock colors, strolling arm-in-arm, chanting mantras together.

A scantily dressed couple on a bench feeding each other tasty treats off smeared fingers.

Two pre-pubertal girls, one fair and the other ebony, one of them clothed and the other not, spinning cartwheels down the grassy boulevard.

Mosshard Garden didn't have a clearly-defined boundary. Block by block there were fewer buildings until the buildings were gone and Vala found herself in a pastoral setting—rolling meadows, small stands of trees, and multiple stand-alone plants that reminded her of dwarf Saguaro cactuses, but without the prickles.

Kri'Zhalee pointed to one and said, "Those are mosshards."

"As in, 'Mosshard Garden?'" Jahangir asked.

"That's right. And 'M-sap.'"

"That man those people were dancing around? He looked deeply aroused. What was that, an erojoule production strategy?"

"That," Bree said, "was a Priap. They're sex priests, one level below High Priests and Priestesses. And yes, that is, among other things, an erojoule production strategy."

"What do Priaps do?"

"Most of the time," she answered vaguely, "they do *that*."

The Treegarden co-housing pod was hidden in a thicket of trees that rose like a spiky crop of hair from the crest of a sloping lawn. Vala and her companions followed a stone path into the woods and soon found themselves in a meadow that was surrounded by trees and open to the sky. A man and a woman were entwined there in the shade of a high parasol. Vala sighed deeply, looked up at the sapphire ring of sky, and returned her gaze to the meadow. They were in the missionary position. He was short and slender, with pale skin and sandy hair. Vala could only see the woman's shapely legs, which were wrapped around the man's thighs, and her slender hands, each gripping a fistful of buttock. Her fingernails and toenails had been painted obsidian.

"It's Vadeen!" Bree proclaimed. "I'd recognize that cute butt anywhere."

Neither he nor his partner were moving. Little "I'm trying not to come" squeaks emerged from the shadow beneath the man beneath the parasol.

"Who's the woman?" Jahangir asked quietly.

"Ool, I think," she answered.

"Yes, Ool," Wyldermon confirmed more loudly. "Her *gev'da* is unmistakable."

"Her what?" Jahangir asked.

"Her *gev'da*. It's the Erotopian word for any on-the-edge-of-coming sound. Erotopians have an entire vocabulary for sex sounds."

"What's the word for a not-on-the-edge-of-coming sex sound?"

"A *da'zel*."

"And for when a person is coming?"

"*Da'fzhun*," Cymanthea chimed in. "Its literal meaning is 'roof-off prayer.'"

"Vadeen and Ool, your guests are here," Kri'Zhalee said crisply.

New vocalizations emerged from the two, speaking this time to embarrassment, not arousal. They hastily disentangled themselves and were on their feet moments later. Vala tried not to notice Vadeen's slender, still-hard *ba'da* as it came sluicing through the air toward her.

"I didn't realize. So rude of me," Vadeen said. He was about Vala's height, with intelligent green eyes and a curl of light-brown hair that made a comma on his forehead. She liked him immediately. He bowed and sowed seed in their direction. "May the Great Ones be with you, in their wisdom and their power."

Ool had a porcelain complexion, a wasp waist, big saucer eyes and an outsized bosom. She was tiny, five feet tall at most. Her hair cascaded like a black waterfall down to her lower back. She offered her massive breasts in the now-familiar greeting. "Greetings, Earthlings! May the Great Ones be with you, from their place of perfect knowledge!"

She was probably in her late teens and certainly not over twenty. Vala recognized her type from the twinkle in her eye. She'd known girls like her in high school. Ool was the good-hearted sexy one with a mischievous wild streak who was always getting her girlfriends into sticky situations. A fun-loving soul, naughty and slutty, perky in more ways than two.

She hated Ool's breasts immediately. They seemed impossibly firm for their size—they hadn't a hint of sag or droop to them. "Do you do breast implants on Erotopia?" she whispered in an aside to Bree. She hoped not. Implants felt unfair to her, like cheating.

"No, we celebrate all shapes and sizes here."

"That's her actual body, then?"

"Yes," Bree nodded, "as it came in the original packaging. But her body is her art form, too. She's spent years perfecting it. When you're a Fuckstarter, you want to have a gorgeous body."

"A Fuckstarter?" Vala asked. "What's that?"

"Fuckstarters get the water boiling. They inspire people to have sex. It's how they contribute to the We."

When Ool caught sight of Darius, she froze like a pointer. Her big brown eyes got even bigger. She aimed a long, black-lacquered fingernail at him and said, "*That* is an Earthling?"

Nods of assent all around. She floated on her tiny ballerina's feet to Darius and came up close to him, well beyond the invisible line that on Earth defines right social distance. Her eyes took him in from north to south, then moved up again. "Wow," she said. "Talk about dreamy!" She held her palm out to his crotch. His body bucked, then bucked again. "How cool is that!" she exclaimed. "A sensitive!"

She took a deep breath in and released it with a long, throaty round-mouthed "Ooh." He responded with a fresh barrage of body-shaking *kriyas*. Moments later they were running energy together.

"Ool's also a Provocatrix," Bree whispered to Vala.

"What's that?"

"A person who tests edges. We don't want boundaries to harden into dogma. When you have dogma, you have people who want to overthrow it; they're expressing their impulse for freedom. When you have attackers, you get defenders—you get conservatives and radicals—you get a society torn in two. Provocatrixes help us keep our boundaries organic and real. They inspire us to examine them, to not take them for granted. They're one of the ways we keep our culture from becoming stultified; you don't get stuck in certainty when you keep asking questions. That hand she put so close to Darius without first asking his permission? Very Provocatrixsie."

A steel fist squeezed Vala's heart as she watched Ool and Darius dance orgasms together. Unlike Zhay'rih, this woman wasn't fat; she was a total hottie. Vala's mouth twisted into a frown as she felt her jealousy run through her. She hated, she just *hated*, how insecure she could still get. After all the personal-growth work she'd done, you'd think she'd have gotten past all that. Vala wasn't insecure about her looks. She knew and often enjoyed how men ogled and desired her. But she had to be honest; Ool had her beat. Her curves were more bodacious, and her face kept pace with the rest. She had better hair, even!

And bad-ass, bad-girl black nail polish.

Darius's and Ool's *kriyas* faded and the two went still. Another Provocatrixsie move followed—she put her hand on his chest. He reciprocated, and while his hand landed on the narrow space between her breasts, not directly on them, Vala couldn't help but notice how the sides of his hand made contact with her dramatic up-curves left and right. Her grimace deepened. Now he was touching her breasts, sort of. Wasn't he? If it hadn't been okay for her to be upset before, was it okay now?

It was Ool who finally broke the silence. "Can we do *tra'ba'da* sometime? Pretty, pretty please with all kinds of sugar on top?"

"*Tra'ba'da?*" said Darius. "What's that?"

"Full-on penetrative sex."

"Well, sure," he answered and then looked nervously at Vala.

"People say the nicest things about my *tra'da*," Ool said. "I think you'll really like it."

"Well, I have a really big cock," Darius said and preened.

"No worries," Ool said. "I'm sure we'll have fun anyway."

Vala could feel herself flushing. *He's mine,* she thought. *You have no right.* She was furious with Ool and even angrier with herself. She knew full well that Darius had every right to be doing what he was doing—they'd traveled to this distant planet to have sex with the natives. But that was the thing about jealousy. It didn't answer to fairness or reason.

The Fuckstarter went onto her toes, brought Darius's head down to hers, and kissed him. Vala flushed and looked angrily away. Here was yet another transgression—what did Ool not get about possession?

The woman was a menace.

A menace, and a shameless bitch.

THE UNDERSTORY WRAPPED AROUND three sides of the meadow where they'd happened on Ool and Vadeen. The space was set up for easy socializing, with comfy chairs and sofas, tables to accommodate groups large and small, carpets clumped on the wood floor, and thick mattresses for cuddling and playing. Vala sat with her companions at a table whose top appeared to be made of smoked glass. The ceiling above her head was a latticework of leaves and branches, and the walls were the shadows of the forest. Small monkey-like creatures were stirring up a fuss here and there, mostly in the cooking area—Vala counted five in all. Bree pointed them out (they were called *x'ings*) and explained that they were as populous in Mosshard Garden as squirrels were in Central Park. They were fun companions—smart and clownish, sociable and friendly.

Wyldermon and Cymanthea said their goodbyes. He was off to meet a group of prospective Wild-venturers, she was expected at a death party. Cymanthea proudly displayed the gift-card she'd prepared for the soon-to-be-departing one, whom she described as one of her aunties. It read, *May Your Death Be as Grand as Your Life Has Been.*

Vadeen and Ool emerged from the food prep area with steaming mugs of herbal tea. Darius's drink had been customized to support his recovery from his *kri'lashö*, Jahangir's would zero out any remaining vestiges of M-sap, and Vala was given what Vadeen described as a "soul-grounding" blend. She was unclear what that meant, but sipped willingly. She liked the taste, which reminded her of root beer.

"You've arrived at a great time," Bree said. "Our summer solstice celebration is a week and a half away. The Union of the Two Delights—we call it Union Night for short. I do hope you'll join us."

"I'm sure we will," Jahangir said in his careful diplomat's voice. "Please tell us about it."

Inquiring looks around the table. "You're the philosopher, Vadeen," Kri'Bondai said finally. "You explain."

From his place at the head of the table, their slender host collected his thoughts, then began. "Our culture celebrates four delights.

They're strung along two separate axes." He drew a line on the table with his finger, then intersected it with another. When he removed his hand, the marks were still there on the smoky glass, shimmering and luminous.

"There you have it. The Cross of Love," he said.

"What do the two axes represent?" Jahangir asked.

"Power and consciousness," Vadeen answered. "The power axis runs from Power Over to Power Under, and the consciousness axis runs from self-awareness, us knowing that we're us, to our pure animal nature. In other words, to pure unconsciousness."

"Those are the four delights?"

"That's right. Power Over and Power Under, and self-awareness and our animal nature. We celebrate the latter two on Union Night."

Jahangir pointed to the image. "Which axis represents power and which represents consciousness?"

"It doesn't matter." Vadeen enclosed the two lines in a circle. "The Cross of Love is the Wheel of Love. See?"

"The Wheel of Love is in constant motion," Kri'Zhalee said. "It pulls the world along with it."

"It's one of our most important symbols," Bree said. "Those cartwheels those girls were doing on the way here? They're reminders of the Wheel of Love."

Vala overcame her shyness and spoke up. "How is Power Over a delight? Power Over is a problem. Power Over has been suppressing women and people of color since forever."

"Ah, but you're talking about pathological Power Over," Bree said. "We don't let that establish a foothold here."

"It's a danger?"

"Yes, a constant one. Some people come into the world with a will to power that's unhealthy. We do everything we can to love that impulse out of them. Our entire culture is built around offering a better alternative."

"If you don't succeed, what happens then?"

Bree said, "We take steps."

"Decisive ones," Kri'Zhalee added.

Silence followed, a conspicuous failure to elaborate. "What about Hagorrhs?" Vala asked with a kind of grim fascination. She felt like she was picking at a wound.

"They're the external form of the threat," Bree explained, "but most of us have an inner Hagorrh. Our entire culture is dedicated to keeping it under control, to keep it from taking the wheel."

"We don't do bullying or coercion here," the High Priestess said. "The only Power Over we allow is Power Over with consent."

"Can you give an example of that, please?" Jahangir asked.

"Vadeen," said Kri'Zhalee, "would you fetch a cup of tea for me?"

"Of course, *Tsh'kiva*," he answered and stood up.

"There you have it," said the High Priestess, "Power Over with consent. Vadeen, no need to bother with that tea."

"Consent," Kri'Bondai volunteered, "is the grease that turns the Wheel of Love."

"Tell me more about Union Night," Darius said. "Is it, like, an orgy?"

Vadeen turned to him and said with a gentle and unreadable smile, "That depends on how you define the term. Sex happens, and there are lots of partners. But Union Night isn't only a sex party; it's a sacred celebration. We celebrate our highest self, our self-awareness, and we also celebrate our original nature, our animal self. We celebrate where we've come from, and we celebrate where we're going. The descent and the ascent, you might say."

"When you put the two together, that's when sex gets over-the-top good," Ool volunteered.

"That's true," Vadeen agreed. "When Ool and I were doing *tra'ba'da* just now, we were doing a spiritual sexual practice. A *bha'troun*. We were being as still as we were because we were practicing awareness—we were totally focused on paying attention. It's a wonderful experience, and it's also very different from the one you'd have if you surrendered fully to your animal sensations. That's what you're saying, right, Ool?"

"It is. *Bha'trouns* are great, but"—she fixed her big eyes on Darius—"me, I'm a crazed monkey-fucking kind of girl."

"The Cross of Love isn't only about sex, though," Kri'Zhalee noted. "It's a philosophy of life. The consciousness axis is about consciousness generally, about being self-aware and making the best choices we can."

"It's about the pursuit of wisdom, in other words," said Vadeen, "which just happens to be the path I've committed to. As a philosopher-in-training, the central issue I work with is how best to be in service to the We while fully engaging our pleasure."

"Which is, of course, our other delight," Kri'Bondai chimed in. "Pleasure. Pleasure in our bodies, pleasure in sex, pleasure in our capacity for understanding, pleasure in our capacity for wisdom, pleasure in our capacity for creativity, pleasure in art, pleasure in everything."

"Philosophers follow the wisdom path. Sexual priests and priestesses follow the pleasure path," Bree elaborated.

"The two aren't mutually exclusive, of course," Vadeen hastened to add. "They need each other. Wisdom without pleasure isn't actually wisdom, it's too ungrounded and theoretical for that; and pleasure without wisdom is empty and vulgar."

"It can be fun, though!" Ool chimed in, smiling saucily at Darius.

"Well, yes," Vadeen continued, "but only because we know we're being naughty and transgressive. Without that, it's just tacky."

"So let me be clear," Jahangir said. "The Union of the Two Delights celebrates the merging of wisdom and pleasure?"

"That's right, and more broadly, it celebrates cosmic opposites. Sun and moon, light and shadow, the male and female principles."

"Union Night rocks," Ool said. "It's an erojoule factory." She turned to Darius and ran her pink tongue around her lips. "You and me, Big Guy, we'll tank up."

F OR THE LAST MINUTES, Vala had been growing sleepier. She stood up, resting her hands on the table so she wouldn't keel over on the spot. "I need to rest," she declared. Her eyelids felt like they had weights on them.

Kri'Zhalee was eyeing her closely. "Yes, rest is what you need," she affirmed. "Sleep will do you good."

"I'll show you to your suites," said Bree, standing up. She indicated a beautifully handcrafted wooden spiral staircase that wrapped around a thick tree trunk and disappeared above the ceiling canopy. "Follow me!"

"'Suites,' plural?" Jahangir interjected.

"That's right. Here, everyone has their own quarters."

"Can we have one suite for them both? I need them to be in full couple mode for *The Erotopian Chronicles*."

Bree gave Kri'Zhalee a questioning look.

"Is that what you'd like?" the High Priestess asked Darius and Vala, who shrugged their okay. "If that's what you want, I don't see why not."

Vala turned to Darius. "Coming?"

He shook his head. "I don't think so. I'm not feeling tired."

"Stay with me! We can play!" Ool said.

Darius looked at Vala pleadingly.

"No," she said firmly. "Absolutely not. You need to rest and recover."

He turned to Kri'Zhalee in mute appeal.

"Resting sounds right," she confirmed.

He stood up reluctantly from the table. "Well, if you say so."

"Rest up, Mister Hunky. Rest up good," Ool said.

Relentless. She was relentless. As she turned to follow Bree, Vala resolved to have sex with Darius as soon as possible. Giving him a taste of her chichis would remind him who his woman was, and it would also ease the way into the discussion she'd pledged to have with him about her nascent romance with Jahangir. The conversation would go better if they'd just had sex and he was feeling powerful.

They left the spiral staircase at the first landing. Bree led them to a door with a cheery painting on it, goats kicking up their heels against a cerulean background.

"Your quarters," she announced.

The door opened onto a corridor. The walls were made of slatted wood. They were painted turquoise and teal and covered with a happy mural. People dancing, bright birds with broad wings, an infant asleep in a cradle. Vala kept her feet moving by imagining herself sleeping like that baby. *Dios*, she was tired. But she felt good about her plan. She'd get refreshed and then she'd do Darius. She'd moan about how big he was, her go-to move for when she wanted him to come. And then she'd broach the topic of Jahangir.

She came to a room with a bed in it. Beneath its gauzy canopy was an inviting fluffy quilt, which opened to reveal a voluptuous cream-colored bottom sheet. She tumbled onto it, surrendered to its embracing softness, and fell promptly asleep.

Something To Say No To

"Erotopians are specialists in boundaries. Their lives unfold within a highly nuanced matrix of lines, transitions, and consent."

—Bree's Tavendish's Journal

-VaLa-

VALA IS AT A GLORIOUS OPEN-AIR BAR. *There are orchids everywhere, also hibiscus, birds of paradise and flowers whose names she doesn't know. The place is ablaze with hothouse colors.*

The joint is called The Snake and Apple. Kri'Bondai is the bartender. Through his energy cloak, she gets the occasional sighting of his broad, muscled chest, the smooth ripple of his abs—and, despite trying not to look, his erect ba'da *below.*

He's got cocktail shakers in both hands and is mixing up a storm. He's the Best Bartender Ever.

"What'll you have?" he asks.

She gives it thought and says, "I'd like a smart, sexy, self-aware man who knows how to please a woman and wants to do exactly that."

Kri'Bondai nods. "Sure. A Romance Novel. I can do that."

Someone slides onto the barstool to her right. It's Darius.

"And you?" Kri'Bondai asks him.

"Can you mix me up a beautiful, smart woman who loves sex, knows she loves sex, and wears that knowledge proudly?"

"I sure can!" Kri'Bondai says. "I've done a million of 'em. That's a Slutty Lady."

He gets to work. A shot of this, a snifter of that—he's like a scientist in a liquor laboratory. Soon two magnificent cocktails are lined up on the bar before them.

"Not quite done," Kri'Bondai says.

He brings his hands down into his energy cloak and does something near his groin. When his hands emerge, they're holding a crystal perfume bottle. Carefully, oh so carefully, he releases one drop and then a second into each of their drinks.

"It's Spirit of Shamelessness. I just harvested it from my genitals."

"I'll drink to that," Vala says and hoists a toast in Kri'Bondai's and then Darius's direction.

She sips. Everything she's ever known spins away. Her physical surroundings, the structures of her psyche. She's everywhere and nowhere, whirling down a tunnel without end.

How long she's there, she cannot say.

When she comes to, it's Jahangir who's behind the bar.

"How are the drinks?" he asks.

They've turned into wine. She sips, and her eyes grow wide. Words cannot describe.

Her gaze wanders over to Darius. She's amazed at what she sees. He's not a problem; he's perfect. He's the very man she ordered up!

He's looking at her like she's looking at him.

His body shudders. She feels his energy come into her, crotch and heart and head. She shivers and sends the kriya *back his way.*

The prince and princess, together at last.

They tumble into each other's arms, mouths meshing in a forever embrace.

Something was worrying at her lips. She wanted it to go away. It was interfering with this amazing, not-in-this-lifetime, once-in-an-eternity kiss.

Why can't I stay in the Snake and Apple forever? I don't want it to go away! Please, can I stay?

That whatever-it-is was still bothering her, still doing that thing to her lips.

It wouldn't go away. It wouldn't stop doing that *thing*. The last wisps of her dream were floating away; she gave up the quest as lost and reluctantly opened her eyes.

It was Darius's cock. It was hard. His hand was around its base and he was painting her lips with it, trying to tease her mouth open so he could slide it in.

"Welcome to Awake Land," he said. "It's me, Darius Di Selva, doctor of dentistry. Time for your appointment, dearie. Open wide!"

Abruptly and fully awake, she jerked her mouth away. "Jesus, Darius, do you know how gross that is?"

"Not gross. Sexy. The word is sexy."

"Ugh. The word is 'ugh.' You have no idea."

"No idea of what."

She'd been planning on having sex with him. Now she'd just as soon have a rattlesnake inside her. "How disgusting you can be. Jesus, Darius, you've really blown it."

"I was hoping you'd be doing the blowing, Mouse."

"Good luck with that. And stop calling me Mouse. I'm not your goddamn mouse."

Moments earlier, she'd been in a fabulous embrace with a perfect man. Then the real-life Darius had whipped out his dick and spoiled everything.

She could taste him. Usually she was okay with it. Right now, though: *Yuck.*

She hadn't wanted his cock there. He hadn't asked for permission and she sure as hell hadn't given it. The more her sleep fog lifted, the angrier she grew. This was the Darius she'd come to know too well. The Darius who didn't respect her. The Darius who was clueless and vulgar. Darius the borderline abuser.

"Jesus, Vala, I was just trying to have some fun."

"It didn't work. Did you notice?" She remembered that they were recording. "Cameras *off*," she said angrily. "*All* cameras off. *That* was disgusting. *This* is totally private."

"Jesus, Vala, how was I to know? Do you remember that time on Catalina Island?"

Indeed she did—she recalled it all too well. They'd been up drinking at the hotel bar most of the night, multiple rounds of a frou-frou absinthe drink with a fancy name, the Parisian Parrot or something. She'd passed out upon getting up to their room and a few hours later had been brought out of sleep and into a raging hangover by Darius's thick shaft gliding in and out of her mouth. She'd gone ahead and obliged him then. It had seemed easier than putting up a fight when she had a splitting headache and the alternative was dealing with a sulky baby for three days or however long it would take for him to rise up from the pouty dead.

"That was then. This is now."

Darius rolled his eyes. She knew what he was thinking, the age-old trope—*Females! Fickle!*

"I was just playing, for fuck's sake. And your lips. Jesus, your lips!"

"My lips were asking for it, right?"

Her gut was spinning in wild somersaults, her mind galloping in full flight. He'd never get it. That was it! He'd never touch her again. The most generous word she could come up with for what he'd done was klutzy, and not even that excused him. Angrily she thought: *The flower doesn't care why the foot stomps it. It gets crushed, regardless.*

She didn't dare look at him. If she did, she'd probably see the bad-puppy, mock-remorseful expression he slipped on when he was trying to wriggle out of something. It was totally phony, about as persuasive as a cheap costume-shop mask—you'd think a professional actor could do better. She abhorred that look of his. It spoke to her of his contempt—it told her he believed she was too gullible or just too plain dumb to notice that he was pretending. "Until further notice," she declared, "my body is off-limits."

"C'mon, Vala. I meant well."

"Yeah, well, outcomes aren't intentions. Choices have consequences."

He stared down at his knees. "Fuck. For how long?"

"Until I can tolerate your touching me."

"How long will that be?"

"What am I, your emotional weather-girl?"

"Jesus, Vala, you can be a bitch."

"Ah, the B-word. I've been waiting for it."

"Yeah, well," Darius began and fell silent.

She heard the words he hadn't said as clearly as if he'd uttered them: *You deserve it.* Vala recognized the moment; he wanted her to zing him again. It was his masochistic streak; he was inviting the stroke of the lash. "I'm not a bitch," she said, happy to oblige him. "I'm a woman with standards. And you just got a failing grade."

A weighty silence followed. Vala was seized by the desire to get away—away from this conversation, out from under their web of lies and half-truths, out from under the suffocating grip of their relationship. Her next stop? It had to be the Understory, down there with her new friends, down where anything was possible but this.

She stood up. "We're done for now," she proclaimed. "You have to start respecting me."

She went into their dressing room and checked out the collection of casually sexy clothes she'd brought along for her adventure. Tight tees, peek-a-boo blouses, microskirts, short shorts. She chose a bronze-colored halter top with an exposed midriff and plunging neckline, and a pair of tight cut-off blue-jean shorts a-dangle with frayed threads. She added makeup—a hint of eyeliner, a touch of blush, twin slashes of dramatic crimson lipstick—and completed the ensemble with a pair of dangly blue and red feather earrings.

Darius was lying on the bed, staring at the wall and fondling himself distractedly. He didn't look at her.

"I'm going downstairs for a while," she announced.

He didn't answer. She gave him a moment, then made for the door. As she was opening it, Darius's voice came at her from behind. "A blow job, maybe, before you go?"

She slammed the door behind her and stormed down the stairs.

-Vala-

CAMPFIRE WAS BURNING in the meadow. A dozen Erotopians were sitting cross-legged around it and dipping handmade wooden spoons into brightly lacquered bowls. An ancient man was there with the ruddy complexion of an Australian Aboriginal. A young woman looked Scandinavian; she had a chocolate-colored toddler affixed to her breast. Vala was especially struck by a beautiful young woman with dark hair, an olive complexion, and almond-shaped cocoa-colored eyes. She looked about fifteen and combined the guileless expression of a child with the curves of a grown woman.

Vadeen and Kri'Zhalee were at the far end of the fire. The philosopher-in-training waved, and she settled in between them. Introductions all around. This was Vala, one of the new Earthling visitors—these were members of the Treegarden pod. Seed was sown around the circle. She was met with easy smiles that were free of pomp. Their behavior confirmed von Zeitler's report—she'd get no special treatment as an Earthling.

"Help yourself to dinner," Kri'Zhalee invited Vala.

The dishes looked unfamiliar. "Some guidance, please?"

"Taste away," the High Priestess said. "Trust your intuition."

Vala chose a thick reddish stew and a bright yellow grain. "Ah," said the High Priestess. "Relaxing and rejuvenating. A fine combination."

Vala mixed them together at her guide's suggestion. "Delicious, too," she said. The taste reminded her of beef burgundy.

"It's a balmy evening," she said to her companions. "Why are you gathering around a campfire?"

"The fire circle reminds us of our history," Vadeen answered. "It invokes the spirit of community."

"It certainly means all that on Earth," Vala answered. "Fire kept us safe in our earliest days. It scared off wild beasts and provided warmth and comfort."

"Just like us," Vadeen said. "We have the same prehistory."

"You do?" Vala was dumbfounded. "Then why did you come out so differently?"

"We had the Great Coming Together. Our planet embraced nonviolence—*radical* nonviolence—while yours made peace with violence. We learned to harness erojoules instead of enslaving people and the planet."

Vala thought it over and decided that yes, that was a fair statement. Horrific events like wars could only happen if violence was considered legitimate, even if only as a last resort. The only people who refused to participate were pacifists, and they were few and far between. She shook her head sadly. Violence was everywhere on Earth.

Including, she thought with a pang, in her relationship with Darius.

"Tell me," she asked, "is a boundary violation violent?"

Vadeen nodded. "Yes, by definition."

"Even if no actual physical violence is involved?"

He nodded again. "Violence doesn't have to be physical. Any transgression without consent is violent."

"Can a person be violent just with words?"

"Absolutely. Bree's told me how you use language to attack people back on Earth. You tell people what's wrong with them—you call them ugly names. Those are all boundary violations."

Vala nodded sadly. It was as she'd thought—both she and Darius had been violent. What choice had she had, though? She'd obeyed one of the first rules of her world. *Fuck with them as they fucked with you.*

"'Radical nonviolence,'" she said eventually. "What's that?"

"Bree's told me about your freedom marches, when people put themselves in harm's way and let themselves be dragged off without fighting back. That's nonviolence, right? Resisting the urge to strike back. A person can stand their ground more actively than that, though, without resorting to violence. There's a middle ground between passive disobedience and striking back."

"I don't get it," she said, baffled.

"You actively invoke the power of love."

"How in heaven's name do you do that?"

Kri'Zhalee caught the eye of the beautiful teenaged girl with the cocoa-colored eyes. "M'dani, would you tell our guest the story of the Great Coming Together?"

"I'd be honored, *Tsh'kiva*."

She smiled at Vala, who felt like a beam of sunlight had been lasered into her. Then she cleared her throat and began, her voice a warm contralto.

"Once upon a time, many thousands of years ago, Erotopia was a wild and savage place, with danger lurking everywhere. The Wild hadn't been separated and protected yet. The world was wild and the Wild was our world. Fearsome creatures—*tszelbuts, h'qorns* and *bharat'sey*—roamed free everywhere.

"Equally menacing were tribes of our own species that were bent on domination and enslavement. Two types of people roamed the planet then. The Dominants' highest pleasure came from controlling others. Their drug was Power Over—Power Over without consent—and they were badly addicted. The Gentle Folk had no interest in imposing their will on others. Their impulses were collaborative, egalitarian and erotic.

"The Gentle Folk were easy marks. They camouflaged themselves as best they could, blending in with the deep jungle. But hiding can keep you safe for only so long. When a powerful chieftain named Akh'Hagorrh united the vast majority of the Dominant tribes in a grand alliance, the fate of the Gentle Folk seemed sealed. How could they withstand such a mighty force? Universal enslavement—even eradication—seemed inevitable.

"Thus was the stage set for the Great Coming Together. The Gentle Folk had been flushed from the jungle. The campfires of

Akh'Hagorrh's army were burning brightly on a hill above the narrow valley where the last Gentle Folk tribes were gathered. At their Council of the Elders, the mood was dark and opinions were divided. Some argued for mass suicide. Better to die free than live in slavery! Others proposed sending a special delegation to Akh'Hagorrh. They would prostrate themselves, beg for mercy, do whatever it took to survive. Become their slaves, if it came to it.

"Of the twelve gathered elders, only one raised high the torch of hope: Mkh'Danaï the Savior.

"It was true, she told them, that we had no technologies of destruction. We did have a weapon, though, and it was a mighty one. The universe had a beating heart, and it was powered by love. Mkh'Danaï then laid out a path to survival. It was narrower than narrow, but not entirely impossible.

"When she'd finished, she went around the Council fire. 'Do you believe in love?' she asked the elders one by one. Challenged to confirm their most cherished value, they had no choice but to cry out, "Yes!"

"Mkh'Danaï's proposal was approved unanimously.

"'Shall we burn the fires brightly?' Mkh'Danaï asked the Council.

"Again, the elders cried out: 'Yes!'

"'Shall we call forth the drums of love?'

"Even more loudly this time: 'Yes!'

"The Gentle Folk were about to practice radical nonviolence.

"Soon the fires were burning high and the drums were beating loud in their encampment. From their observation points nearby, Akh'Hagorrh's scouts sent word back to their commanders. The enemy appeared to be having an orgy. They were coupling in every possible combination, then dancing and singing around the campfire, then returning to coupling again. There were men with women, men with men, women with women, everyone with everyone.

"Akh'Hagorrh's officers were already aware of what was going on; the *da'zels* and *da'fzhuns* of the Gentle Folk were rising into the night, drifting over the vast camp of the Dominants. The brass was uniformly dismissive. The Gentle Folk were probably having a last grand party on this, the eve of their destruction. What they were doing was pathetic but harmless. The scouts should observe, but otherwise ignore.

"And so observe they did, along with many of the soldiers who might otherwise have been readying their weapons further up the hill. They weren't supposed to be forward with the scouts, but that was an orgy going on down there, all lit up for the watching, and why not? It wasn't like tomorrow's engagement would actually be a battle. Blood would be shed, but not their own. There was much light-hearted banter among the watching soldiers about body types and sex styles, more than a little opining about which of the women merited a spot high atop the rape list, and also a fair amount of self-relief there in the wooded shadows.

"Akh'Hagorrh's usually strong military discipline had gotten a small tear in it.

"As the fires burned out, the orgy calmed too, and eventually wound down entirely. Akh'Hagorrh's soldiers crept back to their bedding, their minds on fire with what they'd seen. Women on their knees, women riding men, women with other women, sometimes men with other men, people in their pleasure fully. Now Mkh'Danaï launched her second salvo. Under cover of darkness, the Gentle Folk's most alluring men and women made their silent way across the narrow no-man's land and into the beds of the enemy. The women went to the straight men and the men went to the gay ones (all of whom, of course, were closeted). It was obvious to the trespassers which were which—it was a simple matter of tuning in to their energy. That night, Akh'Hagorrh's soldiers were introduced to the extraordinary sexual talents of the Gentle Folk people.

"At first, Akh'Hagorrh's soldiers thought they were dreaming. When they realized that what they were experiencing was actually happening, they went silent and received. Back home, their women, who were somewhere between servants and slaves, serviced them perfunctorily. Any pleasure the women derived was mild, irrelevant, and fleeting. Orgasms were as rare for them as snow in the Midriff Wild. The Gentle Folk, in contrast, were enthusiasts. Not a single soldier called the guards. What they were experiencing was too good, too special, too improbable to share with their superiors.

"Without exception, the soldiers orgasmed silently. If Akh'Hagorrh found out, all hell would break loose. The men were supposed to be raping the Gentle Folk's women tomorrow, not lying with them tonight, or worse yet, lying with their men.

"Back in the Dominant villages, after a man's needs were met, the woman removed herself immediately. She'd done her job—one more item off the checklist, another chore completed. Not these sex guerrillas. They lingered, squeezing and sucking, extracting every drop, having *kriyas* all the while. Then they were done and it was time to go. They lifted themselves off their partners, kissed them gently, and whispered the words they'd been told to say. 'The love you've enjoyed tonight is the love of a free person. If you invade us tomorrow, you'll never have sex like this again.'

"The soldiers spent the night awake, gazing into the star-studded sky, great cracks appearing in their map of the world.

"Dawn broke bright and clear. Akh'Hagorrh's men awoke to a new orgy of lovemaking by the Gentle Folk. More *da'fzhuns*, more *gev'das* and *da'zels*, more images seared into their minds. When Akh'Hagorrh gave the order to attack, the battle cry that emerged from their troops was muted enough for him to share a worried look with his henchmen before they waved their weapons and joined the charge.

"Neither before nor since have so many people brought so much passion to a party. For the Gentle Folk, it was literally do or die.

"Mkh'Danaï's intuition proved correct—it was the Gentle Folks' pleasure that saved them. A giant transparent bubble materialized out of their bliss and rose up high around them. Thirty feet high and perfectly spherical, impossibly thin and perfectly impregnable, it swayed like an entranced dancer in the heat of the roaring fires. Again and again, Akh'Hagorrh's troops raced up to it with their weapons held aloft, bounced off it, and looked at each other mystified.

"Eventually they stopped trying and stood in a circle, looking in. Thousands upon thousands of them, barred from access to the Gentle Folks' pleasure, their bloodlust melting into a desperate yearning to be part of the party they were witnessing. And then, from out of nowhere, a simple foot soldier slipped in. His name was Gar. The night before, a slender woman with a sensationally muscular vagina had given him the two biggest orgasms of his life. His defenses were down, his loyalty flagging. When his heart opened fully to a mutinous thought—*I want to be with the Gentle Folk!*—the bubble opened and let him in.

"Gar's rebelliousness was infectious. One after another, the soldiers of Akh'Hagorrh opened to love, slipped through the bubble and joined the celebration on the other side.

"The contest, such as it was, was soon over. Spears were set down; the women welcomed the mutineers into their arms. One Dominant even went so far as to fellate a Gentle Folk man; this was an act of rebellion, squared.

"Akh'Hagorrh and his top lieutenants were surrounded by their former troops and brought, bitter and resistant, before the Gentle Folk's Council of Elders. What to do with these harsh men? Punishing them with torture or death, as some of Akh'Hagorrh's former colleagues recommended, was of course out of the question. Yet they clearly could not be set free. They still had a will to Power Over, and they still had their women. They could go home and breed more soldiers. They could regroup and renew.

"Again, it was Mkh'Danaï who came up with the answer. She herself would make love to Akh'Hagorrh—that would bring him around. When she first approached him, he was dismissive. She wasn't a virgin or even young—she had crow's feet, and her breasts hung down to her belly. His resistance faded at her touch. She extracted five huge orgasms from him, one after the other, over the course of a long hour. When they were done, he pledged lifelong fealty to her. He'd never felt pleasure like this before, not with any of his women, not even raping and killing.

"The Dominant soldiers were invited to join the Gentle Folk tribe. A handful refused; they preferred the old ways and were allowed to depart with a solemn pledge never to attack the Gentle Folk again. They went off, leaderless and bedraggled, looking to unite with one of the handful of Dominant tribes that hadn't been swept into Akh'Hagorrh's horde. There were too few of them to seem a threat. In this way, the two tribes became almost completely one. We've been living in harmony ever since."

The story had come to an end. The girl M'dani fell silent.

"Have the Dominants repopulated? How many of them are there?" Vala asked, picking at the wound again.

"We don't know," Kri'Zhalee answered. "The Wild is the Wild, and it must remain so—we can't be running around trying to count them. We believe the numbers are growing, but still small."

"Are they dangerous?"

"Potentially, yes. But our culture has thrived for thousands of years."

Somewhere along the way, Vala had gotten snuggly with Vadeen. His arm was draped around her, and her head was on his shoulder. He kissed Vala gently on the temple. "Did you like the story?"

"It made me happy, and it made me sad." Tears came into Vala's eyes. "Why haven't we had a Great Coming Together on Earth?"

"You have a Savior," Vadeen said, perplexed. "Bree's told me about Him."

"Yes. I was raised to worship him."

"What went wrong? Your Savior didn't save?"

"Not enough, apparently. We don't know how to practice love."

"And you? Did He save you?"

Vala wiped away another tear and shook her head no. "I'm so ashamed of who I am." Why had she been so harsh with Darius? *Dios*, she could be horrid! "My heart is still so violent." A radical notion occurred to her: What if she'd given Darius what he wanted?

What if she'd let him have his way with her mouth and then had a loving heart-to-heart with him? It wasn't like he'd have been hurting her physically. Why had she been so quick to hit back? And why that ugly, angry lust to mete out proper justice? She shook her head sadly. And she called *him* Mister Clueless …

Kri'Zhalee brought her hand to her lips and kissed it. "You're not clueless," she said. "You're learning."

Vala looked at her, startled. Was the High Priestess mind-reading? She decided not to ask. "I'm learning to hate myself. That's what I'm learning."

"No," said the High Priestess gently, "you're learning to see through the mirror."

"The mirror," Vala echoed with only a vague sense of what Kri'Zhalee meant. What mirror? Whose mirror? She gazed into the High Priestess's eyes and wondered what she was seeing.

Lovebirds On the Wing

"Erotopians long ago jettisoned guilt and the complex of concepts associated with it. For them, culpability, sin and evil are passé, psychologically unevolved, and ultimately morally predatory. On Earth, we've weaponized these notions. We tell ourselves we need them, that we need the bad to know the good, but the Erotopian experience suggests otherwise. Erotopians have darkness, they have light; they have ups, and they have downs; they have challenges, and learning. Evil, it turns out, is optional."

—Ulrich Von Zeitler, *First Report to the Senate Select Sub-Committee on Intergalactic Affairs* (2049)

-Vala-

DINNER HAD ENDED. VALA, HER TWO HOSTS AND the beautiful young storyteller M'dani had transitioned to the Understory, where they were cuddling on a plush carpet. Vadeen was lying between the Earthling and Kri'Zhalee with his arms draped around their shoulders; M'dani was sitting cross-legged across from them. Vala's sadness had passed. She was feeling relaxed and happy.

"I can't stay long," M'dani said. "I've got to get to my learning intensive."

"Our teenagers go away together on quarterly retreats," Kri'Zhalee explained. "They spend a week together, focusing on a specific subject."

"I love going on retreat," the girl said. "And I also love spending time with my family. Vadeen's, like, the best uncle ever!"

"Your uncle, eh?" Vala looked at one, then the other. Vadeen looked about ten years older than the girl. The Earthling did some quick calculating—that would make him the much younger brother of her mother or father. "If you're the uncle, who's the mother?"

"You're looking at her," Kri'Zhalee said. "I'm her blood-mother."

"*You* are?" It hadn't occurred to her that the High Priestess might be a mom; it seemed somehow incongruous. Now that she'd said it, though, the family resemblance was unmistakable. "So you two are brother and sister!"

Kri'Zhalee and Vadeen looked at each other and laughed. "Bree had the same confusion when she got here. We do mating and child-rearing differently from Earth," she explained. "When I was in my early twenties, I decided to bring a baby into the world, so I unwrapped my ovulation cycle."

"Meaning you went off birth control?"

"Not exactly. We don't need Earth-style contraception here. We have special meditation practices that allow us to control our hormone production and keep ourselves from ovulating."

"Mind control instead of birth control, you're saying."

"Pretty much."

"Have you developed this ability, M'dani?"

The girl nodded. "If you're Erotopian and you own a uterus, you can wrap your ovulation."

"When you unwrapped your cycle, Kri'Zhalee, did you do it in partnership with a man? Did you and he decide together to have a baby?"

The High Priestess shook her head no.

"So how did you find him? Who is he? Did you and he get married?"

By the time she'd finished her string of questions, Vadeen was laughing outright and broad smiles were creasing M'dani's and Kri'Zhalee's faces. Vadeen brushed a stray lock of hair off Vala's forehead and kissed her lightly on the patch of skin he'd exposed. "We don't do marriage here," he said.

"Why not? How do you raise a family, then?"

"In community," Vadeen answered. "We live in pods like this one. All adult members of a pod share child-rearing responsibilities. I'm in M'dani's pod. That's why I'm her 'uncle.'"

"You and she aren't blood relatives, then."

"That's right."

"We have circles of kinship," Kri'Zhalee elaborated. "Parents and pod-relatives. When I announced my intention to have a baby, two men offered to be the blood-father and two women volunteered to be milk-mothers. The five of us are her parents. The other pod members are her relatives, also known as aunties and uncles."

"Which of the two men is the blood-father?"

"We don't know," Vadeen answered, "and we don't want to. Our kids do better when they bond with the tribe, not by blood. Their hearts go wide as easily as deep."

"The decision to have a baby isn't always individual," Kri'Zhalee added. "Sometimes a tangle of lovers decide to parent a child and collectively choose the blood-mother."

"You don't need marriage for child-rearing, then," Vala said. "What about for sex and love?"

"Not for that, either," Kri'Zhalee answered. "From what Bree tells me, your marriage contracts are about sexual ownership. 'You can have sex with me, but no one else,' right? This confounds us. How can you corral attraction? How can you own another person's yearning for connection? Bliss powers the universe—why deny it? Why try to squeeze it into a cage with room for only two?"

"You don't do monogamy on Erotopia?"

"Sometimes we do," Vadeen corrected Vala gently. "When it's what the heart wants."

"Kavonti is the only person I've been with for the last six months," M'dani said. "It doesn't mean anything long-term. It's just how I'm feeling right now. And there won't be any blaming when we decide on something else, which I'm sure we eventually will. It won't change how we feel about each other."

"This family business," Vala said cautiously, "it's confusing. On Earth, there are rules about who you can have sex with. Family members are out. But you have non-blood relatives as well as blood relatives. How do you manage that here?"

"All incest is totally taboo," Vadeen said. "It's strong *ba'ya'sa*. No blood-relatives and no pod-relatives, either."

"*Ba'ya'sa.* What's that?"

"Anything that involves the inappropriate crossing of boundaries. If something is strong *ba'ya'sa*, it's a cultural hard no."

"If they can't have sex with their podmates, how do kids find sexual partners?"

"From other pods—Kailara has thousands of them. And then, when they're older, sixteen or seventeen, they move out and join other pods."

"How about adults? May adults have sex with teens?"

"It's a sort of sliding scale. A forty-year-old with a fifteen-year-old would be hard *ba'ya'sa*. But twenty and seventeen—sure, why not."

"And sex with preteens? How about that?"

Vadeen's eyes widened in horror. "You mean, before they reach puberty? That happens on Earth?"

She nodded.

"That's not hard *ba'ya'sa*. That's utterly unimaginable."

He looked like he wanted to vomit.

"It's hard *ba'ya'sa* for us," Vala said. "But we have our share of perverts."

"They sound like Hagorrhs," M'dani said. "Hagorrhs who are specially twisted." She stood up. "I must be off. I don't want to be late to my learning intensive."

Hugs all around, an incandescent farewell smile to all, and she was gone.

Vala lay with her head in Vadeen's lap—Kri'Zhalee was sitting cross-legged beside her. "What will M'dani be studying at her retreat?" the Earthling wondered.

"Resilience," Vadeen answered. "It's one of our main soul muscles."

"'Soul muscles?' What are they?"

"Physical muscles help you navigate the physical world. Soul muscles help you navigate the moral, emotional and interpersonal worlds."

"Resilience," said Kri'Zhalee, "is the soul muscle we call on when storm clouds arise."

Vala blinked. "All these new terms! What's a storm cloud?"

"Bad things happen to people," the High Priestess answered, "even here. A loved one dies. Someone oversteps a boundary. Someone is more skilled than you at something, and you're envious. Painful feelings are storm clouds, negative feelings that arise in daily life."

"Would it be a storm cloud if, say, your boyfriend stuck his *ba'da* in your mouth when you didn't want it there?"

"It could be," a voice from behind Vala said. It was Bree—Vala had been so caught up in the conversation that she hadn't heard her approach. She added her muscular frame to the jumble of bodies on the mattress and addressed Vala directly. "Did Darius actually do that?"

Vala nodded. "Just before dinner. I was sleeping when it happened."

"Had you consented?"

"How could I? I was asleep!"

Vadeen said, "Did he have reason to believe it might be okay for him to do that?"

"I don't know. Maybe. I sure hadn't said 'whenever,' though."

"You felt violated, is that right?"

"I still do. And disrespected."

"Ah. Two of your basic storm clouds. Are you pleased with how you handled them?"

"At first I was, but now—no."

"Could you have done better?"

Forlornly, Vala nodded. "I could have made an effort to be nice."

"Our Fourth Guidance," Bree volunteered with an empathetic nod, "is, 'Cultivate kindness.'"

Kri'Zhalee had been watching Vala intently. "You've got a lot going on right now, don't you?" she said. "You seem upset."

Vala's eyes teared up. "It's Darius. He and I may be breaking up."

"Ah," said the High Priestess. "The heartbreak of innocence."

"What does *that* mean?" the Earthling asked sharply.

"It means breaking up is hard to do. I may be able to help ease your pain. May I touch you?"

"Please do," said Vala. "I need all the help I can get."

The High Priestess brought her hand to the Earthling's brow, so lightly that Vala couldn't be sure that she was actually being touched. Her eyelids flickered shut. When she opened them again, Kri'Zhalee was gazing at her so tenderly that Vala went still, closed her eyes again and inclined her face for a kiss. Moments later, their lips met. Kri'Zhalee's touch was soft, sweet, and gentle, but what Vala was most struck by was the utter lack of noise in the High Priestess's presence. It had none of the freight that weighs down Earth kisses. Vala could detect no ego, no uncertainty, no arrogance, no neediness, no shutting down or showing off. With each passing moment, the Earthling's body relaxed and her anxiety washed away. By the time Kri'Zhalee took her lips away, Vala's spirit was in a temple where the geometry was sacred and she felt seen and safe.

A low thrum of vibrations was coursing through her body, the lightest of electric buzzes. Tears were streaming down her cheeks. From out of nowhere, she began to sob. When she opened her eyes again, Kri'Zhalee was gazing at her lovingly. "There," she said. "How was that?"

"I, I'm speechless."

"How do you feel?"

"Lighter. Washed clean. Like I've been baptized."

"Your eyes are so clear." Kri'Zhalee kissed her hands, gazed at her fondly, and at last stood up. "I'm off to visit Darius. I owe him a full Watering."

"Like, now?" The High Priest's comment had set off an alarm. It wouldn't be right for Darius to have sex with an Erotopian sex goddess, not so soon after his transgression.

"Not yet. I just want to get to know him better."

A shudder ran through the High Priestess's body.

Vala blinked. "Excuse me, was that a *kriya*?"

The High Priestess nodded.

"Why? Where did it come from? Lord knows I'm not that good a kisser!"

"I'm a cumpath," Kri'Zhalee answered.

"A what?"

"A cumpath. A person who's so empathic that it gives them orgasms. I felt so connected to you when we kissed that, well, you can see the result."

"You came from connecting to my suffering?"

"More like, I came from connecting to everything about you." The High Priestess hoisted a declamatory finger as another *kriya* coursed through her. "To Darius!" she proclaimed and headed toward the spiral staircase and the Overstory.

-DARIUS-

D
ARIUS WAS LYING ON THE BED in the room he'd been relegated to after his blow-up with Vala, staring at the slatted wooden ceiling and brooding about how badly things were going. There was no getting around the fact that he'd been getting shortchanged since setting foot on Erotopia. Vala and Jahangir had had successful Welcome Waterings—his had been aborted. They'd had whopping orgasms—he'd been handed a pair of blue balls the size of the fucking Ritz. And then, when he'd taken the entirely reasonable step of trying to right the imbalance, his woman had shamed him for it. Shamed him, and blamed him. Called him a rapist, basically. When all he'd wanted to do was play!

He pursed his lips unhappily, closed his eyes, and went back to the first time he'd laid eyes on Vala. It had been at the Limelight Club. He'd had an hour to kill and why not do it there? The dancers were killer, and a good-looking guy could get lucky. He was sitting at the horseshoe-shaped bar with an overpriced margarita in front of him, his entry fee for a close-up view. Two was his magic number. Two loosened him enough to put on the moves without rendering him incapable of performing.

A woman he hadn't seen before came onto the stage. Her body was trim and fit and, even better, her breasts looked real. He loved them big, but not when they looked like glued-on beach balls. She danced proudly and pleasurably—she was sexy, and she knew it. She saw him staring and a slow smile crossed her lips. She tweaked her nipples up and down for him (did it, quite clearly, for him and him alone), then turned away and danced on.

He promptly called for another margarita. Soon she was dancing in front of him. He stuffed a fifty in her G-string, said, "You're really special—do you know that?" and asked if she'd go out with him. She eyed the money and then him, and eventually nodded a cautious yes.

He placed his hand on himself, sadly and gently, and closed his eyes again.

It's later that first evening. He and Vala are at the twenty-four-hour diner across the street. He's drinking battery-acid coffee, she's nibbling at a bowl of rice pudding. She dips a finger into her dessert and holds it out to him. He sucks it off her, grain by grain. He's never tasted better.

He started stroking himself, more to keep himself company than with serious intention.

He's escorting her to her car, a tired ancient Honda, when he has what feels to him like a revelation. It lands like a thunderbolt; this is the woman he's meant to be with. She's just the right height—she fits so snugly there beside him, there at his elbow, perfectly. She's fully present, but not in a loud way—there's still plenty of room for him. She's stylish, gorgeous and good-natured—she'll look great on his arm. She has a body to die for and a face to stun a room. She's smart, she's thoughtful, and she's fun. She's been quite the eye-opener, this Latina from a strip club.

Just before he opens her car door for her, he takes her hand and kisses it. He's not playing the cavalier—he means it. "May I see you again?" he asks.

"I'd like that," she answers, smiling shyly up at him.

They hadn't fucked until their fourth date, a personal record for him going back years. There'd been necking, more necking, and finally a full and proper conversation over dinner about condoms and other boundaries. Only after they'd been through all that had they gone back to his place and made love. That was how hard he'd fallen for her—he'd done it by the book. And the hell of it was that it was years later, and he still loved her. He could feel his love welling up for her right now, soft and moist inside his chest. Sometimes he wished he didn't because there was a lot about her that he didn't love. She'd seemed so sexy and free, but she'd turned out to be uptight in bed. She was reserved and cautious, not playful or experimental. No fun, like when he'd tried to play dentist. She was also critical, and a complainer; sometimes he was left feeling like a cartoon Henpecked Husband. Vala had been a problem for some time; now Erotopia was disappointing him, too.

Naps often sailed him past angry snags; he decided to give it a try. After twenty minutes of tossing and turning, he abandoned his mission; he was too upset. He put his hand on himself again and decided to go with Plan B, masturbating, his go-to source of consolation since a little boy.

He closed his eyes, relaxed his mind, and called his perfect harlot in. His spirit soared when he saw who it was—Ool his new crush, Ool with her long black hair, Ool with her stacked body, slutty spirit, and tiny hoistable frame. He sighed with pleasure, started stroking himself and surrendered to the images as they unfurled in his mind.

Ool on her knees, whimpering lightly, begging to have it in her mouth, really and truly asking for it.

He honors her request and shoves it in. She whimpers again, this time gratefully.

He's fucking her mouth. Her eyelids are quivering with arousal—the rest of her is motionless, docile, obliging.

Two hands appear and grip Ool's skull, keeping it captive and immobile. He looks up and it's Kri'Zhalee! She shares a conspiratorial smile with him.

His ba'da *is deep inside the Fuckstarter's throat. It's amazing that she can squeeze him into her wee mouth at all, even more improbable that she can take him down so far, and positively miraculous that she can kneel there so obligingly with his* ba'da *tickling the back of her throat.*

"Do whatever you want with me," her stillness is saying to him. "I exist for your pleasure only."

Kri'Zhalee steers Ool's mouth up off his shaft, then starts sliding her mouth back down it, up and down, up and down, cautiously at first and then faster, harder, deeper until every inch of him is inside her.

The three of them share a common understanding. Ool is a tool, a willing tool—her mouth a mere object, a fuck-sleeve for his pleasure.

There's no tension here, no gender conflict or confusion; the two women want this as much as he does.

He was getting close to coming when a crisp rat-tat-tat came at the door. "Goddamn!" he exclaimed and removed his hand.

It would probably be Vala. Well, good for her, despite the timing. She'd probably seen the error of her ways and come to apologize. But then he opened the door, and it wasn't Vala, it was the High Priestess—and there he was, all six foot three of him, standing stark naked across the narrow threshold with his *ba'da* more stiff than not and aiming weakly at her.

"May I come in?" she asked. She seemed not to notice his erection.

"Oh, it's you. I hadn't expected."

They continued to contemplate each other, with a narrow door saddle and a small slice of history between them. "May I?" she asked again.

"Of course," he answered, and with a gallant self-mocking bow made way for her to come in.

They got settled alongside each other on a sofa with a view of greenery and branches through the wall-length window. She'd come calling, she told him, because his Watering had left her feeling sad. She wanted to do it over and this time get it right—she wanted him to feel deeply happy and fulfilled. For this to happen, though, she'd have to get to know him better. She found him—she hesitated briefly—a bit opaque. Probably, she added hastily, because he'd come from such a great distance. "If I know how to please you, I can give you more pleasure than you ever dreamed possible."

She said it matter-of-factly, without a trace of arrogance. He believed her—she was a High Priestess. "So how will you get to know me better?"

"Through time-shafting."

"What's that?"

"It's a psychotherapeutic technique—it releases memories from the penile unconscious."

"From the what?"

"The penile unconscious. *Ba'das* are the greatest repository of cellular-level memories in the male body. Formative events are stored there in their original emotional intensity. We use time-shafting to access them."

"And how exactly do 'we' do that?"

"We do it with my hands and mouth. I listen like a safecracker—I find the hidden memories." She fell silent and then said, "*Ba'das* are like trees. They contain history. When I time-shaft you, I'm examining the rings."

"You're proposing blow job therapy?" Darius asked, goggle-eyed. She nodded yes.

"Fuck yeah," he said. "Let's do it."

-Vala-

WHILE KRI'ZHALEE WAS UPSTAIRS with Darius, Vala was spooning downstairs with Bree and Vadeen. She dozed off. When she came to, she was pulsing her haunches slowly and steadily into Bree's groin. Shame arose and was promptly dispatched; this was Erotopia. Yes, Erotopia, she thought as her heart soared, Erotopia where Lola was queen. She took Bree's free hand and placed it on her breast.

"Mm," said Bree and squeezed her areolae. Once, then a second and a third time. "Do you like that? Do you want me to continue?"

She reached behind her and laid a hand on her friend's thigh. "Yes," she said. "I would."

Minutes passed with Bree steadily, lazily stimulating her nipples. "What's going on here?" Vala said eventually. "Is this friendship? Is this sex?"

"What does your heart say?"

"It's friendship."

"And your *tra'da?*"

"Sex."

"Well, there's your answer, maybe. Sex and friendship, it's a moveable feast." After a pause, she said, "Erotopians have a word for a friend you have sex with: *Da'zha'yo*. It's not exactly a friend with benefits, and it's not a fuck-buddy, either. It means a friend you feel an especially close connection to because you have sex together."

"A *da'zha'yo* is a fuck-buddy with soul. Have I got that right?"

"You do."

Vala covered Bree's hand with her own. She wanted it on her breast, but not the dizzying distraction of her areola play. There were things she wanted to discuss. "I'm not sure how I feel about casual sex," she said. "I want it to be special, I guess."

"Sex is as basic an activity as it gets," Vadeen interjected. "How can it possibly be special?"

"Even educated fleas do it, right?" Bree said.

"Yes, but that doesn't change how it can feel. Or how I want it to feel."

"Sex can do that to a person," Vadeen affirmed. "It's the most everyday act in the world, yet it can make you feel amazingly special."

"When those educated fleas are done," Bree said, "I'll bet they say to each other, 'You're the one. Let's get married and make flea babies.'"

Vala felt frustrated—they'd missed her point. "Let me try again," she said. "When I have sex with someone, I want them to view *me* as special."

This time Bree nodded in understanding. "You want to feel chosen, right? Lifted up …"

"Exactly. Like I'm in a little protected bubble where there's only the two of us and we're totally special."

"I get it," Bree said. "Believe me, I get it. I was like you back on Earth. I don't need that validation anymore, though. When I make love here, I don't do it to feel better about myself. I do it to celebrate who I am. I do it because I know that my partner and I are very special cells in a very special universe. I finally get it—I'm *actually* special." She kissed the nape of Vala's neck, sending shivers down her spine. "I'm not saying I'm *more* special than anyone," she continued. "We're all special, all equally special. I knew that on Earth, of course, but only intellectually. Emotionally, I needed to feel *more* special. I needed to feel *chosen*. I needed to feel lifted up because I was always down. When an attractive man wanted to have sex with me, I felt *elected*, like I'd been crowned the prom queen."

What Bree was saying was painfully familiar. Over the course of her life, Vala had had sex with seven men, every one of whom she'd said yes to, at least in part, because of the hand out of the muck they'd seemed to be offering her. She was no one, they were someone; erotic alchemy would lift her up; by sharing bodily fluids with them, she'd improve her status in the world. "*Dios*, we're screwed up," she said.

"You're right," Bree said with a sad smile. "You are. You're primates who haven't grown up yet. You're still hung up on power, on gaining privileged access to food and sex."

"Which would make Erotopians what, clued-in primates?"

"Not quite—we're post-primates," Vadeen chimed in. "We've replaced the will to power with the will to pleasure. We've done a global find-and-replace."

"The only thing we're interested in having power over," Bree added, "is our own selves."

The three lay spooning silently. "I've got an idea," Bree said eventually. "Vadeen, why don't we give Vala the full Erotopian treatment?"

"You mean, like we gave you after you arrived?"

"That's right."

Vala caught her breath. "Was that what you described in the Tavendish Manifesto?"

"It was. It'll be just the two of us, not four, but I recommend it highly. Orgasms await you. Many, many orgasms."

"I'm not a many-orgasm kind of girl."

"Not yet, you're not. May we spoil you?"

She wanted to say yes. This was why she'd come to Erotopia, after all, to test edges; and it would make great material for *The Erotopian Chronicles*. But she couldn't help herself; she hesitated. Vadeen was pretty much a total stranger; she'd only been with a woman once (drunk, very drunk, in a back room at the Limelight Club); and the only time she'd been with two people had been that same day at her Welcome Watering. It all seemed a bit much, and so she tried a technique she'd learned from Zack, something he'd called the Great Leap Forward. She imagined herself physically coiling into readiness, took one deep breath, then another, and on the second exhale sprang into action. Words emerged: "Now there's an offer I can't refuse."

There—it was done. She slipped off her cut-offs and halter top, and settled back onto the mattress. She closed her eyes and visualized her breath going in and out. "Ready when you are," she said.

"Well, well, well," a voice said. "What have we here?"

Vala's eyes shot open. The Universe was good, the Universe was kind. It was Jahangir; he was smiling upside-down at her.

"How lovely to see you! Won't you come join us?" she said and teased her nipples for him, one time only, her go-to move from her Limelight Club days.

HE STARTED OFF SITTING CROSS-LEGGED nearby, watching as Bree and Vadeen warmed Vala up. They started off with deep massage strokes, feathery touches, little nibbles and kisses, delivered slowly and deliberately across the full expanse of her delighted flesh. Jahangir inched closer as Vala dissolved into her pleasure. By the time they'd reached her *tra'da*, he'd settled in behind her and hoisted her willing head onto his lap. He stroked her hair and watched as Vadeen and Bree transformed her from the Vala she'd always known into a moaning, sighing, writhing soul whose body was on fire.

She could feel his hard cock against the back of her head. She let her head fall back onto it and gasped as pleasure waves one after the next tumbled through her. The humble housecat she'd always known had become a roaring tigress. Bree and Vadeen massaged her labia, pressing deep under the skin. They worked the ropey ridge just above the head of her clitoris. They inserted fingers into her lower holes (Bree the front one, Vadeen the rear) and from opposite sides plumped up an erogenous zone she'd never known she had.

Bree asked Jahangir, "Would you like to join us?"

He said with a smile, "I most certainly would," and then addressed Vala. "Did you speak with Darius? Are you quite sure he's okay with this?"

Dios, he was a Boy Scout. She flushed and said, "We're good." She felt guilty about the less-than-candid answer, but this wasn't the

144

time to be splitting moral hairs, not with her arousal at a solid eight and her new flame about to join in.

"May I go down on you?" he said.

She caught her breath. Would her scent be a turn-off? Would how she looked be okay? But then she said, "Be my guest," and opened her thighs to receive him.

He made himself comfortable between her legs and stroked, kissed and licked his way from her thighs to her crotch, working his slow way from the outside in. Vala's trepidation evaporated as she grew familiar with his touch—he was clearly attuned and adept. With his mouth fully on her, he proved to be inventive, exploratory, and curious. And, better yet, he seemed to get really turned on by turning her on. She couldn't help noting how different his style was from Darius's, who was totally outcome-oriented when he went down on her. Blondie approached his work as if he'd been given a job—make her come—which he then pursued with a single-minded intensity of purpose that often had the reverse effect. He liked to home in on her clitoris and, once there, give it a relentless working-over. He especially liked rapid-fire lizard-licks, a move he'd probably learned from porn. Sometimes his approach worked, usually it didn't, and there were times it backfired so badly they'd have to start over again.

Jahangir was a sensualist, not a strategist, and—another strength—he moved easily into Power Under. Every one of his licks, kisses, sucks and nibbles felt undertaken in service to her. She was royalty being attended by a devoted retainer. Because she felt no pressure, it was easy to relax into pleasure. Soon after he went down on her, a fantasy popped into her mind. She was a Renaissance queen, from Spain or Portugal maybe. Her grand gown had been thrown high over her shoulders—his *ba'da* had burst out through his tights. Moments later, she had her first orgasm.

As Jahangir showcased his oral talents, Vadeen attended to her feet and lower legs while Bree showered attention on her upper body—breasts, neck and face. At one point, Vala looked down to where the main action was, and Jahangir's head was right where it should be, buried between her legs, but his hand had gone rogue—it was wrapped around Vadeen's *ba'da* and pumping it vigorously.

She couldn't help herself—she felt put off and disappointed. She'd known from the first that he was bisexual, but it had slipped her mind as the romantic pull between them grew. Her surprise soon made way for concern. What did his fondness for men mean for them as a twosome? Would she have to make room for other men? And, hmm, was she for it or against it? She shooed away her ruminations and surrendered to the feel of their hands and mouths on her, especially Jahangir with his warm, wet tongue.

She had another orgasm, and another. Then he stopped and pulled away; she felt him go up onto his knees. She opened her eyes and looked into his eyes and at his hard cock, which was long-ish, slender and slightly curved. He said, "I want to fuck you. May I fuck you?"

"I thought you'd never ask," she somehow found the breath to say.

-ᗡᗩᖇIᑌᔕ-

VER THE NEXT DAYS, Darius and Kri'Zhalee spent so much time together that they might have been taken for a couple. They hung out at Treegarden and talked. They explored Mosshard Garden and the neighborhoods beyond. The pop-up markets, the public squares with their whimsical statuary, the planetarium with its spectacular view of the heavens (there seemed to be two sorts of constellations for Erotopians, representations of the Great Ones and of sex positions). She took him to taverns where she introduced him to Erotopian cuisine. Wild game from the mountains, delicately-flavored fish from the Midriff Ocean, grain dishes from the plains that were anything but plain. They took a day trip to a working farm on the city's outskirts; it put him in mind of a kibbutz. She played tour guide for him at the Temple of the Divine Nectar, sharing its hidden recesses and erotic statuary. They lay on their sides and eye-gazed—and she time-shafted him enough for the process to become almost routine. This was their only genital contact, and it barely felt sexual to him. He did get an erection every time, though. All that snake charmer had to do was lay her hand on his belly, work her arousal magic—her hand would twitch once or twice—and Monster would start rising up to meet her, as if obeying a Higher Power, until its thick head was grazing her palm.

Once full erection had been achieved, she'd place her free hand beneath his ball sack and pulse her finger into a small circular area that, she informed him, was called the million-erojoule spot.

"Do you like how this feels?"

"God, yes."

"It's a sexual energy center."

With two fingers pressing down there, she'd run her thumb and forefinger down his shaft from top to bottom and then back up again, with the same non-sexual, listening-for-something quality of attention she'd brought to their Welcome Watering. She'd continue until she found what she was looking for, then her fingers would ring him more tightly, her mouth would start sliding up and down his shaft—just so, just so—and his dive into the past would begin. And then, when it was over, he'd come back into the present and there she'd be, waiting for him with open arms. Sometimes he'd be weeping, sometimes he'd be raging—and she'd be having *kriyas*, always *kriyas* of compassion, for she was a cumpath and had been with him throughout.

-KAI'ZHALEE-

FROM THE HIGH PRIESTESS'S CLINICAL NOTES:
For our third time-shafting session, first contact was made two millimeters north of penile center, Grip Intensity 5.

Geo-Location: The living room of a generously appointed apartment in a large city a few hours' drive from Darius's home. Leather sofa and lounger, framed wildlife photos on the wall. A place for liaisons early on, now Pops' permanent residence after his separation from the Mater.

Chrono-Location: It's Darius's sixteenth birthday. He's a strapping but less than full-sized version of his current self. Pops has invited him to come visit for the weekend. He has plans for the boy.

Get hard, goddammit!

She's so obedient. Pops can get her to do anything.

And why is he still here? Stop watching! Go away!

A young woman is on her knees in front of Darius. Her name is Katarina. Light brown, shoulder-level hair cut in bangs low on her forehead. She's popped her breasts out of her bra. They're big. Geez, Pops! You really scored. Katarina is smiling up at Darius with a kind look in her eyes. It's like a secret alliance, the two of them against Pops, Pops who's watching them from the leather lounger, leaning forward with a bright glint in his eyes. This is awkward for me too, she's saying.

Pops stands up, approaches Katarina from behind and hoists up her microskirt so her slender buttocks are revealed. No panties. "Maybe this will help," he says. Then he goes back to his lounger and resumes gazing intently.

He's staring down at Katarina's naked tits and ass, and her mouth is around his cock like he's dreamt of since forever, and he still can't get hard. God, it's embarrassing. What's wrong with him? Why won't his dick behave?

Katarina stands up, returns her microskirt to its intended location, and goes over to Pops. She leans over to talk to him. Darius can't take his eyes off her long and slender legs. She leans over a bit further—and there it is! Her naked pussy. The first live one he's ever seen. She's whispering to Pops—he can't make out the words.

Eventually the old man stands up. "Have fun, kids. I'm going out now."

He pats his pockets for his keys and goes out the front door.

Katarina comes back to him and goes down onto her knees. "Now, where were we?" she says.

Kri'Zhalee's clinical notes continue:

We're lying on my bed at the Temple of the Divine Nectar. I remove my mouth and he emerges from his memory. His lips are trembling and his eyes are bloodshot.

"Who was Katarina?" I ask him. "What was her role in your father's life?"

"She was just passing through, one of many after Pops and the Mater separated. He called her his girlfriend, but if so it was barely. They weren't together long. She'd been a call girl—that's how he met her, I believe. I don't know if he was paying her to do this, and I guess it doesn't matter. Either way, she was Pops' gift to me."

"How did you feel about that?"

"She was hot. I was a virgin. It was a whole lot better than a new skateboard."

"How about her being your father's girlfriend?"

"That was kinda weird, I guess. But, hey, for years I'd been wanting to have sex with a real live woman, and now here she was. Nothing else mattered."

"And your father's wanting to watch you two have sex—how do you feel about that?"

"She was his girlfriend and he'd put her up to it. Paid for it, maybe, even. He had a right, I guess. Didn't he?"

"My opinion doesn't matter. What do you think?"

150

"She was like his gift to me. Of course he'd want to watch me open it. And he was proud of Katarina too, more than of me, now that I think about it."

"Why was he so proud of her?"

"She was young. She was hot. But you were there with me. What did you see?"

"A man who was proud of his girlfriend's looks and youth."

Darius nods thoughtfully. "It sent out a message about him, right? 'This, world, is a man.' Did you see anything else?"

"I did. He wanted to make you happy. He believed he was being generous. Benevolent, if you will."

"Believed he was being generous? He was being generous! That was quite a birthday gift for a sixteen-year-old boy."

I shrug, the gentlest of negations. "Who was the gift for, really?"

A storm cloud flits across his strong-jawed face. "Him more than me, I guess. He was showing off, wasn't he? What a hot young girlfriend he had. And how powerful he was." He shudders and gives me a horrified look. "What the fuck was that about? Wanting to watch me with his hooker girlfriend."

I pull back my da'yo and hold my arms out to him. "Come."

"It wasn't ever about me, was it? It was always about him."

He's shuddering, and on the edge of weeping.

"Come," I repeat. My kriyas have started up again. "It's just us two here, you and me."

He buries his face in my breasts. He's mumbling and ranting into my chest, sobbing as I hold him tight, stroke and kiss his thick blond hair.

-ᗡᗋᖈIᑌᔕ-

TWENTY MINUTES LATER, it occurred to Darius that the High Priestess knew him better than anyone ever had in his entire life. He was astounded by how many secrets he'd revealed to her, and how fast. She was utterly trustworthy, and that wasn't the only wondrous thing about her. There was also this—she saw him perfectly clearly and yet still deigned to be kind. In a mere few days, she'd become everything to him—his good mother, his best friend, his perfect therapist, his witness and companion, too. And then there was her sexiness, her outrageous sexiness. Go through Door Number One, the sex door, and she had to be the best lay ever. This was a woman with the heart of a Mother Theresa, the sex skills of a Cleopatra, the face of a passionate angel, and the tits of a billionaire's whore.

He pictured himself back on Earth, at a Hollywood black-tie charity ball. The paparazzi were there, and their cameras were flashing—the High Priestess was wearing her *da'yo* and looking tanned, curvy and glorious on his arm. As they worked the crowd, person after person dissolved into *kriyas* just by being near her. She was the talk of the party, the talk of the town, the talk of an entire planet. And he, of course, was right up there alongside her. Darius the Glorious, Darius the Woman-Tamer, Darius the envy of the whole wide world.

The High Priestess was half-asleep and holding him. He loved how safe he felt, wrapped up snugly in her arms. And how she smelled, of musk and spring rain.

His eyes shot open.

The thunderbolt—it had happened again.

He'd fallen in love with Kri'Zhalee.

- Vala -

ALA SPENT THE NEXT DAYS with Bree, Vadeen, and Jahangir. She felt like she was on holiday. With each passing day, she saw more clearly how pent-up and unhappy she'd been with Darius. Life with him seemed horribly claustrophobic. Here with her new friends, she could breathe.

She and Darius were still an item, but they were an item on hold. They ran into each other occasionally, but their exchanges were minimal and perfunctory. "How you doing?" "Things good?" Like acquaintances passing on the street.

At one encounter, she decided to tell him about her new lover. It seemed a courtesy, and only fair. "Did you know that I'm seeing Jahangir?"

"I see Jahangir, too," he answered.

"I'm seeing him as in fucking him," she clarified; the blunt verb emerged as a familiar surge of annoyance welled up in her.

"Oh," he answered, his face a mask. "Like, I should be surprised?"

Kri'Zhalee had probably told him. Vala was happy! She was praying! Back home, he'd have been freaked out by the news. *This* Darius barely seemed to care. Vala was pretty sure she knew why. Since they'd gone their separate ways, she'd seen him a good half-dozen times with the High Priestess. Every time, a look of enraptured devotion had been plastered on his face. That dopey expression had told Vala all she needed to know about him. He was totally fixated on the High Priestess, obsessing about her, longing for her admiration and her love.

Her intuitions about the state of Darius's heart were confirmed at the seasonal Cleansing of the Nest. When Vala descended the spiral stairway from the Overstory into the Understory, the Cleansing had been underway for some time. Kri'Bondai was sitting up straight-backed with his legs crossed at the ankles, and Kri'Zhalee was on his lap with her legs wrapped around his hips. They weren't actively thrusting, but they weren't completely motionless, either. Their bodies were shimmering in non-stop energy orgasms and they were chanting together, riding their simultaneous long, slow out-breaths with their voices, he in his thrumming baritone, she in her throaty contralto.

A mist had spread through the Understory; it had plainly come from the two lovers. Awestruck, Vala watched them through the haze. That their coupling could produce this fog was extraordinary enough—and was she only imagining things, or were their bodies fading and flickering, his first and then hers, before re-emerging as firm flesh? Their vapor smelling faintly of roses.

It was then that she saw Darius, who was lurking in a distant corner of the Understory. He was watching the coupling lovers with a terminally forlorn look on his face. There could be no misreading the message on that tragic mug. It had to be agonizing for him to be watching his beloved coupling with another man, especially one who was vastly more skilled sexually than he could ever hope to be with his porn-fed all-American ways. Yet Darius kept watching. His masochistic streak, she guessed.

Right now, thank goodness, Darius wasn't her problem. Kri'Zhalee could do whatever she wanted with him. Adopt him, train him, teach him to beg, roll over, get fisted. Vala was having a grand adventure. She'd be damned if she'd spoil things with thoughts about *him*.

When Vadeen happened along moments later, she surprised him with a long, slow kiss.

VALA'S ONLY UNSETTLING EXPERIENCE during this time occurred at a sex-toy market she visited with Vadeen not far from Mosshard Garden. It was a cloudless day, and a mild breeze was blowing. She was contemplating a table stacked with bicycle seats that were rigged out with erojoule-enhancing add-ons—vibrators, dildos, the two in combination—when a voice came silkily at her from behind.

"Hello there, you. People call me Hoor Ut'chi."

She turned and saw a man with full lips, silver hair and remarkable violet-colored eyes who looked to be in his early thirties. He was striking and attractive, but something about him made her nervous, too. He was standing a bit too close to her. She looked around for Vadeen, but he was nowhere to be seen.

"I'm Vala," she answered cautiously and scanned for Vadeen again.

"Well, Vala," Hoor Ut'chi said, "you are one fine-looking woman." He eyed her up and down and said, "I'd like to tie you up nice and tight. Then I'd like to flog you, give you a really good whipping. I'd like you to love it, and hate it, and beg me to stop, and beg me to keep going."

Vala turned away, shocked by his matter-of-fact tone as much as by the content. A memory surfaced, the time a few years ago when a man in line behind her at a local cafe, a total stranger, had whispered in her ear from out of nowhere, "I'd like to tap your ass on that sofa there." She wondered if she should slap Hoor Ut'chi like she'd done with the guy back home (it had sounded like a whip-crack; the entire café had applauded when she'd told them loudly why she'd done it). But physical violence was probably a bad idea, so she turned back to face Hoor Ut'chi and flung words at him instead. "What is wrong with you? How dare you speak to me that way?"

"How do I dare?" he echoed disbelievingly. "Have I no right to seek companions in pleasure?"

His response took her aback and got her wondering. Erotopians weren't bashful about sex; they didn't mince words and were straightforward. Maybe Hoor Ut'chi hadn't been misbehaving; maybe he'd been, by his lights, healthily direct and unencumbered.

Vadeen appeared at her side, a bit too late. The two men sowed seed cautiously, then Hoor Ut'chi turned back to Vala. "My offer stands. You'd enjoy it. I'd take care of you."

"Thank you," said Vala carefully over her pounding heart, "but I don't think so."

"Be careful with that one," Vadeen told Vala when Hoor Ut'chi was out of earshot. "He's a possible Hagorrh."

"A possible Hagorrh, and a certain creep. He said he wanted to do things to me. Tie me up, whip me."

"That's no surprise. He's hardwired for dominance; it's the only way he can get turned on. He's hoping you're a Server who will want to be a slave for him."

"Like that'll ever happen," she answered. But she couldn't help noting, even as her words emerged, the tide of arousal that was rising in her body.

- Vala -

I T WAS THREE DAYS AFTER the Cleansing of the Temple. Vala and Jahangir were in Mosshard Garden, picnicking in the shade of a massive *z'denda* tree with flowering magenta blossoms and thick above-ground roots. They'd brought bread and cheese along with substances new to them—a moist, energizing wafer called *dra'ndel* and a creamy, mildly intoxicating drink called *ma'zdhi* that tasted like a cross between maple syrup and pineapple wine.

They'd shed their clothes. Why not? It was a balmy day, nudity was normal, and for the last four days they'd been unable to keep their hands off each other. They expected to have rousing sex, but the spark didn't ignite. Vala blamed herself. Sex in public parks got you arrested back home. She kept hearing police whistles.

He went down on her. One last try; it didn't work. They commiserated briefly about their inability to achieve liftoff, then he set out on the return trip northward to her face. The *maz'dhi* had made her silly. She intercepted his face between her breasts.

"If you want to travel further, you must pay the price!" she said in a comical mock-German accent. A playful breast massage followed. Rub-a-dub-dub, two tits in a tub, followed by exaggerated smacks to his cheeks.

The *maz'dhi* had made him silly, too. He worried loudly about facial bruising.

"Stop whining," she commanded, "or you'll get it worse!"

A couple strolling hand-in-hand looked their way with concerned expressions before laughing in relief and moving on.

Now the horseplay was behind them. Jahangir was lying with his head on her belly and they were chatting. A light breeze was fanning their naked bodies and rippling the latticework of leaves and blossoms above their heads.

"Doesn't it feel like we've been here forever?" Jahangir said. "How's your time here been so far?"

"It's been unbelievable. It's like"—she hesitated—"it's like I was always just reacting on Earth, trying to hang in and survive. It feels like I'm starting to take charge of my life."

He furrowed his brow. "I'm not sure what you mean."

"It's like there's a switch, a self-switch, and I'm finding it. I'm discovering my personal operating system. It's like I was always reacting before. Now I'm taking the initiative." She stroked his hair. "What about you, sweet man? Are you blossoming, too?"

"I'm having the time of my life," he said.

Now it was her turn to look puzzled. "So am I, but that's not what I meant. What about your inner life? Are you growing, changing?"

"Not particularly," he answered with a shrug. "You may be asking the wrong person, though—I'm not a personal growth kind of guy. When someone says, 'Something changed deep inside me,' I can't relate. I look down deep and I don't see a there there. My soul feels more like a pond than an ocean."

"Maybe you don't see yourself clearly."

"Why wouldn't I? Aren't I the person who knows myself best?"

"In some ways, sure. But we all have blind spots that others see."

"You're describing a blind *continent*, not a blind spot. A vast territory that's invisible to me."

"Personal growth is all about surfacing repressed material. Don't you want to be the best and wisest person you can be?"

Jahangir fell silent. Eventually he said, "You're politically liberal, right?"

"I am."

"Which means you believe in diversity, right?"

"Of course I do. Just look at me—I've got skin in the game."

"Then why aren't you into *personality* diversity? If white, black and yellow are equally good, why is it wrong for me to have a psyche that's indifferent to personal growth?"

Now it was her turn to fall silent. She felt vexed. She was quite sure that she was seeing a flaw—his first one. This sweet and gentle man was in denial. Of course he had unconscious material; everyone did. Of course he'd be more complete—happier, really—if he put some serious soul-sweat into dealing with it. But things were so sweet between them; now wasn't the time to challenge him. Eventually she would, maybe, if things evolved as she hoped they would. Like someone had said at one of her workshops: The True Lover helps their partner be the best person they can be.

"You're a beautiful man just as you are," she said carefully. And she meant it. She ran her fingers through his chest hairs. "And you're deep too, in your way. You're kind and your kindness runs deep." She felt relieved not to be confronting him. "You're wise and your wisdom runs deep."

"Thank you," he said. "I appreciate it." He rolled onto his belly and said with a firmness that belied his gentle tone, "Let me be clear—I like myself just fine. I don't feel at all deficient. I just try not to overthink things, that's all. There's so much beauty in the world." He kissed her lightly on the lips. "I mean, just look at you! I don't need to go deep."

Vala's hand went still and rested on him gently. "Maybe shallow is wise," she said.

Embraced by the gentle air, they cuddled together, as comfortable in their public nakedness as if they'd been in a private hideaway. Eventually she said, "I love it here, but I feel saddled with a problem. A big one."

"What's that?"

"I still want to get back with Darius, and my heart won't let me. I'm too mad at him." She hesitated. "Do you mind my talking about this?"

"Not at all. You and Darius is why we're here."

"I can vent, then?"

"Please do. Tell me why you're angry with Darius."

"Because he's an ass. Because he's selfish. Because he's never met a boundary he won't test. Back home, there was Roxy LaRue and all the other Bimbos of Los Angeles. And now he gets here and the first thing he does is try to mouth-rape me."

"Any ideas about how to get past your anger?"

"I don't know. Play catch-up, maybe."

"Is that what you're doing with me?"

"Maybe," she acknowledged, "just a little. But we're more than that—we really are. You know that, don't you?" They fell silent. Then she said, "He's had hundreds of partners. I've had eight. It's one more imbalance on an endless list. He's had so much more than me in so many ways." She waited for him to respond, and when he didn't, she said, "May I be completely honest with you?"

"I hope you will be, always."

"I'd like to do anything I want, anything and anyone, while he gets absolutely no one. I get the smorgasbord, he gets *nada*."

Jahangir's eyes widened. "That seems harsh."

"But if it's for one night only?"

"Oh—that's different, not out of the question. What were you thinking, Union Night?"

"Yes." A silence followed, She wondered if Jahangir was thinking ill of her and was relieved when he mused uncritically, "It would be great for the ratings."

"Yes, there's that, too." she said. "The damn thing is," she continued, encouraged by his answer, "I love the big baboon. I want to be with him, and I don't want to hurt him. But that doesn't change the fact that he needs to be put in his place—he needs to be taught a hard lesson. I need to not be a sap; I need to get him to pay attention." Her voice tightened and grew louder. "Jahangir, it's who he is, not what he does, that really gets my goat. He's white, he's male, he comes from money—his privilege shows up in all the ways he relates to me. He just can't help himself; he sees me as his 'little woman.' He makes all the right liberal noises—I wouldn't be with him if he didn't—but underneath all that, he sees me as his servant. Holes and soul, I'm there to serve him." She shook her head bitterly. "And the damn thing is, he doesn't see it. It's like there's a law in his head, an unwritten law that needs breaking."

"A law about what?"

"A law that's about power, about privilege, that says to hell forever with equality and fairness. A law that says, 'I'm up, you're down, and that's okay.' That's what has to change if we're to stay together."

"And you propose to do that by playing sexual catch-up?"

"For starters." She looked at him plaintively. "Do you think I'm horrid?"

"Not horrid," he said. "Human. How will you get him to go along? He'll push back. I promise you."

"You're right, he will. Make nice to him, I guess, and hold off on pitching him until we're on better terms with each other."

"Set and setting matter," he agreed. "But how are you going to sell it?"

"I don't know," she said. "But we've got three days to figure it out. You and I, we can do this."

They fell silent. Feeling warm and contented in the glow of the day and the *maz'dhi*, she reflected back on their conversation. It had been a good one; she'd talked tough and clear, and he'd met her as an equal and hadn't made her wrong. Which told her, in turn, that she was right about her relationship with Darius; the imbalance and unfairness between them ran brutally deep. It badly needed correction.

But then a line from Zack's workshop popped into her mind: *Whatever you're saying about the other person, say it about yourself.* She tried it ("There's a law in my head, a law that needs breaking") and was stunned at how quickly her blindness was revealed to herself.

You must stay small.

Don't take the lead.

She had no right to finger-point. She was as guilty as he was; she worshipped false idols, too.

Two men and three women were strolling their way. A happy band, chattering cheerily. Vala's heart tightened. Did these people have any idea how fortunate they were? They'd been inhaling positivity their whole lives while back on Earth, she'd been getting "thou shalt not" worms injected into her brain. She shivered with horror. She hadn't known it, but she'd been living in a science-fiction nightmare.

How dare you think about yourself?

Don't speak up.

You have no right to pleasure.

From out of nowhere, it dawned on her that she'd been making a beginner's mistake. She'd been assuming that if Darius shucked off his sense of privilege, that would fix everything. Now that seemed profoundly misbegotten. Their relationship problems were real, but they weren't only his fault. Darius might be *a* man, but he wasn't *the* Man. The Man was all those nasty laws, those toxic worms, and they lived inside her as well as him. For their relationship to be successfully re-launched, hers would have to be flushed out, too. And only she could flush them.

Dios, she realized—she was a carrier! She'd come to Erotopia with a bad case of soul-parasites. What if she infected her new friends? She'd be the Spanish introducing syphilis to the New World, the trappers bringing smallpox to the Native Americans. She had to exorcise those mind-worm demons, and she had to do it now. But how?

She knew the answer immediately. *Step into your courage. Claim your power.*

Something shifted deep inside. It felt like a gear locking into place. Yes—she could do this. She could decide to not be dominated any longer—not by the white man in her bed, not by the mind-worms in her head.

Don't stand out.

Don't be a slut.

"I want to go down on you," she said. "Right here, right now. In front of these fine people."

Jahangir's eyebrows arched. "For sure?"

"Gimme," she said. "Gimme."

"Now there's a change of heart! Explain."

"I saw the light. I'm done with cops." Hoisting her fist in a power salute, she said, *"Viva la revolución"* and wriggled her face down toward his *ba'da*, which had seen into the future and was stiffening.

- ᐯᗋᒧᗋ -

HE NEXT TIME VALA SAW DARIUS, she crossed an important
boundary—she made nice to him. They were in their suite;
he was doodling. "I'm looking for my next superhero," he
said without looking up.

She went up to him, grasped his chin between her thumb and
forefinger, brought his gaze up to hers, and said, "Hello."

"Hello, indeed," he answered cautiously. "What's up? Are you
getting tired of Jahangir?"

"It's not that," she said. "I just want to be friends again."

"Friends with a wanna-be rapist?"

"Don't be that way. Don't stew in it."

"Like you haven't been doing that for the better part of a week?"

"Moods are moods. They come and go. But I still want to be
with you, Darius."

"Enough to come to bed with me?"

"Not that. Not yet."

With his eyes still on his drawing, he said, "Well, let me know
when you're ready. I'm not going anywhere."

For a first conversation, it had gone well; by the end, he seemed to
be softening. Over the next days, things grew more relaxed between
them. They got to sharing about their day along with the occasional laugh. The day after their reconciliation had been launched, he
made a passing reference to her feelings for Jahangir, and she didn't
get triggered by it; she mentioned his love for Kri'Zhalee and he
seemed to take it in good humor, too. They said out loud their love
for each other, reluctantly the first time and more generously afterwards. But it wasn't until a full three days had passed and it was the
afternoon before Union Night that she felt comfortable enough to
propose her starvation-diet concept for the evening.

"I've got a proposition," she said. "Darling."

"Oh?" he answered with distrust gleaming in his eyes. "Pray tell, what might that be?"

She plunged straight in as she'd resolved to do. "I get to have sex with anyone I want tonight. You get to have sex with nobody." Then came the sugar coating. "It would be just for Union Night. Just for one night only."

He emitted a humorless laugh. "So I came to Erotopia to be a monk! I hadn't realized. What is this, more punishment because of the Great Mouth-Fuck Betrayal of the other day?"

"It's not about a single incident; it's about the structure of our relationship. It's about righting the scales between us at a deep level." He didn't answer. As the silence grew awkward, she filled it with more explanation. "Jahangir thinks it's a good idea. He thinks it would be great for our ratings."

"Jahangir thinks a lot of things are good ideas. Like banging you, for instance."

He sounded pained. She said, "My having sex with Jahangir doesn't make you not my guy."

"You're not leaving me for him?" he said in a plaintive tone that told Vala everything she needed to know about what he was telling himself. Jahangir was her new true love, her next escape hatch, her free ride to the American Dream.

"You great big silly, no, I'm not."

"Have you ever considered leaving me?"

"A person considers a lot of things."

"Yes," he agreed, "a person does." He sighed and shook his head mournfully. "Go ahead, I'm listening. A man should keep an open mind. You've got this one shot to sell me."

"Fair enough," she said. "Let's start with this: Do you remember our Towel Boy game?"

"*Remember* it? How can I forget it? You pretending to take on one guy after another, and me, Towel Boy, standing by and cleaning up after them."

"You made a great Towel Boy. I loved how docile you were, and obedient!"

"It was easy," he said. "It was just a fantasy, and I was the one doing the fucking. But if you've gotten it into your head that we'll play that game on Union Night—sorry, it ain't happening. That was a private game, for the two of us only." A smile slipped out and he added, "You sure did make a great slut, though."

"I don't want you to play Towel Boy," she said. "I mentioned it because it's an example of a scene we did. Tonight we'd do another one. You'd be playing the role you were born for."

She had his full interest now. "Tell me more."

"You're the lead in a romantic love story. You're a knight in shining armor, Lancelot to my Guinevere—I'm the damsel to be wooed and won. You want me more than anything in the world, and of course I want you too, but I'm an old-fashioned girl. I won't open my legs for you until I've opened my heart to you, and that won't happen until you've proven yourself worthy of my love."

"And how do I do that?"

"By wanting me more than anyone else. By turning your back on temptation."

"It's one night only, right?"

"It'll be over before you know it."

"And why is this the role I was born for?"

"Just look at you! God built you to play Prince Charming. You play this role, every woman who's ever read a romance novel will want you."

Darius fell silent. Then he said, "If I understand you correctly, if I play along, you and I could get back together as soon as tomorrow?"

She nodded. "It could happen."

"And so I woo you?"

"You woo me, and you wow me, and you win me."

"Nail the role, nail the girl." He nodded thoughtfully. "I like it. Sir Knight, the adoring suitor."

"Adoring is good. Paying attention is more important, though. Lots and lots of attention."

"What, like never take my eyes off you?"

"No. I want this to be romantic, not silly—and I don't want you staring at me like a stalker. I do want to know that, if I look around the room for you, your eyes will find mine before long. I want to know that you're there for me. I want you to be my knight, my prince—steadfast, strong and true."

"How about smoldering? Do you want smoldering, too?"

"Duh, what girl doesn't?"

"The Sir Knight game, a romance novel for a lonely world," he said ruminatively. "And it's open season starting tomorrow?"

"Freedom," Vala told him, "is just another word for a whole wide world to fuck."

"Goddammit," said Darius and smiled ruefully at her. "I wish I didn't love you so much."

-Vala-

ALA'S BEDROOM HAD BEEN TAKEN OVER by clothes on loan from her friends. A black latex catsuit hung over one chair, and a small mountain of chiffon and velvet scarves shawls lay piled up on another. Glittery nipple and *tra'da* jewelry was laid out on the bed. Just out of sight in the dressing alcove, a small battalion of microskirts, filmy dresses and feathery capes was lined up on hangers awaiting her review.

Lola's Boutique, she'd started calling it. She tried on one sexy getup after another and eventually settled on a lacy off-white figure-hugging bodysuit with cutouts at the nipples and a tear-away crotch. Makeup-wise, she kept it simple. A dab of carmine lipstick, smoky eyeliner, rouge on her cheekbones and her nipples. She added oversized gold hoop earrings, jangly bracelets on each wrist and, for the hell of it, half a dozen toe rings. She checked herself out in the mirror and presented herself to Darius, who was in the next room doodling.

"I got inspired," he said and held up his sketch-book. "Meet Sir Darius Lance-a-Lot, Superhero!"

Vala saw a blond square-jawed face, a body sheathed in plate armor, and two lances, a standard-length one in his right hand and a bigger one extending out from his crotch. He was facing a dragon who was straddling a damsel atop a pile of gold.

He pointed at the woman and said, "That's you."

She laughed and said, "No, *this* is me. How do I look?"

His eyes went wide. "M'lady," he said and went down to one knee on the floor.

Beyond the Body

"Our home is a house with three stories.
(This map carves the world into words.)
The chatter of matter, the bridge from the body,
The eternal soaring of birds."

—Translated from Vervi M'chani,
The Bridge and the Body

-Vala-

ALA SETTLED ONTO A PLUSH purple high-backed sofa and looked about. The Understory was mostly empty. A man and two women were busy in the food prep area. The guy was naked except for a glittering golden mask that probably represented the Great One called Kaz'nakh, the male principle, the noonday sun. The women were covered in body paint from their necks down. One was a spiral swirl of rainbow colors—a thick-bodied serpent was wrapped around the other. A pair of *x'ings* were at their feet. One was rooting for scraps, the other was trying to mount his companion and getting no help from the lady.

Alone and wishing she wasn't, Vala started to feel anxious. Tonight would be an orgy, and she wasn't an orgy kind of girl (or never had been, anyway). She looked about for Jahangir. She wanted his reassuring presence—she loved how consistent he was, how unflappable and reliable. But he was nowhere to be seen.

A deep voice startled her out of her reverie. "May I?"

Vala's heart did a loop-de-loop. "Of course!"

She'd had a crush on Kri'Bondai for some days now. She'd even come up with a special name for him. The High Priest was Lord Superfuck, an aristocrat among lovers, a superstud among men. As he settled in alongside her, she remembered the time Bobby Bolton had pinned her up against her locker and blocked her, more than not, from going. He was two years older than she, he had blond hair and green eyes, and he was probably going to be the starting quarterback on the varsity football team next year. He was the boy every girl in the high school wanted—and he wanted her! He hadn't touched her, just let his energy ooze all over her, and that had made it even hotter. She'd gotten goosebumps everywhere. A couple of

171

hot necking dates had followed, then their relationship had imploded when, on a moonlit blanket in the Sonoran desert, he put his hands between her legs, she froze up, and he drove her home and never texted her again.

Kri'Bondai's voice brought her back to the present. "How are you feeling?"

"A little shaky. I've never done anything like this before."

"There's absolutely no need to worry. We'll be looking after you, myself and everyone else who's here. Nothing will happen without your eager consent."

Vala looked about. The Understory was starting to fill up. Vadeen had come downstairs and was doing something in the kitchen area. He was decked out in a gold lamé vest and a matching pair of thigh-high sheer stockings. A woman she didn't recognize was wearing a bright bird's mask—her entire body was painted fire-engine red. Wyldermon made his entry down a nearby spiral staircase. He was wearing knee and elbow pads and had what appeared to be a fox tail sprouting from his ass. She shivered as a premonition of what lay ahead ran through her. It seemed way beyond her comfort zone.

Kri'Bondai had been watching her closely. "A *chik'tash* tea. That's what you'll be wanting," he said. "It's one of our liberation teas. It'll take the edge off. Will you have one?"

He returned from the kitchen minutes later with an inky concoction that bubbled like a witch's brew. "How long will it take to kick in?" she asked as she raised the cup to her lips.

"It's very subtle. You won't even know it's happened."

The drink was pleasantly sweet—it tasted like molasses. Her fear faded rapidly—she felt relaxed and renewed. She turned and in the clear light of her newfound peace of mind contemplated the man sitting next to her. *Dios*, he was something. So strong and clear and sure and true. She wondered if they'd make love that evening. She tried to picture herself in his arms, but couldn't quite do it. A girl like her, a guy like him. He'd explode her into a million pieces. A woman could die from too much pleasure.

She squinted, as if trying to see through a tangle in her mind. A confusion, a paradox, had arisen. Kri'Bondai was a special man (the most special man she'd ever met), yet he also wasn't special at all; in fact, he was totally typical. He was all men—he was Everyman. He was every guy who'd ever been and every guy who ever would be. He contained eternity.

The one and only Lord Superfuck, she thought to herself, *is also Mister Perfect Forever.*

"This tea," she said, "it's really something."

If Kri'Bondai was Everyman, then who was she? She looked down at her body in its bodysuit and cutouts and settled on a clear answer. She was female. *But that's not all I am,* she thought to herself. *I'm a child. I'm a daughter. I'm a woman becoming more woman. I'm a woman being reborn as Lola.*

She looked at the backs of her hands, at the familiar caramel skin with its faint blond down, slender elegant fingers and neatly manicured nails. It was all Vala, all indisputably Vala, and yet right now her body didn't feel like hers. More like something on loan to her, a piece of clothing or a bangle.

An irresistible impulse seized her—she took Kri'Bondai's hand and kissed it. It felt like normal skin, which surprised her. It was soft and smooth, and crisscrossed across the back with deep blue veins. A new paradox arose. How could this person who was so unique and so eternal also be so all-fired normal? She brushed her lips across the back of his hand and looked up at him, perplexed. "Who did I just kiss?" she asked. "Was it you? Was it no one? I'm confused."

"You're not confused. You're doing fine," he said.

"I feel like I'm coming apart. I feel like I'm melting."

"No, *l'kivo.* You're ascending."

"How do you know?"

He said, "Because I've already melted."

-ꙴꙵꙶꙷ-

A T LAST—THERE WAS JAHANGIR, descending the stairs in a white linen outfit. He came up to her, took her in from north to south, said "Wow," and plunked down next to her. His eyes were rimmed with kohl; his lips had been stained a dark scarlet. They shared a slow sensual kiss. When they were done, she turned to Kri'Bondai and astonished herself by saying commandingly, "You're next."

The High Priest's eyes probed hers. He seemed to be wondering how much she could handle. At last he smiled and said, "It would be my pleasure."

The touch of his lips entranced her immediately. When his tongue touched hers very gently, tip to tip, every semblance of thought ceased. She went hurtling down a rabbit hole and was gone. When after thirty seconds, or three minutes, or a lifetime, she came back into her body, she felt dizzy and disoriented, as if she'd come back from a very long journey. "What was *that*?" she asked him.

He shrugged and said matter-of-factly, "A kiss."

She pointed to his energy cloak, which was swirling more actively than before. "And what is *that*?" Her breath was coming back. "I've been wanting to ask since I got here."

"My *da'yö*? It's me in my energy aspect." She looked at him blankly, and he elaborated. "We Erotopians believe that the psyche is a house with three stories. The first level is physical, the second is energetic, and the third is archetypal. As a High Priest, I inhabit a space midway between the physical and energetic."

"Does that explain your energy cloak? Because you're not entirely of the material body?"

"That's right. I'm starting to dematerialize."

"So that kiss we just shared …"

Kri'Bondai finished her sentence for her. "Exactly. It took you out of your body and spun you into energy."

"Since you have this, uh, semidetached relationship with your body," Jahangir said, "can you perform miracles? Walk on water, things like that?"

"Why would someone want to do that?" Kri'Bondai asked. "What is that, a party trick? We High Priests and Priestesses can do things you Earthlings would be astonished by, though."

"Like what?" Vala asked.

"My body can be in two places at once. It's called space-shifting. Shall I demonstrate?"

"Please do."

Kri'Bondai's lips promptly landed on hers. She started to spin out of her body again, but his touch vanished as quickly as it had arrived, and she was just as abruptly back in the Understory, back amidst physical matter.

"Reality check, please," she said to Jahangir. "What did Kri'Bondai just do?"

"Nothing. He was just sitting there. Talking with us. Looking at you."

"Well," she said, "while he was sitting there doing nothing, he was also kissing me." She turned to Kri'Bondai. "You must have been quite the scamp at teenage make-out parties."

"What other magic can you do?" asked a plainly astounded Jahangir.

"We don't do magic here. We do virtuosity."

"Virtuosity, then."

Kri'Bondai said, "What's your preferred *ba'da* size?"

Jahangir said, "I don't have one."

Vala blushed. "I don't know. I've never given it much thought. Darius is too big sometimes."

"Let's say you liked eight inches for your *tra'da*, but something smaller for your Rear Gate. I could do that for you."

"You can adjust the size of your erection at will?" Jahangir asked open-mouthed.

The High Priest nodded.

"So what you're saying," Vala said slowly, "is that you have a perfect *ba'da* … for every person. And for every hole."

Sheepishly: "Something like that."

"You are truly gifted," Vala said to the High Priest, "and I feel so silly, not knowing what *ba'da* size I prefer! If you and I were to have a date"—she flushed again—"I'm not saying you'd want to have a date with me, of course, but if we did, it would be like I was in a *ba'da* restaurant and I didn't know what to order!"

We'd figure it out, I'm sure," he said and smiled at her so radiantly that for a moment she feared she might faint.

A THOUGHT OCCURRED TO HER—A HUNCH. "Is the archetypal realm where a person's Inner God or Goddess lives?"

"It is," Kri'Bondai said.

Aha! Then it was as she'd suspected. Darius scorned her fascination with all things Goddess, but Kri'Bondai had just ruled in her favor, and Lord Superfuck would know. All men were gods, all women goddesses. "Thank you," she said. "That was useful."

She relaxed into the sofa and took Jahangir's hand. Her body felt warm all over. She imagined Darius upstairs in their Overstory suite and felt her heart open up toward him. She saw it in broad cartoon form, the organ spilling out of her body and extending up toward him through the interlaced web of branches. It pained her to acknowledge it to herself, but the truth was that she still loved Darius—she loved him *deeply*—and yearned to connect with him. He could be awful; in many ways, he *was* awful; but right now none of that mattered. He was her guy. They had history, and that was the thing about relationships—a person got hooked, regardless.

In her mind's eye, she saw a ball of tangled yarn. It was as big as a desk globe, and it was floating in the air at shoulder level. It seemed to explain everything. Life presented you with a vast jumble of confusion and, outside the confusion, clarity. The purpose of human existence, it was plain to her at that moment, consisted of one thing only—learning to step away from the hall of mirrors that kept people from connecting authentically with each other. Their notions of you, your notions of them, your notion of their notions, endless recursive echoes that kept you imprisoned forever.

She imagined encountering Darius outside the Tangle. That's where they'd been when they fell in love. She saw no reason it couldn't happen again, maybe as soon as tomorrow. If that happened, they'd meet and make love again as God and Goddess; they'd dive through each other's eyes into another hall of mirrors, this one bottomless and good, where they'd see themselves as they truly were, one and indivisible, together forever beyond the Tangle.

And if that never happened, if it was God's will for them never to meet again in that holy and illuminated space, that would be sad but not tragic. There'd be pain, but no suffering. Life would go on— *she* would go on. There would be others—lovers, children, elders, friends. That was the thing about the universe—it didn't know how to stop giving.

She squeezed the hands of the men on either side of her. "*Santo Dios*, I'm in a mood," she declared. "I want to make love to everything."

-Vala-

REE WAS ON THE FAR SIDE of the Understory, nibbling on a dripping piece of fruit. Vala waved to her and she joined them. She was wearing thigh-high leather boots, fingerless lace gloves with a burst of frilly lace at the wrists, and nothing else. Her strawberry-blonde hair hung down to midback.

Kri'Bondai stood up. "Here, take my place. I've got to oversee the preparations."

A heavy thunderclap sounded overhead, followed by a flash of lightning. Fat drops splashed down onto the meadow. "Uh-oh," Vala said. "Will Union Night be called on account of rain?"

Bree shook her head no. "A retractable dome covers the meadow. It's probably being rolled out now."

The thunder grew more distant and the rain disappeared. A man and a woman wearing sweatsuits came onto the meadow. They were attractive, early 30s, fit. He had a square jaw, a hawk nose, and straight black hair that fell down to his shoulders; she had curly chartreuse locks and was model-slender. They started stretching, seriously, professionally, like athletes preparing for a track meet. Calf stretches, hip rotations, downward dogs. They were impressively flexible.

Bree said, "That's Vix'han and Daruna. They're our resident Priap and Holy Fountain."

"They're what, sex priests?" asked Vala.

"That's right. They're above Celebrants and below High Priests and Priestesses on the hierarchy."

"Can they space-shift or size-shift?" Jahangir asked.

"No," said Bree, "that's a High Priest and High Priestess specialty. They do have impressive skills, though. Fountains excel at gushing, and Priaps at *not* ejaculating."

"Are you telling me Priaps are celibate?"

"Not at all. Where would the pleasure be in that? Or the celebration? Vix'han can have all the sex he wants and he can also have all the *kriyas* he wants, but he can only have wet orgasms twice a year. The rest of the time, he builds up his erotic energy so that when he finally does ejaculate, he does the moment proud. Kri'Bondai ejaculated for fourteen minutes when he was still a Priap. It's one of the things that got him promoted."

"Priaps develop their capacity to control, and Fountains to surrender," Jahangir offered. "Do I have that right?"

"You do." Bree nodded. "Priaps teeter on the bank, Fountains swim in the river."

"And that special occasion," Vala hypothesized, "when the Priap finally gets to ejaculate, that would happen during grand ritual events like, let me take a wild guess, this evening?"

"Right you are," Bree answered. "Tonight there shall be rain."

Their stretching complete, Vix'han and Daruna slipped out of their sweat suits and stood naked facing each other. As they gazed into each other's eyes, they synchronized their breathing. In due course, she dipped into an athletic back bend—he went onto his knees and buried his face in her—a loud *da'zel* emerged from her immediately. Vala could sense no passion in their connection; these were professionals getting ready. He stood up, carefully slipped two fingers inside her and worked them vigorously. He pulled them out, and the Fountain responded with a long spray of amrita.

Moments later they'd swapped positions and Daruna was busy with her hands and mouth. A baritone version of her *da'zel* followed. She stood up and gave his *ba'da* two sharp slaps, from left to right and back again. It stayed stiff and barely quivered.

"Successfully attuned and entrained," Bree said. "All systems are go."

The Priap and Holy Fountain shared a sociable kiss, locked arms companionably, and ambled off the meadow.

A thick obelisk-shaped boulder emerged from beneath the meadow and rose up to about twice Vala's height. A second cavity opened and this time it was water that emerged, gushing up almost as high as the boulder. Two men and a woman toted a piece of furniture onto the meadow. It looked like an oversized round bed with a big pie-shaped wedged cut out of it.

"That's a *tra'zen*, a sex divan," Bree whispered. "You can raise it, lower it, tilt it. It has hydraulics."

It looked sexy and comfortable. Vala wondered if she'd end up lying on it. The crew positioned it near the spouting water and returned moments later with a wooden cross whose beams were joined in an 'X' pattern. The crew placed the cross midway between the sex divan and the obelisk, then made their way offstage.

"On Earth, that's called a St. John's Cross, I believe," Vala whispered to Bree. "Darius brought me to a kink club once. I only watched, and I made him watch, too—we had a big fight afterwards. They had a St. John's Cross there. It was very popular."

"This one looks modified," Jahangir observed. "Do you see the hole that's been carved out at the center where the beams cross? It looks like anal penetration will be in someone's lucky future."

Vala nodded distractedly. She was still imagining herself on the *tra'zen*, and now she had Jahangir up there too, kneeling in the wedge with his face between her legs.

The lights dimmed in the Understory—the meadow remained bathed in light. Vala squeezed Jahangir's hand and felt the adrenaline coursing through her. Union Night was about to begin.

-Vala-

A PERSON IN A SHARP-ANGLED black-and-silver mask shambled onto the meadow. The body was hidden by a long shapeless robe. But the feet were delicate—it was probably a woman. She was holding a sledgehammer in one hand and a broom in the other. After carefully laying the broom down, she picked up the mallet in both hands and started swinging it wildly about her head. Its weight pulled her all about the meadow. She seemed to be breaking something up, something invisible in the air, something invisible that was everywhere. Once the shattering and smashing was done, the woman put down the mallet, picked up the broom, and swept the meadow clean of the invisible debris her efforts had deposited there. Then she picked up her tools, paused as if to contemplate her handiwork, and shuffled off the meadow.

"That's Zhivonye," Bree whispered to Vala. "Zhivonye the Spell-Breaker."

"What spells does she break?" Vala whispered back.

"The spell of language. The spell of spelling. The spell of the ground floor of the three-story house." Bree stood up. "I have to go," she said. "I've got me some dancing to do."

Vala followed her athletic frame as it disappeared into the dimness of the Understory. A few minutes passed, and then the Holy Fountain Daruna came onto the meadow, leading a row of people into the bright light. She was naked except for bands of purple corded velvet that were wrapped around her neck, wrists and ankles. Vala recognized some of the people behind her. Cymanthea was there, wearing nothing but an oversized strap-on dildo that wobbled wildly in its harness—it looked like an elephant's trunk. Wyldermon was there. Bree was immediately behind him and clinging to his foxtail for some reason. And there was Darius, bare-chested and squeezed into tight matador pants; she'd been wondering when he'd make his appearance. He was with Ool at the end of the line. The Fuckstarter hadn't bothered to wear anything, unless you counted a figure-eight of taut scarlet elastic pulled tight around her breasts and an identically colored bowtie that was held in place by a black velvet band around her neck. Her belly and crotch bore the bodypainted image of a snarling big-toothed feline. Vala's initial annoyance at seeing the two of them together passed as she realized that it was actually a good thing. She wanted Darius to be tested; Ool would give him all he could handle.

Darius peered out into the darkness of the Understory and bowed grandly in Vala's general direction. She leaned into Jahangir, pointed toward Darius, and whispered excitedly, "Did you see that? He's playing!"

"It's like dog training, isn't it?" Jahangir responded after a short silence. "You're teaching him not to chase after squirrels."

She said, "That's right. It's obedience training."

Sometime in the last minutes, the lighting on the fountain had shifted from white to multicolored—indigo, golden, emerald, red. The people on the meadow linked hands in a generous circle around the spouting rainbow waters. They bowed their heads and waited silently. First in an undertone and then more dramatically, a glorious a cappella women's chorus emerged from the surrounding darkness. The celebrants began to dance. They started off holding hands but soon transitioned to solo. As the music's tempo accelerated, their footsteps quickened. They spun, they dipped, they clapped their hands. By the time the trumpets came in, adding their triumphal notes to the soaring female chorus, the celebrants were whirling and twirling around the fountain with their voices lifted ecstatically and their arms raised heavenward, too.

The only person on the meadow who hadn't switched to dancing solo was Ool. She was totally preoccupied with Darius, coming on to him outrageously, dancing tight circles around him and rubbing up against him. Vala gawked with disbelief as she went into a deep squat that just happened to bring her mouth to *ba'da* level, the little slut, then raked his thighs with her fingernails as she rose up again.

"Poor Darius," she whispered to Jahangir. "At what point does he just throw her down and take her?"

"The man," he answered with a nod, "is being sorely tested."

Darius was trying to spin in a circle—Ool was making it difficult. She'd climbed onto him from behind. Her arms were wrapped around his waist, her heels were hooked around his legs, and her body was pressed up against his back. He was peering with a distressed look out into the Understory. *I didn't ask for this,* he seemed to be saying. *She's making it damn hard for me.*

Vala was thrilled that he was playing—and *Dios,* he was beautiful! She wanted to be angry with him for wanting Ool so visibly—she was quite sure she *should* be angry with him—but she was unable to summon the requisite indignation; she figured it was probably the tea. Of course a man like Darius would want a woman like Ool. Men had as much control over their arousal patterns as they did over their mortality. *See woman, hunt woman.* The directive was hardwired.

For a brief moment, Vala's surroundings slipped away and she found herself gazing upon a scene from prehistory. A man with stooped shoulders and a Neanderthal brow was loping with a spear in his hand. He was on the African savannah, and he was tracking. The camera zoomed in; it was Darius. She flashed back to the first days of their relationship when she was the one he'd been hunting. God, she'd loved it! He'd focused in on her like she was all he cared about in the whole wide world—she'd felt totally special.

A new possibility occurred to her—she'd been getting it wrong about infidelity. It was an embarrassing likelihood, but there it was—growing meant shedding; it meant shedding old patterns and old stories; and sometimes shedding hurt. She'd been defining betrayal as having sex with other women, and to a lesser degree as *wanting* to have sex with other women. But that, she now realized, missed the point. The true betrayal lay in the dishonesty, not the desire or the deed. Sin was a real thing, but it wasn't sinful to be open and honest. Sin was like a maggot; it lurked and bred inside the lie. And here was the thing—Darius's lack of transparency wasn't only his doing; she was as guilty as he was. She'd brought the hostility and small-mindedness that had basically forced him to lie.

Jesus, she thought, *you're taking his side now? What's next, lining up dates for him with the Bimbos of Los Angeles?*

THE MUSIC GREW QUIETER, the fountain shrank in size and the dancers' activity slowed. Silence descended on the Understory—the dancers filed off the meadow. A single celebrant remained. Daruna. She touched herself—her arms, her shoulders, her belly and her breasts, and finally her *tra'da*. Her breath grew shorter, higher. She lowered herself onto the spouting water and emitted a high-pitched *da'zel*. When she stepped away, liquid was fountaining from her in a steady rhythm.

Squirt pause pause squirt. Squirt pause pause squirt.

The Holy Fountain extended her arms straight out to her sides and stood there, squirting and waiting. The man in the Kaz'nakh mask came onto the meadow, escorted her to the *tra'zen*, and fastened her to it with the bands of corded velvet that were wrapped around her wrists and ankles. When he left, Daruna's arms were stretched out above her head and her legs were bracketing the two sides of the cut-out wedge. *Amrita* continued to spout from her. *Squirt pause pause squirt.*

The lighting expanded to include the half of the meadow with the cross and boulder on it. A new procession emerged, this time with Vix'han in the lead. He was wearing an ankle-length, hooded cloak that completely covered his body except for crotch-level openings fore and aft. A new dance unfolded, this time to a soundtrack that was all jungle drums and thudding bass notes rising up as if from underground. The dancers pounded the turf—they grunted and cried out. The music wound down and the celebrants departed the meadow one after the next until only the Priap remained. He extended his arms out to his sides. Two women emerged and strapped him onto the X-shaped cross with his face toward the Fountain twenty feet away. His *ba'da* was hard and poking through the hole in his robe. He was having full-body *kri'yas*.

A new *da'zel* emerged from Daruna. Her ejaculate fountained higher and further, and the pace of her gushing picked up. *Squirt pause squirt. Squirt pause squirt.*

"It's their energy fields. They're connecting," Jahangir whispered.

"I'm getting goosebumps," she whispered back.

"Me, too," said Jahangir. "But maybe not because of them."

Vala followed his gaze and there was Kri'Bondai, gliding silkily toward them. He came up to Vala and held out his hand. "May I have the honor of this dance?" he asked.

She sailed into his arms without saying a word. Shivers cascaded from neck to crotch. He escorted her up to the meadow.

-Vala-

RI'BONDAI STARTED THEM DANCING before she could hear any music, spinning her as he held her in his strong and solid frame. *So this,* she thought, *is what it feels like to be with a master dancer.* She had ample freedom to move and yet he also had her; he really, really had her. A man as sexually gifted as Kri'Bondai, of course he'd be a great dancer. By the time he'd spun her half a dozen times, her thinking, witnessing brain was gone, erased by all that whirling, erased by the erotic energy passing through her. What remained was a Vala who could respond to cues—left foot, right foot, follow the leader—and a Vala who was swimming in arousal. Every part of her that could be engorged was. Even her nostrils were flaring.

The energy fields of Daruna and Vix'han came sweeping into her front and back. His was deep and pulsating—hers had a higher frequency and register. As the two waves came crashing together inside her, she gasped for breath and went shooting up the arousal ladder.

She and Kri'Bondai moved easily together. They *flowed*—she felt no tension or uncertainty whatever. By the time the music reemerged from the Understory, the drums providing the bass note for the celestial women's chorus, they had a great groove going. As he swept her around the meadow, she felt blissed-out, blessed, and overwhelmed by gratitude. Goddess, she was lucky! To be in the arms of this magnificent man, and more broadly to have been so lifted up—her, Vala Cortes, the little invisible daughter of illegals, a nobody girl from a nowhere town on a tortured faraway planet.

"May I touch you sexually if the moment wants it?"

Her heart skipped a beat. She bobbed her head.

"The word," he said. "I need to hear it. 'Yes.'"

"Yes," she managed to get out. It sounded so good that she said it again, more firmly this time. "Yes."

Daruna's eyes were glazed over, her eyeballs rolled back in her head. She was lost inside her arousal trance and gushing, gushing, gushing. *Squirt pause squirt. Squirt pause squirt.* When Kri'Bondai twirled Vala out toward the Fountain, she knew intuitively what he wanted her to do. And so she leaned over and drank.

She'd never tasted female ejaculate before. Daruna's was delicious, mild and fresh. It didn't taste at all of pee. She took down all she could in two big swallows, then followed with a third—and when that still didn't feel like quite enough, she tore off the thin strip of material that covered her crotch and straddled Daruna so that the Fountain's *amrita* splashed directly onto her *tra'da.*

The blast shocked her with its intensity. A loud *da'zel* emerged from her as she spun back into the High Priest's arms. When he whirled her out toward the Priap, she was ready. Two full pirouettes took her to him on his X-shaped cross. She went onto her knees, cradled him between her hands, and slid her mouth down him as far as she comfortably could. She stayed like that for a long moment, awaiting guidance from somewhere, someone, anything. Eventually it came as she'd known it would, a call to hum into Vix'han's shaft from deep down in her throat. A fresh *kriya* shivered his body; white-hot energy poured from him into her mouth, traveled into her chest, and from there throughout her body. Somehow she managed to stand up and stagger back to Kri'Bondai, who spun her into a new set of grand-waltz whirls that left her dizzier and more aroused than ever.

Dimly and distantly, she could sense that others had come onto the meadow. Some were surrounding the Priap, others around the Fountain. It was all a daze, a vast confusing whirl. Was that Jahangir on his knees before Vix'han? Vadeen, penetrating the Priap from behind? Cymanthea stepping between Daruna's legs, wielding her wobbling dildo? All around Vala there arose a new song, the sound of *gev'das* and *daf'zhuns* rising. Then a sharp cry rose above the hub-bub. She knew immediately what it was. After six long months of holding out, Vix'han the Priap was coming.

Moments later, a new *daf'zhun* split the air. Vala could sense the source of this one, too—it had come from the Fountain Daruna.

She closed her eyes so she could experience her sensations more deeply. The Priap's energy was spinning clockwise inside her body, the Holy Fountain's counter-clockwise. She was in an ocean, and the ocean was rising. She opened her eyes and there was Jahangir, facing her from inches away, his expression a mask of tender desire. Surprised and delighted, she surrendered to his gaze and felt her heart open up to him.

They were gazing transfixed into each other's eyes when she felt something press against her *tra'da*. She was quite sure that it was a penis.

The *ba'da* (if that's what it was) began to rotate in slow steady cir-cles, painting her lips and clitoris, swelling them more with each new loop. She moaned and her eyelids fluttered shut again. Her breath was coming quicker when it dawned on her, in the shrunken part of her mind still capable of thought, that she didn't actually know whose *ba'da* was pleasuring her. She'd been assuming it was Jahangir's because he was the only penis owner in the immediate vicinity. But it could be Kri'Bondai, working his space-shifting magic.

Her uncertainty left her feeling even more disoriented. A depth-less crevasse opened up, and she went tumbling down it.

A voice inside her head said, *Just say yes. Don't try to know. Be present to the song, not the story.*

This voice, this insight, was what tipped her. Her orgasm didn't start in her clitoris or in her *tra'da*, or even in her body. It entered from above and it entered from below, and when the two energies met inside her—sky and soil, bank and river—Vala exploded. Every inch of her, every ounce of her, every neuron in her exploded.

The *da'fzhun* that emerged from her was even louder than the ones that had come from the Priap and the Fountain. She heard it with a rising sense of wonder. It was the song she'd been waiting all her life to hear. It was the song of Vala the Woman, the song of Vala the Goddess.

The next thing she knew, she was down on her knees and still coming. She became aware of an odd, exquisite sensation coming from deep inside her pelvis. This time, she looked down and was met with yet another shock.

Squirt pause squirt. Squirt pause squirt.

She, Vala Cortes, was ejaculating.

It didn't feel like she was doing it on her own, though. More like the universe was squirting and she was its agent of transmission. The *amrita* hadn't originated in her and it didn't belong to her, either. It belonged to Source and it was returning to Source. She was just spraying it forward.

She had no idea how long she came. An eternity, it felt like. When it was over, she opened her eyes and looked around. The meadow was emptying, and the lights had gone on in the Understory. *Ohmigod*, she thought—*Darius*. She'd forgotten all about him. She looked about and there he was, nestled between Ool and Kri'Zhalee on a crimson sofa deep in the Understory. He saw her looking at him, smiled at her, and waggled languid fingers in her direction.

Aww. He'd been there for her. He'd stayed present and faithful throughout, despite its being Union Night, despite the blandishments of Ool, despite the relentless temptations. Vala waved back weakly as a new type of bliss washed over her, this time a bliss of the heart. Maybe she'd been reading things wrong. Maybe her man was a good man. Maybe his being a hunter was good; maybe *everything* was good. Maybe her guy was a keeper.

The Mother
Of All
Connections

"There is a complex and intimate relationship between transgression and transcendence."

—The Provocatrix Handbook,
32nd edition

-DARIUS-

D
ARIUS WAS A VERY HAPPY MAN as Union Night ended. He and Vala had such a gift for making the other miserable. Had all that suffering been worthwhile? Now, for the first time, he knew the answer to that question. Yes, absolutely yes, as a newly liberated Vala watered the turf with her *amrita* and he sat watching proudly, sandwiched between two of the hottest babes a man could find on this or any planet. He'd been sage, he'd been strategic, and the hand he'd played had been a winning one. Things couldn't have gone better.

Union Night had started at a gallop for him and not eased up for a second. After that hellacious tease on the meadow, Ool had led him to a distant nook of the Understory where she'd gotten comfortable on a sofa, plunked him on the floor in front of her, and started running her hands all over her body, a private show for his eyes only. She'd just begun to rub the nose of the ferocious feline on her *tra'da* when a tanned hand landed on his shoulder. He looked up; it was Kri'Zhalee.

"Hi," he said weakly. He felt embarrassed; he could feel himself flushing. His heart was ricocheting around his chest.

She smiled at him and said, "How about tonight for your do-over Watering?"

His eyes widened. "For real?"

"I know you so much better now. I'm sure I can water you wonderfully."

"I'm sure you can," he said and looked around nervously. There were dangers here, big dangers. Yes, a thousand times yes to being watered by the High Priestess, yes to being watered by his new true love, but he couldn't have Vala busting in on them and catching him in what for her would be a sublime betrayal. Right now his

193

girlfriend was up on the meadow being spun around by Kri'Bondai. She looked totally blissed out, which was a fine thing; she wouldn't be thinking of her boyfriend, much less keeping an eye out for him. And even if she did happen to look around for him, the Understory was in shadow and she probably wouldn't see him. "Can we do the Watering here?" he asked.

"We can do it wherever you want to."

"Can we do it now?"

"That's what I was thinking."

The perimeter needed securing going forward, too. That meant no footage. "Cameras off," he told his rig.

"You don't want to take a memento home?" Kri'Zhalee seemed mystified. "This is an important occasion."

Darius didn't see a choice; he lied. "I'm feeling shy."

The High Priestess looked at him closely and said, "Then shy and in the shadows it shall be." She bladed her hand against Darius's naked belly. "May I? Before we start, I need a bit more information."

He raised his arms as if to block her. "You're not going to time-shaft me, are you?"

"You'll be fine," she reassured him. "I'll be sex-shafting you, not time-shafting you. Sex-shafting takes you into your fantasies, not your memories. Into your pleasure, not your pain."

"You'll be taking me on a sex trip? Is that what you're saying?"

"Not quite. I'll be sampling your fantasies. A snippet of this, a frame of that."

"And why will you be doing this?"

"So I can understand you better. So I can learn how to please you more."

"Well, then," he said and unbuttoned.

Her hands were around him for less than a minute, her mouth even more briefly. By the time she looked up, his face was flushed and his *ba'da* was pulsing toward the vertical. "That was perfect!" she said. "I can see clearly now." She turned to Ool. "Would you help out with Darius's Watering?"

The Fuckstarter put her hand to her heart and exclaimed, "I'd love to!"

"Excellent! Then here's what I want you to do," Kri'Zhalee said and whispered in the young woman's ear. Ool clapped excitedly when she was done. "Oh boy," she exclaimed, "that sounds like fun!" But then she hesitated. "Are you quite sure I can manage? Those are high-level skills."

"You'll be fine," the High Priestess said. "I'll be there to support you."

Ool turned an adoring gaze on her mentor. "It sounds so exciting. May I come? I don't want to be a distraction."

Kri'Zhalee ran a thoughtful finger along her lower lip. "Yes, you may," she said at last. "But only when I say."

Darius looked from the High Priestess to Ool, then back again. His mouth opened and flapped shut. He wanted to say something appreciative, but he couldn't find the right words. Nor could he go public with what he was thinking; he was fretting about coming too soon. Ool's request for permission to come had already made him stupid with lust, and his Watering hadn't even started yet. What if he couldn't handle what awaited him once the curtain was drawn? Pussy power was on the loose, pussy power in overdrive, and it was barreling toward him.

He resolved to handle it as best he could. He'd think about baseball if he had to.

Or maybe they'd be kind and show mercy.

-DARIUS-

KRI'ZHALEE PULLED BACK her *da'yo*. "My breasts," she said, like she was introducing them.

"What about them," he answered flatly. He couldn't stop staring at them; he felt like a dopey teenager.

"My breasts," she said again. "How big do you like them?"

His brow furrowed. "They're amazing just the way they are."

"Thank you. But let's say you could choose. How big would you want them to be?"

"They're fine," he said. "Really."

"You like them big, right?"

He nodded yes with his eyes fixed on her chest.

"As a general rule, would you say bigger is better?"

He head-bobbed yes again.

"Well, then, how about this?"

Her breasts began to swell before his eyes. They had the same luscious firmness, the same wondrous shape, the same lust-inspiring areola-to-flesh proportions as before. They were just ... *bigger*, slightly but noticeably bigger.

He blinked, looked away, and then back. It was actually happening—they were growing.

"Say when," Kri'Zhalee said.

`"Now. How about now?"

"Are you quite sure? You said bigger is better, didn't you? How about ... *this*? Or maybe *this*?"

All right, then—he'd follow his bliss without worrying. "Bigger. A lot bigger."

"How much bigger?"

Porn-anime tits, that's what he wanted. Cartoon-big and cartoon-firm, bigger and better than any he'd seen in the flesh, including Roxy's wildly enhanced ones. "Half again the size of Ool's, please."

"I do declare," the High Priestess said. Time passed. "Like this?"

"Oh my God. Yes, like that. A tiny bit bigger, maybe? Yes, that's perfect."

"Would you like to feel them?"

"Sweet Jesus, yes."

"How lovely! But wait—let me first do this." She reached inside her *tra'da* and probed briefly. Her fingers were glistening moistly when she removed them. She finger-painted the liquid across her breasts, down the steep slopes and into the crevice between them.

"My breasts," she said, "they're soaking wet! Would you be an angel and lick them dry, please?"

-ᴋᴀɪˈᴢʜᴀʟᴇᴇ-

HE HIGH PRIESTESS HAD DAUBED her breasts for strategic reasons. What she had in mind for Darius and Ool would be a stretch for them both, and while she'd be able to coach the Fuckstarter through any challenges that arose for her, the Earthling would be beyond her control if he freaked out, which seemed entirely possible given his failed first Watering. This was a very fragile man. He'd spook and run or possibly get violent if he wasn't at his most laid-back and amenable.

Her first thought had been to dispatch Ool for a mug of custom-blended liberation tea. But then she'd come up with something better—she'd give him her *tra'la'dyo* instead. Over the years, the High Priestess's body chemistry had been dramatically altered by her commitment to compassion. Because she'd been transformed by love, *literally* transformed by love, anyone who came into physical contact with her was transformed, too. Her love juices were especially potent. Her *tra'la'dyo* would be more effective than the most potent liberation tea—and he'd enjoy it more, too.

The High Priestess pressed his head close as he licked her dry. "Take your time, *l'kivo.*"

Her body flooded with a heartgasm as she gazed down on his golden hair. Beneath all that bravado, he was such a sweet sad man. She wanted to help him and was quite sure she could. When he looked up from her breasts, it was as she'd hoped—the defended Darius was gone. His expression was gentle and unguarded, his gaze was soft, his breath relaxed and slow. "You are so beautiful," he purred to the High Priestess. "So perfectly beautiful."

"As are you. As is everything." She drew his face back down to her breast. "Feed."

When he'd been licking her *tra'la'dyo* off her, his touch had felt tentative and uncertain. Now it felt totally tuned in. Making love to her breasts, to the feel and wild curves of them, had become an act of prayer for him. She closed her eyes and pulled him closer to her. A snippet of the ancient roundelay flitted through her mind:

The boy is the man, the man the boy,
And perfect is their pleasure,
In every part, in every port,
By every manhood measure.

Things were falling into place. It was time to unwrap her lactation.

OOL WAS ON HER KNEES in front of Darius. Her *l'shava* was gray and reedy and anxious; she was plainly feeling intimidated. Now, before they got started in earnest, was the time to shore up her confidence. The High Priestess called forth her Teacher self and spiraled into Ool. Energetically and esthetically, her soulscape was very different from the flirty, flighty persona she projected to the world; it was a desert of windblown sands, timeless and fractal, shapely and elegant. She scanned the scene for an entry point, and eventually one emerged. Two plumes spread apart and formed a generous circle. She plunged through it, mind-messaging Ool as she did so: *Dilate it all, girl, from the top down to the bottom.*

Three deep sounding breaths from Ool attested to reception.

A string runs through your center. Strum it. Become it. Surrender!

Again Ool got it, did it.

Surrender, Ool! the High Priestess mind-messaged again.

The Fuckstarter heard her and obeyed, plunging three levels into Power Under. Kri'Zhalee shifted into Witness mode and ran a quick assessment. Ool's dive had taken her down deep enough to do the submitting required of her.

The High Priestess addressed the Earthling in her outside voice. "Darius di Selva, do you choose sex for your Welcome Watering?"

Darius looked from one woman to the other and said nothing.

"We're here to make your dreams come true," she said to reassure him.

Yet he remained silent. Perplexed, she traveled inside him. His nervous system was practically fibrillating with excitement. There was anxiety there, and arousal, and also something more profound—a deep seismic shift, a state-change in his notion of the possible.

None of that could be detected in his answer, which emerged wrapped up in glacial cool. "I'm good with that. Let's get started."

-DARIUS-

RI'ZHALEE PULLED DARIUS'S HEAD down to her breast. "My nipples," she said. "It's time for them now. Suck."

The Earthling cupped the High Priestess's enormous breast between his hands and slipped his lips around the merlot-colored nipple. It felt hard and tight against his lips and tongue. He sucked and released, sucked and released, sucked and released until a steady rhythm was established. Nectar spilled into him. It tasted amazingly good.

He could hear, as if from a great distance, a small dim voice protesting. A real man would be fucking a woman with a body like that, not sucking at her tit like a baby. But the taste—ah, the taste! Which was improbable, magical, like vanilla ice cream churned by the divine. He grew dizzy as the milk spilled down his throat. His adult sense of self vanished inside his disorientation. When he emerged from it, it was with a new identity. He was the baby he'd once been, sucking at his mama's breast.

Baby Darius squeaked happily and settled in for some serious drinking.

Enough time passed for Darius to get lost inside the bliss of the milk passing into him. Then he felt Ool's lips close down around his *ba'da*, and her mouth as it started sliding up and down him. Infant and adult, milk and mouth—it was too much too handle—he was stunned back into his adult body. He opened his eyes and stared down at the Fuckstarter on her knees, at her glorious breasts, at her arms self-pinioned behind her back, at her motionless mouth halfway down him.

"Come back to me," said Kri'Zhalee. "Come back to me now and suck."

He brought his mouth back to her nipple, drew more milk into him, and descended into dizziness again. This time, though, his awareness was split. Above, he was with the breast and the nipple, and the milk that was pouring into him. Below there was the Fuckstarter's eager mouth, which had gone completely still and seemed to be waiting for something. Darius knew exactly where she'd stopped. It was where all but the most gifted women braked, just on the safe side of the gag reflex.

"Ready, Ool?" Kri'Zhalee asked.

The Fuckstarter exhaled a long "Aah" of a yes.

"Excellent." The High Priestess's next words were directed at Darius. "Fuck away," she said. "Keep sucking my tit, and fuck away. Don't hold back. Drink me down, and fuck her as hard as you want to."

He drew more milk into him, pumped his hips and damn if another miracle didn't descend on him as his *ba'da* went sliding past the Great Throat Barrier deep down into Ool's waiting gullet. He had no idea how she was managing it—Ool's mouth was as petite as the rest of her—but there it was, his Really Big Cock in her Really Small Throat, and not only that but he could sense not an ounce of resistance in her. Here was yet another miracle; she seemed perfectly content to have him all the way down there. Did Erotopians have elastic throats? Because she was better than Roxy, even.

"Good girl," Kri'Zhalee said. "Now stay like that with him down there. Stay still until I let you go."

He experienced a brief moment of *déjà vu*. Hadn't this same exact thing happened recently? Then he recalled his fantasy from a few days before. Then, too, he'd had Ool on her knees with a fully submissive mouth and throat, and a crucial supporting actress in Kri'Zhalee. That had to be the fantasy she'd tapped into when she sex-shafted him. But something wasn't quite right here, not quite square. Her hands were around *his* head (he could feel them there), not Ool's as in his fantasy; it was an inaccurate rendering.

"May I fuck her mouth with your *ba'da*?" Kri'Zhalee asked.

Now at last he understood. The High Priestess was space-shifting. Her physical hands were on his head, and her virtual ones were on Ool's. She was reenacting his fantasy in its entirety. He purred his permission into her nipple, a mumbled "mmm" that brought in its wake a fresh milk release. He gobbled it down greedily.

Kri'Zhalee raised Ool's mouth up until it was almost off him. Then she plunged it down again, all the way down, smoothly past the Great Throat Barrier. She repeated the action again and again, a drawn-out suspenseful lifting up followed by a forceful thrusting down.

"Why does Ool have a mouth?" Kri'Zhalee asked. "Why did Source give her a throat?"

All the way up, all the way down, again and again and again. A moan emerged from Ool. It was, Darius realized with a start, a *gev'da*—the wench was on the verge of coming.

Ool moaned again. "Are you requesting permission to come?" the High Priestess asked coolly.

The Fuckstarter responded with a stifled squeal that was probably a yes.

"Not yet," Kri'Zhalee said. She hoisted Ool's head high up off his *ba'da* and held it imprisoned it there. "You will come when I tell you to and not a moment sooner." A new squeak emerged from Ool, even more desperate than before. The High Priestess held her head still for one long extra beat. Then she said grandly, "You may come," and plunged the Fuckstarter's head all the way down Darius.

He first felt the Fuckstarter's orgasm in his *ba'da*. He felt it spread throughout her body. Her throat, her crotch, her heart, her head.

A small miracle then happened. Ool's orgasmic energy crossed into Darius via the land-bridge of his cock and traveled up his body. It streamed into his mouth and from there into Kri'Zhalee's nipple and into the flow of milk beyond. In his mind's eye, he could see the alchemy unfolding, the gold of Ool's orgasm mixing with the white of the High Priestess's milk.

"Your turn now," Kri'Zhalee said and tapped the crown of his head.

The two women's elixir poured back into him, breastmilk transformed into white-gold light that went washing through him, culminating in a vast orgasmic explosion that sent his offering down Ool's throat in wild spurt after spurt after spurt.

When he opened his eyes, Ool was staring at him in wide-eyed disbelief. Kri'Zhalee was laughing and having *kriyas*. "What the fuck?" said Darius. "I believe I just came milk."

They were lying collapsed in a post-orgasmic stupor when Kri'Bondai and Jahangir deposited a weak-kneed Vala at their feet and wandered off arm-in-arm somewhere.

"Oh. My. God," the new arrival said from her place on the carpet. "What. Just. Happened."

Ool sowed lazy seed in her direction. "We have a word for your condition," she said. "Cumatose. You're cumatose."

"*Santo Jesús*," Vala said. "Who knew?" She turned to Kri'Zhalee. "Was it good for you, *Tsh'kiva*?"

"Better than that."

The High Priestess's *da'yo* was back in place, her breasts their normal size again.

"And you, Ool?"

The Fuckstarter stretched lazily and said, "Yum."

"And you, Sir Knight?"

"Oh yes, m'lady," he said carefully. "It's been a grand evening for us all, I think."

Someone suggested that they go onto the meadow. They went there and tumbled onto the welcoming grass. The rain had long since stopped, the roof been long since retracted. They lay cumatose beneath the trees and stars, Darius and his women, this pasha and his harem.

In the Garden,
With a Mosshard

"*Kailara's location was selected for the
abundance of mosshards in the region.
They are a national treasure.*"

—Ulrich Von Zeitler, *First Report to
the Senate Select Sub-Committee on
Intergalactic Affairs* (2049)

-DARIUS-

ARIUS AWOKE THE NEXT MORNING in Kri'Zhalee's chambers at the Temple of the Divine Nectar. They hadn't had sex; they'd only cuddled. She brought him into the temple's enormous kitchen, where they enjoyed a breakfast of *dra'dhero*, a creamy pale-blue porridge with hints of vanilla, honey, and bacon in it. Then they returned with steaming mugs of tea to the scarlet-bedecked sprawl of mattresses where they'd slept.

"There's something I want you to do for me," she said.

"What's that?"

"Go down on me."

"Say what?"

"Go down on me," she said again.

And there she went, blowing his mind again. She'd told him she wouldn't be having sex with him; apparently cunnilingus didn't count. He could hardly imagine a less romantic proposition, but no matter. He was being asked to go down on Kri'Zhalee, a sex priestess and the woman he was madly in love with; he didn't need flowers to say yes.

"You must follow my directions. Do exactly as I say."

The High Priestess's inner lips had ornate folds and were bigger than her outer ones. Her button was larger than average but not dramatically so—he could see it peeking out from under its hood. Her vulva was as swollen and juicy as a succulently ripe piece of fruit.

"Lick slowly up the left side—a bit more to the outside, please— then slowly down the right. Slower. Slower. That's right. Lovely! Now again." She took a deep inhale and with a long rounded "Aah" of an exhale sent the breath down into her crotch. Her body trembled all over. "Slowly! More central this time," she said. "That's right. Yes!" Another breath, another shudder. "Again. Even more to the middle, please."

With each new lick, Darius was transported ever deeper into a fog of pure sensation until finally he was only aware of her taste (like raspberries) and smell (an intensely musky rose).

"Mouth over *tra'la'dö*," she said sharply. "Now!"

He wasn't sure what the word meant, took a wild guess at the urethral orifice, and got there just in time to a receive a blast of *amrita*. He swallowed it down and blacked out.

When he came to, Kri'Zhalee was smiling down at him. Before he could say anything, she tapped him with her forefinger just above and between his eyes.

He went blank again. When he opened his eyes again, everything looked different. "Holy shit," Darius said.

The High Priestess smiled. "Yes, even shit is holy."

"I'm seeing jewels. Emeralds, diamonds, sapphires. The world is jewels. What happened?"

"You're seeing things as they really are."

"It's like a palace, like I'm living in a palace. It's like it's all wearing a crown."

"It's beautiful, isn't it?"

"Words can't describe. God's glory isn't trumpets and hosannas. It's *this*."

She nodded and said, "*'And the angel waved her perfect hand/And displayed for all to see/The sultan's palace/It humbled me.'*"

"Yes, that describes it precisely!"

"Those words were written over two thousand years ago by our immortal poet Vervi M'chani."

"And you, you're my angel. The angel from the poem. You're the one who showed this to me."

"I'm a messenger, that's all. A reminder."

"A stunningly beautiful reminder."

"A stunningly beautiful reminder of a stunningly beautiful world. You're stunningly beautiful, too." She paused and then said, "I asked you to lick my *tra'da* because I wanted you to see what Vervi M'chani saw. Because I wanted you to see what we all see."

She went silent again and then said softly, delicately, "You've been having special feelings for me, is that right?"

"Yes." He hesitated for a long moment and then added, "It's true. I've fallen in love with you."

His exposure left him feeling terribly embarrassed and out of his league, like a teenaged hick declaring his love to a world-renowned beauty. For some time now, he'd been having fantasies about the two of them together. That was her on his arm at an Oscars party, dispensing orgasms like bonbons. That was her decked out in a white *da'yo*, thrilled to tears at their wedding. That was them on a mountaintop, fucking happily ever after. He didn't actually expect any of this to happen, of course, but if there was ever a dream girl, it was she.

Hope got the better of him again. Now was when she'd say she felt the same way about him, or at least blush with girlish modesty.

Nothing remotely like that happened. "You were in love with me before you drank down my *amrita*," she said matter-of-factly. "How about now?"

He suppressed his disappointment and gave her question thought. "It's the same, but different," he answered eventually.

"How so?"

"I have the same feelings for you, but you don't stand out anymore. I was seeing you as truly special. Now it's more like you blend in."

She nodded understandingly. "Do you know why, *l'kivo*? Because romantic love is actually spiritual passion, displaced. When a person 'falls in love' in the romantic sense, they pour the world's perfection into a single person. This is an error, a spiritual error. Source doesn't play favorites. Love isn't a scarce resource. We're all equally beloved."

"Is that why there's so little jealousy here? Because you all feel profoundly loved?"

"It contributes, certainly."

Darius shook his head uncertainly. "It's a very old habit you're asking me to change. On Earth, we're madly in love with romantic love. It's how we feel most alive."

She kissed his forehead. "Romantic love is a confusion, and confusions burn away."

"It'll be an easier attitude to maintain if I'm still seeing the sultan's palace. But I can't imagine it will last."

"You're right—your connection will fade. You'll still have the memory, though. Hang on to that." She brought his hand up to her lips. "May you rest inside your bliss, which never rests."

Darius settled back into his nest of pillows and stared up into the temple's vaulted whiteness. What a morning it had been! He'd tasted the pussy of the woman he loved, and had a close encounter with God. He sighed with pleasure and returned his attention to Kri'Zhalee. She was gazing at him tenderly. Her *da'yo* was pulled back and shimmering, her breasts were swelling before his eyes, and a dewy jewel was hanging from a nipple. . "Welcome to Erotopia," she said. "I'm so glad you'll be staying with us. Would you care to join me for a drink?"

-DARIUS-

"WAS THINKING OF A WALK in Mosshard Garden today," Vala said to Darius. They were sitting in their Overstory suite. "Would it work for you to join me?"

It didn't. He sighed, gazed abstractedly at the tangle of leaves outside the window, and whisked away the wisps of irritation he felt arising. He couldn't keep an ugly thought from his mind. Her proposal was evidence of a small betrayal; she'd pretty much promised him to take him back into her bed if he behaved himself on Union Night, which he'd done, sort of, so far as she knew. But then he remembered the sultan's palace and decided to let the grievance go. "A promenade in the park? I'd love to, m'lady," he said.

"No need to play the Sir Knight game today." She ran her hands through her hair and said dully, "Last night was really something, wasn't it?"

It was odd; he'd expected her to be ecstatic after the wonders of the previous night. "You don't seem happy," he said, confused. "What's up? Why not?"

"Something happened this morning. I don't know if I can talk about it."

"Go ahead, tell me. Let's not have secrets between us."

And so she'd shared. She'd gone back to Jahangir's suite after Union Night had ended and slept there deeply but not long. Over breakfast, he'd advised her that he'd be spending the rest of the day with Vadeen. She'd been looking forward to a lovely romantic day with him, and now he was off having sex with someone else—and a male someone, at that. She was feeling jealous and angry.

"Now you know what it feels like," he said, unable to keep the petulance from his voice. "I've been looking forward to a lovely romantic day with you."

She didn't respond with the annoyance he'd expected. Instead she smiled ruefully and said, "I'm sorry, but I'm just not there yet. I hoped it would be different." She took his hand. "Don't be sad— we'll get there. You and I, we're doing better. When I look at you, I see a friend again."

"May I bring along Kri'Zhalee on our walk today?"

Vala raised an eyebrow. "You want to get back with me, and you want to bring along your new great love?"

He shook his head. "It's not like that."

"You're not madly in love with her?"

"I'm madly in love with everyone, and most of all with you."

She looked at him skeptically. Then her face softened and she said, "*Que extraño!* I actually believe you."

†

-Vala-

THE SKY WAS OVERCAST and the trees were still—the air was thick with moisture. Vala, Darius and the High Priestess strolled along without speaking. Vala's sadness had passed; she'd cheered herself up with her choice of outfit, a tight black corset with dangling nipple jewelry that bounced and jiggled as she walked. Darius kept sneaking peeks. Every time he did it, she felt a surge of pride; she wanted him to be looking.

With each step they took, her anger with Jahangir faded. Without a word, Darius took her hand. Without a word, she let it happen.

Two flightless birds, *kradoos*, were hunting bugs on a nearby rise. They were as big as ostriches and plumed like peacocks. She wondered if a person could ride them. If so, she'd like to try it. There was a mosshard at the crest of the rise the *kradoos* were patrolling. It looked about five feet high; it seemed stark and summoning against its backdrop of silver-gray sky. A wild idea occurred to her. Riding a *kradoo* might be out, but what about a mosshard? Priaps and Fountains played with mosshards regularly, as did your everyday citizens. It really pumped up the erojoules, and it was said to feel amazing. The notion had immediate appeal. It would distance her even more from her current storm cloud; it would give Lola a chance to be outrageous; and it would be mightily just. Darius would get to watch, his reward for being so sweet lately, and Jahangir *wouldn't* get to watch, at least not in real time, which would serve him right for abandoning her for Vadeen the entire day.

She braked and pointed. "Look, a mosshard!" She fixed Darius with a mischievous gaze and said, "What do you think, should I go introduce myself?"

He looked startled, then alarmed, and finally unhappy. "If that's what you want, I guess."

His answer took her aback; she'd expected enthusiasm. He'd always loved her dirty-girl routines, like the time she'd gone to a party with him wearing a vibrating gizmo under her panties, and that other time, very early on, when she'd put on a private show for him with a cucumber, which she'd taken care to make sure was organic.

"I thought you'd like it," she said.

"I don't want to watch you fuck a cactus."

"It's not a cactus, it's a mushroom."

"Whatever. The point is, it's a *thing*. I don't want you connecting with a *thing*. I want you connecting with *me*."

Her answer came out more harshly than she'd intended. "Not today, Darius. I thought I'd made myself clear."

"But, Vala—" he began.

She cut him off. "That's enough. Do knights whine?"

"I thought we weren't playing that game."

"Enough," she said. "I mean it."

Kri'Zhalee had been tracking their exchange like she was watching a tennis match. Now she looked from one to the other and said with a perplexed look, "In the name of the Great Ones, what is going on between you two?"

-KRI'ZHaLee-

AS THE HIGH PRIESTESS WATCHED Vala make her way toward the mosshard, she found herself marveling at Earthling pathology. On Erotopia, lovers grew more affectionate the more they were together. It couldn't *not* happen—it was a spiritual law of nature. The more you were intimate with another person, the more your love for them blossomed and grew. *When adjacent roses kiss the sun/They slowly intertwine*—that was how Vervi M'chani had put it. Then why wasn't that so for these Earthlings? It wasn't only individuals who had *l'shavas*. Couples had them too, and theirs was distorted and chaotic, turbulent and throttled. Love and hate were in there, admiration and frustration, yearning and resentment too. They seemed to have forgotten how to simply love.

So why were they still together? Why were they persisting? The High Priestess squeezed Darius's hand and read the information that flowed in. He was longing for Vala—he was deeply in love with her.

It had to be Vala, then, who was doing the turning away, Vala who was choosing not to intertwine. The High Priestess had used *ya'ma'ya*, sex magic, hundreds of times to help people out of a stuck place. She wondered if she should use it here. The mosshard would be a perfect conduit.

Because *ya'ma'ya* was such a powerful technology, there were strict rules about its deployment. A sex magician couldn't mess with a person's free will—they couldn't do the sex-magic equivalent of making a person cluck like a chicken. You were allowed to intervene spiritually, though, in other words you could conduct what amounted to a heliocentric operation—you could invite them to

215

turn toward the light. *Influence attitude, not action*—that was how the guidance put it.

Two stems emerged from the mosshard; one faced them and the other was directly opposite. Vala wrapped both hands around the closer one and started milking it. Kri'Zhalee knew what would happen next. She'd apply the M-sap to her *tra'da*, and things would proceed with lightning speed from there. The M-sap would overwhelm her, she'd slide the stem in, and she'd plunge from there into the *l'dayo*, the Inner Temple, the place beyond words where there was only pleasure and more pleasure. Transmission of the *ya'ma'ya* would have to take place during the few seconds when Vala was riding the mosshard but hadn't quite tumbled into the *l'dayo*. Timing was everything when it came to sex magic, and it would be even more challenging than usual here because they'd be sharing a mosshard, and M-sap accelerated everything

"Vala! A moment, please," the High Priestess called out and went up to the Earthling.

-Vala-

THE HIGH PRIESTESS WAS STANDING across from Vala with her back against the mosshard's upright and her thighs around the protruding stem. "You start," she said. "I'll follow."

Vala brought her hands to her face and sniffed them. They smelled like honey mixed with pepper. She brought her hand to her *tra'da*, made contact with the pads of two fingers, and gasped. Wildfire spread through her body—her flesh felt like it was rising off her—any moment now and her spirit would join her skin and float away. Then a new awareness came in, an emptiness that claimed her soul and her body, and desperately called out for filling *now*. It was an all-consuming need; all else in her consciousness faded. She got down on all fours, inched backward toward the waiting stem, and wriggled cautiously onto it. Scarcely an inch, no more. Her eyes snapped shut, her chest heaved, and she cried out. She heard the sound of her own self, panting. Then she shoved the stem all the way in.

-KRI'ZHaLee-

THE HIGH PRIESTESS SLID SLOWLY down the mosshard's trunk until the tip of the stem was poised at her Front Gate. She'd slathered M-sap on her *tra'da*, and then on her breasts as well. This would be a tricky one; she'd need all the sex energy she could get. She closed her eyes, visualized Vala with a lighter, healthier *I'shava*, and said to herself the opening words of the sex magic ritual: *As I see it, so be it*. Then she lowered herself onto the shoot and felt the fiery heat rise up to greet her.

She started sliding up and down the shaft, up and down, smooth and steady, not too fast and not too slow. Once she'd gotten into a groove, she went into her Inner Observatory and scanned for Vala. And there she was! With her eyes shut tight, her body trembling, and her arousal blasting skyward. The High Priestess adjusted her tempo to match Vala's slower one, then timed the moment and jumped in. The connection went off without a hitch—she and Vala were conjoined. As the Earthling ascended her mosshard shaft, the High Priestess descended hers. Back and forth they went, pushing each other's erotic swing, creating a lovely shared rhythm.

A new *da'zel* emerged from Vala. It was almost a *daf'zhun*—the Earthling's orgasm was approaching. Now! Kri'Zhalee had to impart the *ya'ma'ya* now! And she had to make it powerful. She squeezed down on her stem as hard as she could. It responded as she'd hoped by going soft and squishy. She squeezed a second time, and met with success again as M-sap gushed from the stem's entire epidermis and shot with firehose force from the tip. Kri'Zhalee's innards were blasted, drenched.

The High Priestess's orgasm had started—she was tumbling into the *I'dayo*. She visualized the magic words, illuminating each letter in bright neon. Once they were standing up strong and sturdy in her mind, she bathed them in two moist exhales, then followed them with a third out-breath that sent them down her central channel into her *tra'da*, and from there into Vala via the mosshard they were sharing.

Three simple heliocentric words. *OPEN. HEART. DARIUS.*

The Earthling gasped and pulled herself up to the tip of her stem, as if she were making room for something. Kri'Zhalee used her last vestige of conscious control to organize her orgasmic energy into a tight bright cylinder and fire it into Vala's *tra'da*. Her aim was true; she succeeded on the first try. From her Inner Observatory, she saw the three words shatter into fragments and go coursing into the Earthling's bloodstream.

Vala slid slowly down her shoot. Her eyes were shuttered and her body was shuddering. Then Kri'Zhalee's view shifted and it was her own self she saw, hanging suspended from her stem. An image came to her, the fishing boats on the Midriff Ocean with their carvings of the Great Ones on their bowsprits. The ship careened down into the trough of a wave and she went diving down with it, into the bottomless *l'dayo*.

- Vala -

OR A BRIEF MOMENT, the Earthling felt nothing, absolutely nothing, not even any pleasure. She didn't know who she was, where she came from, or what had just happened. Then she opened her eyes and there, directly ahead of her, was Darius. His mouth was open wide and his eyes were staring.

An ancient part of her took over. Darius was there and she was here. She had to go there and get him. She extracted herself from the mosshard and set off in his direction. It didn't occur to her to stand up and walk upright; that would require motor skills she was nowhere near possessing. Instead she crawled, inch by slow unblinking inch, across the blue-green turf between them.

MUST. FUCK. DARIUS.

Vala had made it halfway to him when a contrary impulse brought her to a halt. If she went any further, she'd be going into Darius's territory and, worse still, she'd be doing it on her knees. That wouldn't do—no, not at all. He needed to come to her, too. She rolled over onto her back, opened her legs wide so he had a full-on view of her swollen *tra'da*, and lay there waiting for him to come do the obvious.

He didn't oblige her. Instead he tore off his sarong and started stroking himself furiously.

Vala couldn't believe what she was seeing. She was serving up what Darius claimed to want more than anything, a Vala whose entire identity had been reduced to a desperate need to be fucked by him. She'd absolved him of the need for foreplay, even! But he wasn't interested. And then in a flash, she understood. He was operating under old rules—*thou shalt not fuck Vala*—and that was actually fine

220

with him. The scene he was seeing was totally hot; he was in his porn place, watching.

That wouldn't do, no not at all. She smacked her *tra'da* and cried out, "Hey, you! Yes, you! Get over here and do your job. Bring your big dick over here and fuck me!"

-ᗪᗩᖇIᑌᔕ-

ARIUS WAS IN SHOCK. Vala had told him she wasn't ready to have sex with him. Now she was acting like a cat in heat. What the fuck was happening?

It wasn't until she hollered at him that he was startled out of his paralysis. It woke him up; he realized that this wasn't a show—it was actually happening. Vala was being the slut of his dreams; she was waiting there open-legged for him.

Moments later, he was on his knees above her with Monster hard and ready to plunge in. This was their long-awaited fresh start; he decided to memorialize the moment. He paused, looked down at her tenderly and said, "I love you."

She grabbed him by the nipples, pulled him toward her, and said, "Shut the fuck up and fuck me."

Her *tra'da* had never felt so sopping wet or squishy-ready. He thrust away without restraint, delighting in the full freedom her marshiness made possible. Then something completely new occurred. She gazed at him from a faraway place with a look of wide-eyed disbelief, cried out, "Oh God, your cock," and started to come.

The moment broke him open. She'd praised his cock many times before, but this time, for the first time ever, he was absolutely sure she wasn't faking. Nor had she ever come with him inside her, not without active attention to her clitoris.

Her *daf'zhun* sounded loud and long as she fastened around him, squeezed tight and released, and then clamped down again.

"Jesus, your cock," she exclaimed again.

His ejaculation started at the base of his spine, just below his sacrum. Every time he spasmed, she spasmed with him, a call-and-response that inspired a new release from him. Their dance went on

222

and on, squeeze and release, squeeze and release, until he had nothing more to give. They collapsed into each other's arms.

When he opened his eyes some time later, Vala's eyes were gazing into his. "Oh, Monster," she said.

"Oh, Mouse," he answered.

Something big had happened—they both knew it. They'd come together . . . and from fucking. They kissed, closed their eyes, and rested.

Monster was still inside her, limp but contented, when Darius looked up and there was the High Priestess. His eyes went wide; he'd forgotten all about her. She was astride the mosshard and her body was shuddering. He turned back to Vala and whispered with ferocious urgency, "Look. Look now."

She followed his gaze and her eyes went wide. *Amrita* was arcing from Kri'Zhalee's crotch, milk fountaining forth from her nipples.

The Pray Party

"The span between thought and action
Is the arc upon which the Wheel turns.
We choose and we do, or we do not,
And the world we thought we knew burns."

—Translated from Vervi M'chani,
The Bridge and the Body

-vaLa-

OU AND ME. IN BED. ALL DAY. How about it?" Darius proposed. His hand landed on Vala's belly and caressed it.

"No," she said firmly and through the fog of sleep removed it.

They were lying on her wood-framed canopy bed in the Treegarden Overstory. She'd invited him to spend the night with her after their tryst in Mosshard Garden. He rolled onto his belly, stared down at her, and said, "Why not?"

"I'm sorry, Darius. I thought I'd be ready, but I'm not."

Outside the open window, a slow, steady rain was rustling the leaves. "Am I missing something here? Did yesterday not happen? Because you and I made love if I'm not mistaken. We had amazing sex."

Oh. Right. It all came back to her. The mosshard, the High Priestess, her own ferocious urgency, and the grand finale with Darius, that strange and improbable coupling. What wild spirit had possessed her? It hadn't been Lola, more like a fuck-monster come up from the deep. And that strange imperative, which had dragged her crawling across the turf: *Must. Fuck. Darius.* It had all been so odd, so unaccountable. "Pretend it didn't happen," she said.

"But why?" he protested. "Do you remember how we came together? We had our best connection ever."

She answered by taking his hand in silence. "Monster, you're right," she said at last. "It really did happen. But that wasn't really me out there. I'd lost my mind. I was temporarily insane."

"You were temporarily insanely hot."

"Yeah, well, here's the thing—I didn't actually consent to having sex with you."

Darius emitted a barking laugh of disbelief. "You didn't *what?* Jesus, Vala, you directly ordered me to fuck you!"

"Someone ordered you, but it wasn't me. Look: I'm as baffled as you are. There I was with the mosshard inside me"—she shivered—"and the next thing I knew, I was crawling across the grass with one thing only on my mind. I had to have you inside me."

Darius was trying not to smile and failing badly. "I loved it. You looked like a cock-crazed fuck-zombie."

"That's my point. Can zombies consent? I'm sorry, Darius, but it's like I was brainwashed. We had great sex, but it doesn't mean what you think it does. We haven't kissed and made up yet."

"That's not fair," he objected.

"The heart isn't fair. It's got its own rules and rhythms."

"That's just an excuse," he challenged her. "You're hanging onto your anger."

"No, Darius. It's more like my anger is hanging on to me." She made a fist and brought it to her chest. "I can feel it in here. It's red, and it's hard. I can't just will it away. Before we can get back together again, I need to forgive you truly, deeply. I'm getting closer, but I'm not there yet."

"What can I do to help make that happen?"

"Keep being sweet, for starters. Beyond that, I'm not sure. Atone? Repent? Or maybe it's really about me. Maybe I need to get better at forgiving." Her hand found his beneath the sheet. "I want to get back with you, too. So let's try this. Give me some time to think things through. Come back to me this afternoon. I'll try to have a plan by then."

"If that's the best we can do," he said in a voice tinged with sadness. He raised his hand to her lips. "May I?"

"You may."

Some moments passed. She said, "And now you may stop kissing it."

-Darius-

ARIUS WAS WALKING IN MOSSHARD GARDEN. The rain had lightened into a soft mist. A *x'ing* from the Understory was perched on his right shoulder. Darius was glad for the company. The sultan's palace had faded; he was feeling hemmed in by grievances.

His initial impulse upon being turned away by Vala had been to seek out Kri'Zhalee. If anyone could console him, it was she. But she was off doing something priestess-y, and so he'd headed off to Mosshard Garden to walk off his hurt and angry feelings there. As he strolled along, he shared his grievances with the *x'ing*, who seemed more than happy to hear them. A person needed a partner they could trust, and Vala was totally unreliable. A promise-breaker, that's what she was. Always setting new tests, always setting new conditions. Women—Jesus!

He was stewing in the injustice of it all, and his *x'ing* friend was examining the shape and structure of his right ear, when he happened on a Priap who was being serviced by someone on their knees before him. An acid taste came into Darius's mouth when he saw who was doing the pleasuring. It was a man, blond and handsome like himself. He couldn't help himself—he found it just a bit disgusting. It wasn't like he had anything against homosexuals (in fact, he viewed himself as refreshingly open-minded), but there was no getting around the fact that actually seeing a guy with his mouth around another man's dick was unsettling. There was something inherently *wrong* about it—it was like the guy on his knees had two penises. One was where it should be, at his crotch, and the other was in his mouth where it just plain didn't belong. Mister Cocksucker wasn't normal anymore. He was a mutant, an aberration.

Darius averted his eyes, experienced a brief pang of guilt for not being sufficiently liberated, and walked on. And another thing, he complained to the *x'ing*—Priaps were available for whatever, you invariably saw one or more when you went strolling in Mosshard Garden, but not Holy Fountains. Talk about unfair! By all rights there should be women there too, women as available as Priaps were, women laid out as if on a platter, lying there with everything but an apple in their mouth, lying there for anyone in the mood who came along, like, for instance, a certain unhappy Earthling who could really use some random strange right now.

He shook his head disconsolately. "There's a pattern here," he told the *x'ing*, "a dangerous and disconcerting pattern. I may look all worldly and Hollywood, but I'm terminally naïve. I thought a romantic connection counted for something, but apparently it doesn't, not to Vala anyway. What do you think, buddy?"

The *x'ing* didn't answer. Darius didn't take it personally and continued to lament privately. He'd assumed that when he got to Erotopia, he'd finally find himself in a fully liberated society where men and women were treated equally. Well, silly him—he'd swallowed the sucker bait yet again. Was Erotopia woman-friendly? Yes. Gay-friendly? That, too. But *real-man* friendly? *Hale-and-het-man* friendly? Nope. And here was the incontrovertible evidence—there wasn't a Fountain to be found in Mosshard Garden. Where oh where were the equal-opportunity women? If what Vala kept telling him was true, that the universe was a tapestry, injustice was woven into it.

A wooded path opened onto a clearing and a massive festival tent. Banners were raised high on the roof, and unlit torches planted in the ground surrounded the canvas like sentinels. An odd sense of dislocation came over Darius, as if he'd slipped the bonds of time and happened on the traveling quarters of a feudal king.

A naked man was on his hands and knees, doing something with a tent rope. He had milk-chocolate skin and was built like a linebacker. Dreadlocks hung down to mid-back. He looked behind him at the sound of approaching footsteps and stood up. Large hoop earrings adorned both ears; a third and smaller hoop hung from his left nipple. His chest was massive and hairless.

He smiled and said, "My name's Akhmeen. May I help you?"

Darius shook his head sadly. "I wish you could, but I don't think so."

Akhmeen was eyeing him closely. "You're one of the Earthlings, right?"

Darius nodded, and they got to talking. This was the Mosshard Café, a community gathering space. Akhmeen was its manager. He was preparing the place for the evening's Pray Party.

"The what?"

"Pray Parties are regular community gatherings. People congregate at venues like this one for a nationwide erotic improvisation."

Darius perked up. "Tell me more."

"A lead group provides an erotic through note—we beam their lovemaking to Pray Party venues throughout the planet."

"Using what, a hologram?"

"Something like that—a very advanced hologram. Sounds and smells are transmitted. If a lead-group player were to ejaculate, a person elsewhere could get soaked."

Darius nodded thoughtfully; an idea was hatching. Less than twenty-four hours earlier, Vala had taken the lead in an over-the-top sex scene that had culminated in the best sex he'd ever had with her. Tonight's Pray Party, if anything, was a better setup. An erotic tide lifted every ship. This one might get him back with Vala.

"You've done me a solid, Akhmeen," he said. "I'll see you this evening, I believe."

-VaLa-

"'VE GOT A PROBLEM," VALA SAID TO JAHANGIR. They were sharing a table at the Museum of Love's rooftop café under a bistro umbrella that couldn't quite keep off the misting rain. They'd just come from two hours cruising the exhibits. The Mystic Poets, Shades of Love, the Performance Art space with its coupling silhouetted forms. (They'd elected not to join in.)

He brought a glass of *maz'dhi* up to his nostrils, sniffed, sampled, savored. "Lemony with a hint of pine," he concluded and put the glass down. "You have a problem. What sort of problem?"

She gazed at him affectionately. Yesterday's upset seemed far away. "I want to get back with Darius, but I can't bring myself to be sexual with him. I need to get past that. It's really strange, this resistance, considering…"

She paused and grew silent.

"Considering … *what?*" he asked eventually.

Now she'd gone and stepped in it—she had no choice but to tell him about the events of the day before. Falteringly at first but with increasing confidence, she recounted her adventure, starting with her decision to mount a mosshard and culminating in her sex-crazed coupling with Darius.

His smile broadened during the telling. "I look forward to seeing the footage," he said when she'd concluded.

"Lola was in a mood," she answered with a small, proud smile.

He sipped his *maz'dhi*, put it down, and said, "But I'm confused. How can you have had sex with him yesterday yet not be ready to be intimate with him today?"

"Because I didn't choose to have sex with him. It's like I was possessed."

"Demon-possessed?"

"No, slut-possessed."

"Hmm," he said and looked out over the low roofs of the city. "Kri'Zhalee's sex magic, maybe?"

Her eyes widened. "Maybe. I hadn't thought of that. Do you think she was trying to get me to fuck Darius?"

"I doubt that. It would violate their notions of consent. She probably had something else in mind, and for some reason it went awry."

"That makes sense," Vala agreed.

"And now a day has passed. How do you feel about what happened?"

"Both good and bad," she answered eventually. "I'm proud of how bold I was, and I also feel ashamed."

"Ashamed? Why?"

"Because I need Darius to respect me as a woman, and that means seeing me as a full person, not a sex object. And then what happens yesterday? I turn into a bimbo from a sexist wet dream. I became the perfect cock-crazed slut. I feel like I betrayed my gender."

"Maybe you're being too hard on yourself? Lola emerged and did herself proud. You and Darius had great sex. These seem like things to celebrate."

"You don't understand," she said with a frustrated shake of her head. "My relationship isn't only about me and him, it's about all men and all women through all time. There's a voice in my head that keeps saying, 'You're a warrior in an army. Sisters don't sleep with the enemy.'" She refilled her glass, stared somberly into the *maz'dhi's* pink sparkling depths, and said, "The personal is political. The personal is *never* not political."

"He cheats," Jahangir said. "Is his cheating political?"

The question stopped her, but only briefly. "Ultimately, yes. He does it because he has a dick, and he does it because he's the product of a culture where men get to have bimbos and mistresses. It's part of the package that comes with male privilege."

"If he comes around politically, he'll stop philandering?"

"I doubt it. But it would be easier for me to make my peace with it."

"Isn't it philandering you signed up for on Erotopia? Mutual philandering?"

She gave his question thought and shook her head. "No, I signed up for honesty and integrity." She turned to her partner. "You have lots of partners outside your triad. Do you call that philandering?"

"No. Everything is open and aboveboard."

"That's because you've created an evolved post-patriarchal relationship. Your relationship with Jonah and Marie isn't fundamentally corrupt. You've created structural equality. You're not living a lie."

"I had no idea," Jahangir said, "that you're such a political creature."

"I didn't use to be one. But here I am, and I'm glad it's happened. I look back at how I used to be, and I see a sad, solitary and disconnected person. Now I'm a member of a team, Team Woman, and it's not some silly, inconsequential sport we're playing, not jump rope or field hockey. We're riding the arc of history; we're in a great battle for justice." She paused and then added, "A person needs to know wrong from right. A person needs a purpose."

"And Darius, he's chosen the other side?"

"He didn't have to choose," she answered with a frown. "He was born there."

"And now you want him to cross over."

"He can't be my boyfriend if he doesn't." She emptied her glass. "If I truly believed he was on my side, I could probably let his bad behavior slide—I'd be able to forgive him. It would be easier for me to see him as a hunter, not as a pig. But the reality is that he's *not* on my side—I know this man; he's deeply sexist. It's his training; it's his privilege. If we could somehow get past that, if he could shuck off all that history and make me his genuine equal, man meeting woman smackdab in the middle, we might actually be able to have the fresh start we keep going on about."

"What would 'shucking off all that history' look like? What actions would he need to take? What emotions would he have to feel?"

She fell silent and then said, "For one thing, he'd have to show some real contrition. Yes, that's it," she continued excitedly as the tumblers fell into place. "I need him to bow down and plead guilty. I need him to show real penitence. He's been on the wrong side for too long."

"You need a ritual submission. Is that what I'm hearing?"

"I believe it is," she said as her eyes went wide with understanding. "I need him to repent and renounce. I need him to declare his allegiance to *my* tribe."

"You need him to capitulate."

"Let's just say that he needs to own that he's been wrong and I've been right."

"Any ideas how to make this happen?"

"Not yet."

Jahangir fell silent. Eventually he said thoughtfully, "There's a negotiation happening here. Maybe the two sides can make a deal."

"Me and Darius? I don't think so. I've compromised for far too long. No—I've *been* compromised for too long. It's all or nothing for me at this point."

"I didn't mean that. The negotiation isn't between you and him. It's between you and you." She looked at him baffled, and he continued. "There's a part of you that wants to get back with Darius. Your Woman in Love, let's call her. And then there's another part of you that sees your interactions with him in a political and historical context. This is your Empowered Woman. She needs to extract concessions before she'll let your Woman in Love get back together with him."

"Yes, that's it!" Vala agreed excitedly. "I feel surrounded by the ghosts of all the women who've been mistreated by men since forever. I can feel their spirits fluttering around me, here"—she waggled her fingers above one shoulder—"and here"—she repeated the action on the other. "I can't sleep with him because I feel accountable to them."

"I'm wondering if your Woman in Love could have a friendly chat with your Empowered Woman and come up with a mutually agreeable middle ground."

She thought and then shook her head no. "It's not up to either of them, Jahangir. It's up to these flying ghosts of mine."

"Then have the conversation be between your Empowered Woman and those spirits that she answers to. Find out what will get them to fly away so your Woman in Love can be happy again."

She said nothing for a time. Then: "I asked the ghosts and they answered. One more trial, they said, and it has to really put the screws to him. If he passes, it'll mean he's truly penitent and is ready to acknowledge the historical truth of women's suffering. It'll mean that at last he's come around and is on our side. If that happens, the ghosts will stop hovering and fly away." She met Jahangir's gaze with a plaintive look. "I have a problem with that, though. I don't want to be testing him anymore. He's already suffered enough, I think."

"And there it is," he replied, "your creative challenge. How do you honor your Woman in Love and your army of aggrieved women, too?"

She fell silent for a time and then emitted a pealing laugh. "Damn, I think I've got it! Have you ever had a rash?"

His eyebrows went up. "Excuse me?"

"Have you ever taken a hot shower when you have a rash? Do you know how the sensation can be both excruciating and exquisite? That's what we need for Darius. Something that feels great and awful, too."

"The agony and the ecstasy ..."

"That's right. The ecstasy is the gift of my Woman in Love. The agony is what lets my ghosts fly away."

"Do you have a specific notion?"

She said, "Let me tell you about our Towel Boy game."

-KRI'ZHALEE-

AKHMEEN AND KRI'ZHALEE were cuddling on an *amrita*-soaked bed—their eyes were sparkling and ecstatic. He said, "Your Earthling friends will be attending tonight's Pray Party, I believe."

"How lovely! I'm sure they'll have a grand time."

The High Priestess was in an especially fine mood. Yesterday's *ya'ma'ya* with the Earthlings had gone surpassingly well, although she hadn't expected her magical words to route around Vala's heart and go straight to her groin. But that was the mosshard for you; it blasted you into the *l'dayo*. The morning's testosterone training had been successful, too. All eight pups had gotten hard when she'd demo'd a small orgasm for them. She'd then led a lively conversation with them about how best to manage the sex energy she'd sent coursing through their veins. Gently she'd suggested that they'd serve their own erotic interests best by learning to channel their lust into ramping up their partner's pleasure. They'd been attentive and respectful and had understood completely. She'd left with eight blooming boys on the path to becoming skilled lovers. A lovely siesta had followed with her longtime *da'zha'yo* Akhmeen. He was a third-degree Celebrant, skilled and sensitive. She kissed him and tasted her own musky flavors on his lips. An idea came to her: Why not invite the two Earthling lovers to take the lead at the Pray Party? It would send a positive, affirming message: *We love you, we celebrate you, we want to learn from you.* Darius and Vala, raised up and celebrated by the We. She couldn't see why not to do it.

She put her hand on her lover. He was hard again. That was one of his delightful qualities, his short refractory period.

"May I?" She made her way down between his legs and settled into a full-lotus position. She took his thick shaft in her hands and contemplated him for a long moment. Then she offered up a silent gratitude (for Akhmeen, for men, for all creation), leaned forward and started to pray.

- ᗡ ꒐ ᖇ I ᑌ ᔕ -

ARIUS WAS SITTING with Vala, Jahangir and Vadeen at a table that was located midway between the Mosshard Café's canvas walls and its midpoint, where a small, empty stage rotated silently. He felt at an infinite distance from his companions. Those three were lovers, intimate; he was an outsider, nothing. And what made things even worse was how infernally sexy Vala looked. She'd chosen to be topless, and Vala topless was a sight to behold. Below her waist, she was wearing a silver microskirt and nothing else. No panties. He knew because she'd flashed him in the Overstory.

As he gazed across the vast space that separated him from his companions, it was painfully clear to him that Vala had had sex with both Jahangir and Vadeen; the three of them were enjoying the special liquid intimacy that emerges from the sharing of bodily fluids. That she'd also been with the Erotopian was new and distressing information. Jesus, she'd been busy! Sexual empowerment was a fine thing, but a woman should have some self-respect. A woman should have limits.

Vadeen was talking philosophy. "We believe that life is a game, and that the object of the game is to discover what the rules are."

"That makes sense," Jahangir said. "Games make life more fun."

"You're right, they do. And they also call us into self-awareness; they call us into self-witnessing."

The Towel Boy game won't make things more fun, Darius thought, staring moodily at the low platform of mattresses that ringed the tent's walls and was filling up rapidly with laughing, chatting people.

"It's an existential game; we're doing our mapping in the void," Vadeen continued. "We weren't given an operating manual.

Our starting point is this: What's our polestar in the game of life? Over the years, we've come up with two competing answers—two competing questions, really. 'How can I best make the most of this opportunity?' versus 'How can I best be a good person?' Quantity versus quality, Maximalists versus Moralists."

"I'm probably a Maximalist," said Jahangir. "I accumulate experiences. I accumulate money. I accumulate pleasure."

"And I," said Vala, "am probably a Moralist. I want to make myself a better person, and the world a better place. But enough philosophy." She batted her eyes at Jahangir and Vadeen. "You two men, you're so interesting!"

Maximalists, thought Darius. *Moralists. Fuck these categories. Where's your place for just plain pissed?* For the past half hour, Vala had been flirting up a storm with Jahangir and Vadeen, smiling and fawning and coming on to them like they were the most fascinating people *ever*. Meanwhile she'd been ignoring Darius completely. The Towel Boy game wasn't supposed to start until she and her guys got down and dirty, but she'd jumped the gun and was putting him in his place already. He thought back to earlier in the Overstory, when she'd proposed what she'd called their "really and truly one last test." She'd barely gotten the words "Towel Boy" out when he'd cut her off with an abrupt "No way!" But she'd asked to be heard out and, idiot that he was, he'd agreed to listen the same way he'd done when she'd proposed that crazy scheme for Union Night. It would be fun, she told him, like their private Towel Boy fantasy only better because she wouldn't be pretending. "You love me to be slutty," was how she'd put it to him. "I'll be living the dream."

"It'll be humiliating," he'd protested. "Playing Sir Knight is one thing. Playing Towel Boy is another."

"They're both performances," she'd responded, "and people aren't dumb—they'll know it. Sir Knight one night, and now this: You'll be showcasing your diversity."

"I don't know," he ventured hesitantly.

"Would you play a gay person?"

"Of course I would!"

"Well, this is a kinky person. What, it's okay to be gay, but not to be a bottom?"

He had to admit that she had him there; it wouldn't do to come across as anti-kink. And truth be told, he quite liked the idea of being submissive. He'd never gotten up the courage to actually propose it, but he'd brought himself to orgasm more than once with Vala as a leather-clad domme, and him beneath her in cuffs and chains.

"How many men?"

"I don't know. A couple, maybe."

"Not a gang bang, then."

"No, not in spirit or in quantity."

"Hmm. Let's say I'm crazy enough to say yes. Will you and I get back together for real this time? No ifs, ands, or buts?"

"No ifs, ands, or buts," she'd promised. "Except for this one." This was when she'd flicked up her microskirt, bent over and flashed him.

That's what had clinched it, when she'd showed herself to him and pledged absolutely, positively, to be his again if he succeeded at this one last test. But that had been then and this was now, and it was nowhere close to fun, watching her flirt with Vadeen and Jahangir like a dark-skinned Scarlett O'Hara. He couldn't see Vala's hands beneath the table, but he had his suspicions. The two guys were looking mighty happy.

A sex divan had been set up on the stage at the café's center. It was decked out in red and gold velour, and it seemed somehow lonely and incomplete, like it wanted populating. And there, sweet Jesus, was Ool, newly arrived and perched on a sofa in the first row, two short steps distant from the stage. She was outfitted in leather thongs that started with her sandals, crisscrossed her calves and thighs and kept climbing from there, creasing her hips, belly and breasts and continuing up to her neck, where they were attached to a leather collar via O-rings fore and aft. Her outfit, such as it was, was topped off by a black bellboy hat adorned with pink roses that was perched at a sharp angle on her head.

A silver-haired man approached their table. He was new to Darius, who was struck by his remarkable good looks and especially his eyes, which were an exotic purple color that made him seem other, alien and unknowable. He went up to Vala was if the others weren't there and said, "Hello there, you."

"Oh, it's you, Hoor Ut'chi," she said and looked away.

He plowed forward as if she'd encouraged him. "Would you come play with our group tonight? We're looking for another bottom."

"I'm not available," she muttered, avoiding his gaze.

"Not available *now*, or not available *ever*?"

"Please don't," she said with her eyes still on the table.

"Have a lovely evening," Vadeen said with cool finality.

"Yes, a lovely evening," she echoed and for the first time gazed at her tormentor directly.

Hoor Ut'chi looked from Vadeen to Vala and gave a tiny nod of understanding. "To be continued," he said. He sowed seed to the table and strolled away nonchalantly, like nothing untoward had happened.

Darius felt furious, and ashamed. Vala was *his* woman; it was he, not Vadeen, who should have stepped in to shield her. But Vala had cast him as Towel Boy, and that meant staying on the sidelines.

"I was hoping you'd ask Hoor Ut'chi to join us," Jahangir offered. "You told me you might want a third."

"With the right guy, yes—three's not a crowd. But Hoor Ut'chi is creepy." She shuddered. "Now, where were we? Oh, I remember." She crooked a finger at Jahangir. "We were getting ourselves warmed up. Come to me, lover, and kiss me."

They'd settled into a leisurely embrace when Vala reached out for Vadeen's hand and placed it squarely on her breast. The gesture assaulted Darius like a message in neon. *Yes to him and no to you. Vadeen rates—you're untouchable.* He took a deep breath and gazed off into the tent's recesses where more and more revelers were gathering. He felt miserably alone and full of self-loathing. It was incomprehensible to him how, only a few hours earlier, he'd agreed to stand by and watch his woman have sex with other men. Watch, and clean up after them. He'd signed on the dotted line under "Humiliation." But that was the thing about him—he'd do anything to make his woman happy. Crawl and grovel, if it came to that. He shook his head in disbelief. What the fuck was wrong with him?

-Vala-

NCENSE WAS WAFTING THROUGH THE CAFÉ. Musk of Mosshard, it smelled like; it was probably aphrodisiac. Vala's nerve-ends were tingling.

A man was approaching. "Ah," said Vala. "Hmm."

The men swiveled to look. It was Akhmeen. He had on a black-and-gold sarong beneath his naked chest. "*Dios*, that's fine," Vala said.

Men had been objectifying women since forever—it pleased her to be giving them a taste of their own medicine. And she wasn't just pretending—she'd experienced an actual physical thrill at the sight of Akhmeen. She loved how big his chest was, and strong, and hairless, and his chocolatey weathered skin. Most of all, she was captivated by his eyes, which were an unexpected blue and crinkling kindly at her.

When Vadeen introduced them, Vala sandwiched his hand in hers and held his gaze for an extra soulful moment. He accepted her flirtation with an appreciative smile and then turned his attention to the group. He came with an invitation from Kri'Zhalee. Would Darius and Vala do Erotopia the honor of leading tonight's Pray Party? Their lovemaking would be projected to all participants—their erotic artistry would provide the motifs and inspiration.

Panic seized Vala. She recalled what she'd learned at a recent workshop, where she'd been told that the best way to deal with anxiety was by adopting a positive attitude. *Treat every threat like an opportunity.* Next, you calmed yourself somatically. She took three deep breaths like they'd taught her to and asked herself what they'd called The Three Questions: *What is the path of boldness here? Will you be loved and supported as you travel it? Will success bring you closer to your power?* By the time she'd gotten to the third question, she knew what her answer would be. A firm if slightly frightened yes.

But this wasn't only about her. She turned to Jahangir and Vadeen. "You didn't sign up to perform for a planet—you signed up to make love to me. How do you feel about this?"

"I'm fine with it," Vadeen said. "It's not my first lead scene."

Jahangir said, "I've already gone public with my sex life. What's another planet, more or less?"

"No fucking way," Darius broke in. "Absolutely not."

Vala gave him a look. "Since when do you have a say about it, Towel Boy?"

"The sene hasn't started," he said crisply. "I'm still Darius." He looked at Jahangir and said warily, "You think I should say yes, right?"

"Speaking as a showrunner, yes, I do."

Vala fixed Darius with a hard stare and said, "I don't think you get it. This is it, now or never."

"Ah," he said and nodded grimly. "Welcome to the Last Chance Ranch."

As she waited for Darius to issue his decision, it occurred to her that she wouldn't have to wait till the next day to reward him for his good behavior, assuming he continued to play along. Not only *could* she, in fact—she probably *should*. She'd hadn't been treating him fairly or kindly; she'd already put him off for far too long. Sex with her tonight would be his grand reward, his surprise prize, for having successfully played the Towel Boy game.

Jahangir's voice brought her back to the present. "What about you, Vala?"

"The thought makes me nervous, but I think we should do it. We're galactic ambassadors. It would be wrong to decline, don't you think?"

"Nervousness is entirely optional," Akhmeen said.

"What," she asked him with a smile, "you have a tea for that?"

He inclined his head in a gentle yes.

The three Earthlings looked at each other. "Jesus fucking Christ," said Darius. He heaved a sigh and said, "Okay."

Vala said, "We'll have three cups of tea, thank you." Akhmeen gave a small bow and turned to go. "Wait," said Vala and grabbed his arm. "Would you consider joining us? I'm on the lookout for a Mysterious Stranger."

"But I'm not a stranger. You know me already. My name's Akhmeen."

"Your name's Akhmeen. You're Erotopian. That's more than strange enough for me."

"I have an event to manage. I may not be available."

"I'm not hearing that as no," she said.

He eyed her up and down and said, "It's not. It's a maybe."

"Good. I'll call for you when the time comes and hope I get lucky. Promise to listen for me, okay?"

"I will."

"What will you be listening for?"

"My name. Akhmeen."

"Ah," she said, "but that's not right. The name I'll be calling out is 'Next!'"

-Darius-

A GONG SOUNDED—IT WAS TIME. The tea had done its job;
Darius felt relaxed, lucid and fully capable of handling
anything that came his way. He followed the others up
onto the round stage.

Earlier that evening, Vala had dispensed her instructions with
the crisp authority of a military commander. Vadeen and Jahangir
were to slather themselves with M-sap from a nearby mosshard
and bring their bounty to Vala. They were to get her deeply aroused
before proceeding to the main act. When the time for penetration
came, Vadeen would go first, then Jahangir. They needn't rush, but
they shouldn't tarry, either. This was, among other things, a performance; timing mattered. They were to ejaculate on an accessible and
visible part of her body. Breasts or belly would be fine, but not the
face. (Absolutely *not* the face—the face was gross.) Towel Boy was
to watch and clean up on command. No matter how turned on he
got, he mustn't touch himself.

Vadeen stripped without a trace of modesty and stood relaxed
and naked when he was done. Jahangir undressed like he'd rather
not be on the stage, then plopped awkwardly down on the sex divan.
Vala made a bit of a show out of taking off her boots and microskirt. Towel Boy sourly did the same with his tight tee and snug
jeans. He wouldn't have much to be proud of that evening—at least
he could show off his body.

He took up his position alongside a stool piled high with towels,
went still and used what a favorite teacher of his had called "identity
mantras" to climb into character. *I exist to serve my lady. Her pleasure
is my pleasure. It is my honor to do this.*

Coos and sighs filled the tent as the Pray Party participants started kissing and caressing. Vala's lovers returned from the moss-hard, lay down alongside Vala on the sex divan, and started stroking her. Jahangir focused on her upper parts while Vadeen worked his way down to her belly and her thighs. In due course, his M-sap-soaked hand went to her *tra'da*. She gasped and shuddered. When her breath came back, she tapped her mouth and said, "Here, too." Jahangir rubbed M-sap on his lips and kissed her.

Watching, Darius was aware of a profound split inside him. At one level, there was numbing disbelief and, below it, massive agitation. It couldn't quite sink in that this was his woman, his *actual woman*, who was stroking her breasts for the raw pleasure of it as her two lovers kissed and caressed her. That was Jahangir, his *actual friend and business colleague*, with his tongue in her mouth like there wasn't this thing called boundaries, and that was Vadeen, a perfectly nice fellow but a *fucking extraterrestrial for crissakes*, whose fingers on her *tra'da* had her arching her back and moaning with pleasure. It was all too much to process; he couldn't imagine feeling turned on.

With each new *da'zel* that emerged from Vala, reality retreated a bit more. This was a performance he was witnessing, and the three lovers were characters in it—it seemed a sort of Kabuki. But the curtain had a tear in it—reality kept intruding. He couldn't stop staring at Vala's nipples. Physically they were engorged, tight and ruby-red, and narratively they were hot hard proof that she wasn't just faking it. This might be a performance; it might be performance art as well; but her nipples and the rest of her were truly and deeply aroused.

Neither man was attending to her breasts. This seemed a monumental error. Darius could feel in every cell of his body how lonely those two beauties were. In a fairer, saner, better world, his hands would be all over them—his lips would be tasting those hard, tight peaks. But he was Towel Boy and mustn't.

Vala moaned, reached out a hand for Jahangir's *ba'da*, and began to stroke him. Darius was startled by what happened next; his own cock began to get hard. As he stared transfixed at her hand on

Jahangir's penis, his upset made way for arousal. She had a strong, steady rhythm going, with a consistent corkscrewing action and regular detours to the balls. He'd never been big on Vala's hand skills, but he couldn't help but be impressed; a woman had to have quite some talent to maintain her focus and her timing with two of Vadeen's fingers inside her and stirring up a storm below. What she'd predicted was coming true. She was being the perfect slut, and it was driving him wild.

As his *ba'da* continued on its inexorable and unaided journey toward full vertical, an image arose in Darius's mind: Vala covered with cum and having an endless megagasm. *Really* covered: cum caking her belly and her breasts, cum as makeup on her face, cum covering her thighs and *tra'da* like a creamy body-paint version of the micro-skirt she'd had on. Orgasmic sparkling fireworks were shooting off all around her.

SuperSlut—that was her name. His latest superhero. He suppressed a smile and resolved to tell Vala about it when he could, maybe as soon as tomorrow. She'd like it, maybe. He hoped so.

"Vadeen!" his girlfriend called out, louder than she needed to. "Inside me! Now! And hurry!"

-DARIUS-

N RETROSPECT (and a lot of retrospecting would take place over the next days), it was clear to Darius that he'd done the best he could. He'd been battling gargantuan odds, though. He got muddled when upset, and he got stupid when aroused. It was the combination that had done him in.

For a time, during what he would later come to think of as the first act of his Towel Boy drama, he'd wallowed in his woman's lewd performance. It was like he was watching the best porno ever. There was only one thorn on this hothouse rose: He mustn't touch himself. And he wanted to, badly.

Vala had her first orgasm shortly after Vadeen entered her. A second and even more rollicking one followed soon after. Moments later, it was the Erotopian's turn. He pulled out and deposited a copious load onto her belly. "Thank you, Vadeen!" she cried out when he'd finished. "Thank you, Goddess!"

She crooked a finger at the clustering pools and issued an imperious command. "Towel Boy?"

He shuffled over to her and wiped her clean. Contrary to his expectation, it didn't feel humiliating. He actually felt proud about what he was doing. This was a very hot sex scene, and he was contributing. It was only a supporting role, but every actor made a movie great, not just the one or two leads.

A thick glob had fallen short of the mark and was slowing sinking out of sight beneath the narrow hedgerow that bounded her vulva to the north. He spotted it and mopped it up, savoring the feel of her fur as he did so.

"Jahangir, it's your turn!" Vala cried out and startled Darius by looking into her lover's eyes and saying with mawkish tenderness, "How shall we do this, beloved?"

The term of endearment sandbagged Darius—he winced as if he'd been spat on. And then the horrid woman went and did something even worse. She touched her lover's face tenderly with two gentle fingers.

Thus was launched the downward spiral into Darius's Act Two. Her words dragged him away from the best porno ever and transformed him into a Peeping Tom, snooping where he didn't belong. These were lovers; their connection was personal and private. He watched horrified as she leaned in toward Jahangir and whispered something to him.

He gave her a look and said loudly enough for Darius to hear, "Are you sure?"

"Oh yes, I'm sure," she said. "I am Lola the Empowered Woman, and I want you to come on my breasts."

"It's not too much of a money shot?"

"It's exactly the right amount of money shot. I'm doing this for Towel Boy. There's a lesson he needs to learn."

"But I want you to come, too."

Oh, I'll come all right," she said and gazed at Jahangir so warmly that Darius's heart felt shot through with buckshot. "I'll use my hand too, and we'll eye-gaze while we're doing it, and we'll time it so we come together." She pulled his face down to hers, kissed him and said, "How's that? Will that work for you?"

"Yes, I believe it will," Jahangir said as a slow smile spread across his face.

Darius watched frozen with horror. He didn't want to be up there on the stage, he didn't want to be Towel Boy, and he sure as hell didn't want to watch Vala and Jahangir being all sexy and sweet together. Desperately he cast about for a different story, one that would make him powerful again. What if he was a corporate CEO and Vala was the hot hooker he'd hired to land a couple of clients? But then his woman locked eyes with Jahangir and put her hand on her *tra'da*, and his friend began to stroke himself, and Darius forgot all about alternative scenarios.

When Jahangir finally called out "Now!," she raised her breasts in his direction, as if the only thing she wanted out of life was to receive his offering there. He spasmed for an improbably long time, spilling his ejaculate onto her curves, in between them on her breastbone, and (most gallingly of all) on one hard nipple, which it draped like snow on a mountain peak.

Vala came throughout, with long arcing cries and shivers that trembled her entire body.

"Thank you," she whispered to Jahangir after they'd shared a last shudder together. They were locked in a long and languid kiss when she snapped her fingers at Towel Boy and pointed at her chest. Darius bowed his head and went to work. Minutes earlier, he'd fantasized about fondling her breasts. Now he was doing it (after a fashion, with a plush rag between his hands and her flesh), and he was deriving no pleasure whatever. As he wiped up here and wiped up there, a single brutal truth kept bursting in on him. Vala's orgasm had intensified while Jahangir was ejaculating on her, and it wasn't because she was into money shots. It was because she was into Jahangir.

Vala gave him a vexed look and spread her breasts. "You missed a spot."

There it was, a smidgen of translucent cream at the base of her left one. He took a fresh towel and mopped up.

She sat up abruptly and called out, "Next!"

Fuck. He'd forgotten all about Akhmeen.

-ᗪᗩᖇIᑌᔕ-

ARIUS WAS QUITE SURE HE KNEW what would happen next. Vala would slide her body up the sex divan so her head was leaning over the edge, and Akhmeen would slide his big dick in. He'd fuck her in the mouth and he'd fuck her in the throat; he'd fuck her where no man had gone before. The M-sap would make it all do-able. She'd probably come while he was throat-fucking her.

The notion was intolerable. Since their first days together, he'd been trying to get Vala's gullet to receive him. He'd started off by trying to tease it open with his cock. When that hadn't worked, he'd attempted to sweet-talk her into relaxing her throat. When that had proved a dead end, too, he'd encouraged her to study with someone who could teach her how to deep-throat—he'd even gone so far as to research teachers on the holo-web. As a final desperate move, he'd lifted a move from porn and stuck three fingers down her throat. All that had gotten him was thrown up on. She'd soon be offering Akhmeen her throat; Darius was quite sure she was doing it to humiliate him. *Here, Big Guy, help yourself! You can open what Darius can't.* She'd be sending her guy another message. There was this thing called manhood, and Akhmeen had more of it.

A wild and horrific emotion arose in him—it felt like a scream encased in silence. He was being humiliated, fully and deeply, and it was happening before an entire world (no, two!). This was the nightmare scenario, the bogeyman around the corner, that had haunted him his entire life. A public declaration to the world: Darius di Selva was weak and small, despite his muscles and conquests.

He looked out into the audience, scanning for someone, anyone, anything, praying for a miracle to save him.

F ONLY OOL HADN'T BEEN WRAPPED UP in that rawhide netting, a neat little package all laid out on the doorstep for him.

If she hadn't had that small blue dildo peeking out from her Front Gate.

If she hadn't popped out the toy and emitted a squirt of *amrita*.

If she hadn't been so goddamn close, a small step for mankind away.

If none of that had happened, things might not have gotten so derailed. But he was a man in a panic, and she was a miracle cure. As the rotating stage took her out of sight again, it occurred to him that he'd been misreading Vala badly. She hadn't been tormenting him out of spite—she'd been looking after his best interests. *"Show some backbone!"* How many times had she said that to him? Yet he'd repeatedly (and, again, tonight) acted like a total jellyfish. An entirely new and luminously clear explanation for why she'd chosen the Towel Boy game came to him. She hadn't wanted him to submit, she'd wanted him to show some *cojones*—she'd wanted him to call her on her bullshit and take charge. She'd wanted a man, not Towel Boy. Instead he'd bobbed and weaved, and then bobbed and weaved some more, and ultimately bobbled everything.

And now here came Ool around again, wrapped up like Mother Nature's gift to him. She'd spread her legs wide and added a flirty beg to her offer, two prayerful hands between two massive breasts. The dildo was next to her on the sofa.

Darius looked at her, then at Vala, and back at Ool again. A cosmic chasm had opened before him; at long last, it was time to decide. *Claim your freedom or stay a slave? Make your woman proud or ashamed? Get off the wheel or stay on it?*

Thus framed, he could see no choice but one. A great capaciousness filled his soul; he was finally breaking free. He tossed his soiled towel onto the stage, seized his hard *ba'da* with a firm hand, and hopped off the merry-go-round.

-Vala-

ALA WAS FEELING EXUBERANT. Akhmeen hadn't responded to her call, but that was the only way her Towel Boy
scene wasn't proceeding as planned. She'd had magnificent
orgasms with her two lovers, and Darius had behaved himself throughout. Now was the time for his reward—she'd surprise
and delight him by taking him on board.

"Towel Boy?" she called out. "I mean, Darius?"

No response came. She waited an extra moment and was met by
more of the same. "Darius?" she said, more tentatively now.

A vast sense of bafflement arose in her. Where was he? She
looked over to his station by the towels. Not there. She hoisted herself onto her elbows and surveyed the room.

And there he was! Off the stage and wrapped up in Ool. In
her ass, maybe, even, it looked like! Her legs were wrapped around
his neck, her hands were squeezing his muscled butt, and she was
coming and giggling.

Vala levitated up off the divan. Her fists were clenched into tight
balls; a tuning fork of purple veins bulged in her lower forehead.

"Darius di Selva," she cried out, "what the fuck do you think
you're doing?"

He didn't answer, just stared at her with his mouth agape and a
horrified look in his eyes.

"That cock was meant for me. For me!"

"I, I thought you wanted this," he ventured weakly.

"Fuck you, Darius! Fuck you, *fuck you,* FUCK YOU! I swear to
God, I'm going to chop your balls off and feed them to the goddamn pigs!"

Silence throughout the Mosshard Café.

Silence, probably, everywhere.

A hand landed gently on her shoulder. "Are you quite sure, *l'kivo?*" Akhmeen asked. "Castration is forever."

"I'll cut his nuts off," she raged at him over her shoulder. "He deserves it!"

Akhmeen didn't answer; he just stood there with his hand on her shoulder.

In the thickening silence, Vala's mood shifted. She felt abashed and then ashamed and weighed down. She flushed, and her hands went across her private parts. Darius saw her cover up and promptly did the same.

Jahangir stepped in front of Vala and raised his hands as if to shield her from public view. "Show's over, folks," he loudly proclaimed. "Cameras off, goddammit! Off! There's nothing to see here, nothing at all. It's time for you all to go home."

The Coming Together

"Erotopia is an entheocracy. Not a theocracy, an entheocracy. Not black robes, but a hallelujah-singing, consensus-based democracy that's plugged into God-drugs and Source."

—Ulrich Von Zeitler, *First Report to the Senate Select Sub-Committee on Intergalactic Affairs* (2049)

-JAHANGIR-

SOMEONE WAS OPENING HIS SUITE'S front door. Jahangir's heart started racing. The person would be bringing news, and it probably wasn't good.

He'd slept fitfully and upon waking had headed downstairs to the Understory, where he'd been intercepted by a stocky woman who'd advised him that after last night's debacle, everything was under review and would he please return to his suite and stay there. He'd remonstrated briefly. It was just a dustup, he'd told her. Things like that happened all the time on Earth. The ill will would blow over in a day or two. Hell—mustering what enthusiasm he could—they'd probably have great makeup sex!

In the face of her blank jailer's gaze, his oratory had rung increasingly hollow. "Never mind," he'd concluded weakly and headed back upstairs. But then he'd paused and looked back. "Are you sure there's nothing I can do to help? There may be things about us Earthlings that I can help you understand."

"Thank you, no. We have Bree for that," she'd answered firmly, and that had been the end of that.

Later that day, he'd tried the front door and it was locked. He was taken aback at first, and then angry. But as he calmed down, he realized he couldn't blame his hosts. Of course they'd be alarmed by Vala's threat of violence and want to keep a safe distance. Bree had explained Erotopians this way: When you have a soft belly, you need a hard shell. Nor could he complain about being mistreated. He had plenty of food and drink. But he had become their prisoner.

He plunked down on the floor, leaned back against a pink pastel wall, and took stock. He'd walked into an ancient, tragic myth—he'd been cast out of the kingdom. And the ugly truth was that he and his travel mates deserved it. Erotopians didn't only have it good—they had it damn near perfect. Why would they let themselves be soiled by Earthlings' ignorance? Last night's debacle had been based on a big misunderstanding. Erotopians were much more literal than Earthlings. There were no actual castrations in the offing. But none of that changed the fact that the three eronauts were cosmic trash, unworthy creatures of a lesser planet. Of course they'd get the brushoff and be shipped home.

His visitor appeared in the doorway. He sighed with relief when he saw who it was—Bree. They'd have sent Erotopians if they were being deported.

She was wearing a simple muslin shift with a keyhole neckline and no reveals. A slim cream-colored bag hung down from her shoulder. They hugged. Briefly she updated him on what was happening in the world beyond his suite turned cell. Their Erotopian friends had been badly spooked by the previous night's misadventure. "They're deciding whether or not to let you stay." Tears came into her eyes. "I might be shipped out, too."

Jahangir's heart sparked, a single solar flare of indignation. "That's so wrong! I get why they'd send Darius, Vala and me back. You could say we earned it. But you've put down roots here. Damn, girl, you're half Erotopian."

"I agree, and I'm praying it won't happen. I do get where they're coming from, though. They're afraid our ways might be contagious. They've even got a name for it—they're calling it the 'Earth Disease.' Nice, eh? These are loving, gentle people. They'd feel bad about sending us back to Earth, but they'll do it if they decide we're too dangerous."

They made themselves comfortable in the suite's cuddle pit, a large circular affair surrounded on three sides by high pillows. He draped his arm around her shoulder as she leaned up against him with her hand resting on his thigh.

"Have you been asked to testify?"

"I spent the morning answering their questions."

"What sort of questions?"

"What's the deal with us and why are we so unkind to each other and why are we so weird about sex."

"What did you tell them?"

"I told them it was complicated." She shook her head ruefully. "Kri'Zhalee boiled it down, though. She said, 'You spend so much time in the courtroom that you've forgotten how to dance.'"

"I'm not sure I understand."

"The mind is organized into complexes, distinct neural networks of connection. Among them are what Erotopians call the 'debate' complex and the 'celebrate' complex. The courtroom is where people debate; it's the wiring that inspires people to argue about what's true and not, about what's right and wrong."

"And the dance floor," Jahangir said, filling in the blank, "is where people celebrate."

"We need both complexes," Bree continued. "The confusion is about priorities. The courtroom produces hostility—arguments, brawls, worse—when we forget that it's part of the dance."

"Two left feet," Jahangir said sadly. "Weak on the dance floor. That's you. That's me. That's us."

"It's Darius and Vala, mostly."

"Will they be sending us home?"

"I don't know. They're considering three options—let us stay, ship us out, or send us into the Wild."

"Jesus," said Jahangir. "The Wild?"

"That's right, like they do with confirmed Hagorrhs."

"What happens to them there?"

"Nothing good, surely. It's nature in its primordial state. Big scary animals, diseases without doctors, no safe space to call home."

A shiver went down Jahangir's neck. "They're thinking we might be Hagorrhs?"

"That's what they're wondering. Try to see your behavior through their eyes. Darius slapped Kri'Zhalee without her consent. Vala threatened Darius with castration. Erotopians associate these behaviors with Hagorrhianism."

"None of that is raping and pillaging."

"But that's just a matter of degree. The underlying issues are the same, a deep cluelessness about boundaries and the will to punish, to hurt."

They sat quietly for a time. Then Jahangir said, "How will they decide?"

"With a Coming Together."

He looked at her sharply. "Like with Mkh'Danaï?"

"Yes, in the sense that the entire nation participates in an erotic celebration."

"It's a Pray Party. Is that what you're saying?"

"Not quite. This is a political process and the Pray Party isn't that, it is simply a party. That's why we use an entheogen."

"A what?"

"A drug that takes you to the god- or goddess-self within. Erotopians make all their important decisions collectively, and their most important decisions are mediated by an entheogen called *cha'nog*. It connects people directly to Source, and it helps them stay focused on the central question—*What's the right decision here?*—no matter how tripped out they get."

"People take *cha'nog*, and have sex."

"Yes. And sing. And dance. And do whatever it takes to ramp up the erotic energy."

"You party hearty."

"More like, we party with our hearts. We party with a purpose. We connect and come together to find out what is right and true."

"And then? How does all this erotic energy produce a decision?"

"A planet-wide force field is created. Because we've all been focusing on the same question, a group wisdom emerges, a collective intention that requires interpreting."

"Who does the interpreting?"

"The Sheman absorbs the energy, takes it to the Great Ones, and returns with their guidance."

"The Sheman—who's that?"

"The first among the Nine. The one with the most powers."

"So it's the Great Ones who decide?"

"No, it's our decision. But it's also *not* our decision—it's the will of Source. The Great Ones do the deciphering for us. They supply the Source code, you might say."

"When will the Coming Together happen?"

"Today. Soon."

Jahangir had grown pensive. "So it's hanging in the balance," he said eventually. "The We will decide."

"That's right," Bree affirmed. "Individually and collectively."

"I feel so powerless, sitting here waiting."

"That's not our only option. We could"—she paused—"get involved."

He looked bewildered. "We could? How?"

"We could"—she tried again—"get busy." He gaped at her incredulously. "That's right," she continued. "We could participate."

Jahangir looked at her disbelievingly. "Everyone else is having sex, so we should have sex, too? I love sex, Bree, you know I do, but how can you and I possible play with all this"—he gestured vaguely in the air, indicating everything and nothing—"going on?"

She slapped her forehead with the heel of her hand. "Silly me, of course you'd be confused!"

She reached into her bag, took out a small yellow pouch and dangled it between her thumb and forefinger. "There's *cha'nog* in here," she said. "Two doses. One for me and one for you."

Jahangir's eyes widened. "Did you smuggle it in?"

"No, Kri'Bondai gave it to me. He wants us to participate. We're their guests until we're not."

"How about Darius and Vala?"

Bree shook her head. "They're in quarantine—our hosts are worried about contamination. You're in the clear, though, and so am I. So tell me, Jahangir: Do you believe in democracy?"

"Well, sure. I guess."

"In that case," she said, "let's you and me get out and vote."

The prospect of having entheogen-fueled sex with Bree, and in a very real sense with all Erotopia, had undeniable allure. Doubts lingered, though. "It's an intriguing notion,' Jahangir said, "but I'm not sure I'll be able. My friend"—he indicated his *ba'da*—"might not cooperate. He's as stressed out as I am. You can't vote if you lack capacity, right?"

"Don't worry about that." She smiled at him. "We can ramp up the energy just fine without your lovely cock getting hard. We've got our tongues and fingers, right?" She cupped her breasts. "And I've got these." She dangled the *cha'nog*. "And these. Have I mentioned that M-sap is a main ingredient?"

"Oh! That changes everything." He was silent for a time. Then he said quietly, "It would make a great scene for *The Erotopian Chronicles*."

"Yes," said Bree. "There's that."

She seemed preoccupied and a bit unsettled. A low-lying skepticism seemed to have taken root in her, a sort of bedrock uncertainty. Was it something he'd said or hadn't said? He decided to rewind and try again. "And another good thing. My voice would be heard."

She nodded and added, "And your deepest wisdom, too." But then her uncertainty sailed in again. "Which is what? Your deepest wisdom, I mean."

"My deepest wisdom?" Now he was feeling unsettled, too. "I'm not even sure what the notion means. Why do you ask?"

"It's the *cha'nog*. I'm not sure we should be taking it." She looked up, met his gaze, and said bluntly, "There's something about your attitude that I find troubling." She hesitated. "I'm not meaning to sound critical. I hope you don't hear it that way."

"System," he said with a wry smile, "prepare to receive criticism."

"No, I mean it," she said. "It's about effectiveness. We should only take the *cha'nog* if it will produce a positive outcome, and right now I'm not sure it will. Do you mind if I ask you some questions?"

"Sure, go ahead."

"Let's start with this: What outcome do you wish for?"

"That one's easy. To be allowed to stay here."

"Why?"

"So we can keep discovering Erotopia. So we can continue on this grand adventure. So we can go on with the show."

"If we were dispatched back to Earth, how would you feel?"

"Embarrassed and ashamed. Humiliated, really." He paused. "But—it's confession time, I guess—I'd also be okay with it. If we were sent home tomorrow, our trip would already be a success. I've got enough footage for one strong season, and I'd be going home with other revenue opportunities, too."

"Like what?"

"Like M-sap. Can you imagine how it would sell?"

"I'm hearing both shame and excitement. You're ambivalent."

"Not quite," he said, shaking his head. "It's more like I've got consolations if we fail. Make no mistake about it, Bree: I want to stay. But riches await me either way."

"Ah. That explains it, then."

"Explains what?"

"This energy I've been picking up. This noise in the system."

"What noise?"

"The theme that keeps flowing through your 'why.'" He looked at her, uncomprehending. "Have you noticed," she continued, "that all your reasons are about your own needs? Your fear of shame. Your dream of wealth. You've been asking yourself, 'What's right for me?' You've been asking yourself, 'How do I minimize my pain and maximize my pleasure?' You've landed on the shadow side of Maximalism. Where in all that is the We?"

Her words hit him hard. He felt chagrined and foolish. She was right; his motives were totally selfish. His first impulse was to defend himself. "Let's say you're right. Why does it matter? Since when is making one's peace with not getting what you want a problem? I'd like to think that's wise and smart."

"I'm not judging," she reminded him again. "My concern is strictly practical. I'm concerned about how your lack of commitment to the We will play out once we've taken the *cha'nog*."

Jahangir wrinkled his brow. "I don't understand."

"You'll be out of sync with everyone, and it will be happening while you're tripping. You'll be a solitary 'me' in an ocean of 'we's.' I wouldn't wish that on my worst enemy."

He nodded in reluctant agreement. He'd feel alone and ashamed and it would all be orders-of-magnitude magnified, tripping-balls magnified. "I'd freak out, and I'd freak people out. That's what you're saying."

"It's possible, certainly. Erotopians would pick up your vibe and experience it as more Earth Disease. Their guard would go up—they'd start producing antibodies. You'd be tilting the scales against us." She paused. "And it might not work for the two of us, either. It might create friction, energetic cross talk. We could end up under a storm cloud. That wouldn't help, either."

"You're making sense. Too much sense. So what now?" he asked grimly. "Do we sit here and wait for them to decide our fate? Do we flush the *cha'nog* down the drain?"

"I don't want that. Let me think."

Jahangir filled the silence that followed by pacing up and down the room. Eventually she said, "It's like there's a switch inside you that hasn't been activated yet. It's there, but you haven't found it."

He gave her words thought, then nodded slowly. "Yes. The Higher Purpose switch."

"That's right. The muscle of the We."

"You're right," he acknowledged. "Business has always been a fun adventure for me—the pursuit of riches, the thrill of the hunt. I've been ethical by the usual Earth standards, but I've been out to make as much money as I can, not be in service to others. It's not that I have a problem with do-goodism. I've just never seen it as for me."

"Well, Jahangir, if there ever was a time for an attitude adjustment, it's now. I'm thinking you don't quite get the stakes here."

"I believe I do," he countered. "We're about to be sent home in shame."

She shook her head. "That's the risk, the Maximalist risk. I'm talking about the opportunity. The Moralist opportunity."

He stared at her blankly. "I see the opportunity in dollar terms. You seem to have something else in mind."

She nodded. "Erotopians are worried about the Earth disease, right?"

He nodded.

"Well, flip that on its head. If Earth can do unto Erotopia, Erotopia can do unto Earth."

"You mean, if we can make them ill, they can make us well? A dose of Erotopian anti-virus to cure us of the Earth Disease?"

"Jahangir, what if you brought Erotopians' wisdom and knowledge back home with you?"

Jahangir's eyes went wide. "I think I get it. Terrorists wear suicide vests. We'd come in wearing celebration vests."

"That's right," she nodded. "You'd be the ultimate counterterrorists."

"But for that to happen …" he began.

She interrupted excitedly. "That's right—you'd have to live here for a while. Absorb our values and our ways. Become fully Erotopian."

"Which, in turn, would require them to let us stay." They fell silent. Then Jahangir said, "It's a lovely vision, but let's get real. Jesus couldn't save the planet. Why could we?"

"Jesus may have had the soul," she said, "but we have the technology."

Jahangir looked intrigued. "Say more."

"What if you brought home with you the technical know-how to produce erojoules?"

His eyes widened. "Wow," he said, "dig Bree's modest proposal. Replace petroleum with sex. Bring an end to climate change."

"That's right. A pleasure-based economy instead of a carbon-based one."

The vision was opening before him, bracing and expansive. "You're right," he said. "I had no idea. But do you seriously believe we could get this done?"

"I don't see why not. Erotopia will be happy to share; Earthlings will be happy to participate. Sex or oil—it's not really a choice, is it? It's basically a matter of developing the right business plan, one that gets buy-in from all your important stakeholder groups—consumers, governments, and so on."

He nodded and said, "It's ambitious, but do-able."

"If you have the right chops, it is. And you've got them."

He said, "I wonder if I could monetize it."

"Sure you could. You could charge a tiny use royalty. A dollar a year, ten billion times—it could be bigger than your biggest dream. And you'd be saving the world while you're at it."

Jahangir spoke his thoughts out loud. "The R&D is already done. The cost of the technology would be nil. I could serve the We and get crazy-rich, too."

"Yes," she said. "There's that, too. You'd be modeling the new capitalism."

Suddenly, from out of nowhere he got it. We were all microcosms of the whole—we all *were* the whole—and we all shared responsibility for the whole for the very same reason that we were individually responsible for our own private selves. The Me and the We were essentially the same; one was a cell, the other was the body. A person might sometimes feel alone, but that was mere confusion; we were in divine community, always. His shoulders slumped as the insight sunk in. He was feeling grief, and embarrassment too. He'd always thought of himself as a man of grand ambitions—now he looked back and saw small. "You're right," he said. "I didn't get it. Let's do it to cure us of the Earth Disease." He pointed to the pouch with the *cha'nog* in it. "Shall we?"

"Yes," said Bree. She was smiling at him. "But not here, lover. Come with me."

She led him out of his suite and up the spiral staircase, around and around the massive tree. Up and up they went until they emerged just above the canopy into a small and roofless circular space with a padded floor and protective railing.

268

"Welcome," she said, "to the Eyrie."

The view was spectacular. Beyond the shadows of Mosshard Park, lights twinkled out toward the horizon. The Temple of the Divine Nectar was illuminated in a show of shifting colors, azure and crimson and gold.

"Yes," said Jahangir. "This is good."

Bree was smiling at him with a big 'yes' in her eyes when a gong sounded, a sonorous vibration that seemed to spread across the land and then dissolved into silence.

"It's time," she said.

She opened the pouch, removed two small dark candies with rippled tops, and handed one to Jahangir.

"To right intention," he offered, hoisting it in her direction.

She hoisted back and said, "To voting with our passion."

"To a brighter, better future for us all."

He took a tentative nibble, then a bolder one.

She smiled at him happily. "The *cha'nog*," she said. "Isn't it delish?"

To The
Great Ones

On the bridge between what is and isn't,
On the bridge where some stories come true,
The sentinels wait, patrolling their fate,
As never rolls into the new.

—Translated from Vervi M'chani,
The Bridge and the Body

-KRI'ZHaLee-

THE TEMPLE OF THE DIVINE NECTAR was a vast white double-domed space, all soaring arches and marble and columns. At the apex of the domes were circular skylights that were opened on special celebration days so water symbolizing sacred feminine liquids—milk, *amrita*—could be shot into the air.

The Coming Together was approaching its conclusion. Kri'Zhalee, Kri'Bondai, and the other members of the Eight were lying on a sprawl of hassocks, ottomans, pillows and bedding, all arrayed on plush area rugs. They had made love as an ensemble, joining over the course of the hours into twosomes, threesomes and moresomes, then breaking for self-pleasuring before returning to the group. Two piles of puddle pads were alongside. The fresh ones were few and stacked neatly, the soaked ones plentiful and strewn about in haste.

The Eight were lying in each other's arms, depleted and exhausted. The High Priestesses had come for hours and produced gallons of *amrita*. All four High Priests had had ejaculatory orgasms, a rarity for them. This had happened at the end of their trip, simultaneously. In a sort of intuitive inspired choreography, each High Priest had deposited his seed in a different receptacle. Kri'Anael had come in Kri'Gallia's *tra'da*, Kri'Elyon between Kri'Nedali's breasts, Kri'Xaphan down Kri'Calonis's throat, and Kri'Bondai in Kri'Zhalee's Rear Gate.

Such was their artistry.

Such was their civic commitment.

Their orgasms were so intense that the energy-sensitive sky-

273

lights had retracted upon registering their *da'fzhuns*, releasing the Eight's cries into the pleasure storm that was roiling the air over every square inch of Civside, as far south as the Wild.

Kri'Zhalee and Kri'Bondai were lying on their sides, eye-gazing. The High Priest flickered briefly into immateriality, then came back on like a firefly. Moments later, she did the same. They kissed lightly, sweetly.

Kri'Zhalee sat up, newly alert. A familiar presence had joined them. The energy she was sensing was powerful but not oppressive, and utterly lacking in binary qualities—not good or bad, not beautiful or ugly, not strong or weak, not masculine or feminine. It simply was, like the universe itself.

The Ninth emerged into the material realm as zhe usually did, slowly and steadily, deliberately. The Sheman was hairless and portly, with a round face, flat nose and full lips upturned in a slight smile. Zher eyes, which had a slightly Asian cast, were topped off by long eyelashes and gray like the ocean on a cloudy day. Zher pupils contracted and dilated once, twice, three times. When they flickered open for the last time, they'd gone entirely blank and colorless. Whatever identity they'd possessed was gone. A bolt of orange light sparked across zher cheeks. This was followed by new flashes—red, yellow, purple—until zher entire face was crackling and sparkling with rainbow light.

A faint sizzling sound reached Kri'Zhalee's ears, followed by a low whirring, like an engine was starting up somewhere.

From their seated positions, the Eight bent at their waists as low as they could go, and waited with their eyes to the ground.

When Kri'Zhalee looked up again, the Sheman was gone, so completely that it was like zhe'd never been there at all. The High Priestess mind-messaged Kri'Bondai. "It's over now. We've done our part."

"Do you have a sense how this will come out?" he answered in the same mode.

"I saw them in a bright white light. Darius and Vala."

"What meaning do you make of that? "

"I saw them as they perhaps could be. I saw them as they may never be." Switching to her outside voice, she said, "They're suffering. I can feel it."

Again they flickered in and out of view. When they emerged, he kissed her and hovered his hand over her *tra'da*. A puff of moisture emerged. "How about that?" she said. "A straggler."

He brought his hand down the rest of the way. She sighed contentedly and said, "Yes, like that."

He said, "And now, Beloved, we wait."

To be continued ...

Glossary

Ba'da—The penis.

Ba'da'yo—Semen.

Ba'ya'sa—Taboo.

Bharat'sey—An extinct wild animal.

Bha'troun—A sexual-spiritual practice.

Cha'nog—An entheogen.

Da'fzhun—The sounds a person makes when coming. 'Roof-off prayer.'

Da'yö—The energy cloak worn by High Priests and Priestesses.

Da'zel—Your everyday sound of sexual pleasure.

Da'zha'yo—A friend with whom you feel an especially close connection because you have sex together.

Dra'dhero—A breakfast porridge.

Dra'ndel—A tasty and energizing Erotopian wafer.

Gev'da—The sex sound a person makes who's trying not to come.

H'qorn—An extinct wild animal.

Kradoo—An Erotopian wingless bird, a cross between an ostrich and a peacock.

Kri'lashö—A training technique intended to dramatically shift the recipient's emotional and erotic energy.

L'da'yo—The region of the brain that is devoted exclusively to pleasure.

L'kivo—A term of endearment. Literally, "cell in the body." Rough translation: "Beloved."

L'shava—A person's essential energy makeup.

Maz'dhi—A Erotopian beverage, the rough equivalent of wine.

M-sap—The aphrodisiac sap of the mosshard plant.

Prik'tash—A grounding herbal blend.

Sheman—The highest of all the High Priests and Priestesses, a non-gendered/all-gendered being.

Stan'ghetti—A large lizard.

Tra'ba'da—Genital sex.

Tra'ba'na—Light sexual activity.

Tra'da—The vulva.

Tra'la'dö—The urethral orifice.

Tra'la'dyo—Vaginal secretions.

Tra'zen—Sex divan.

Tsel'but—An extinct wild animal.

Tsh'kiva—An honorific reserved for sexual high priestesses.

Tsh'kivo—An honorific reserved for sexual high priests.

Ya'ma'ya—Sex magic.

X'ing—A small Erotopian monkey.

Z'denda—A sprawling shade tree with above-ground roots.

Zhun'ha—Running energy. 'Orgasm-dancing.'

Acknowledgements

I AM GRATEFUL TO EVERYONE who helped get me to a place in my life where I could write a novel (ultimately, a trilogy) about life as celebration. In particular, I would like to thank my family, my friends, and my teachers formal and informal, including the women I've partnered with.

I am deeply grateful to the pre-publication readers of this novel, many of whom were subjected to premature sharing. Thanks to proof-reader Val Vadeboncoeur, copy-editor Eliza Dee, layout ace Tilman Reitzle, cover designer Erin Papa of Turning Mill Design, and developmental editor Nanci Panuccio for her invaluable guidance.

This novel was written over the course of literally years of mornings at Dominick's Café in Kingston, NY. Thanks to everyone there who made it such a congenial community office for me: Dominick, Denise, Rita, Maria, Maddie, Ian, Sylvia, Sophia, Johnny, Destiny, Samantha, and Gina. (My apologies to anyone I've overlooked; I'm grateful to you, too.)

I am indebted to Ernest (Chick) Callenbach, author of the seminal 1975 novel *Ecotopia*. Erotopia can be seen as a sort of Ecotopia 2.0—further out, farther away, and a whole lot bawdier. In the early 1990s, I spent a weekend with Chick at a sustainability retreat on Angel Island in San Francisco Bay. I had no idea that decades later I would be following in his footsteps.

Finally, I owe my wife, the wholistic sexuality teacher Sheri Winston, a very special debt of gratitude. Sheri, when you came into my life, I was unfamiliar with sacred sex and sex-positivity. Thank you for introducing me to this wondrous world. Thank you also for your unique and extensive subject-matter expertise, for the values and attitudes I picked up from you, for your dutiful readings and spot-on editing, for your companionship and good humor, and most of all for your love. As a midwife, you caught over 500 babies. Now you've midwifed a novel, too.